EXILE'S RETURN

"I cannot go home," Emri said quietly. "I would do so if I could, but the shaman, Mandris, has cast me out of the tribe and vowed to kill me should I return."

"We are not afraid of him!" shouted Tusk. "You are not alone anymore; you have a tribe of your own. We would not let him harm you. He would not dare to fight you while we stand at your side!"

There were many such cries, and Hawk and Emri looked at each other with equal parts astonishment and cautious wonder. Never had they thought of returning, except in their own private dreams. Much as it was desired, it had seemed an all but impossible dream.

Dawn looked up at Emri and there were tears in her eyes. "I want to go home," she whispered. "I want to go home."

Proud Bear looked at Emri with eyes that shone with an unusual brightness. "You could return if you wished to do so," he said quietly. "You are not afraid of anything, animal or human. We have witnessed your courage. As you have told us yourself, you are brother to the lion. Take us to the land that does not die with the coming of Cold Time. Take us, Emri, take us home."

SPIRIT
OF THE
HAWK

Rose Estes

BANTAM BOOKS
TORONTO • NEW YORK • LONDON • SYDNEY • AUCKLAND

SPIRIT OF THE HAWK
A Bantam Spectra Book / September 1988

ISBN 0-553-27408-2

Published simultaneously in the United States and Canada

Bantam Books are published by Bantam Books, a division of
Bantam Doubleday Dell Publishing Group, Inc. Its trademark,
consisting of the words "Bantam Books" and the portrayal
of a rooster, is Registered in U.S. Patent and Trademark
Office and in other countries. Marca Registrada. Bantam Books,
666 Fifth Avenue, New York, New York 10103.

This book is dedicated to my friends Mary Gygax, Mary Kohli, and Helen Brandt, who persevered with courage through times of travail.

The research for this book and its two companion novels was greatly aided by help from Diane Gabriel, Assistant Curator of Paleontology and Kurt Hallin, Scientific Assistant at the Milwaukee Public Museum. Also extremely helpful was the medical knowledge, keen comments and extreme patience of Doctor R. V. Both, DVM, Puyalla, Washington. I also depended greatly on Peggy Hayes's vast knowledge of young wild animals and their relationship to man.

Lastly, if there are any mistakes, their information is not to blame but rather my interpretation.

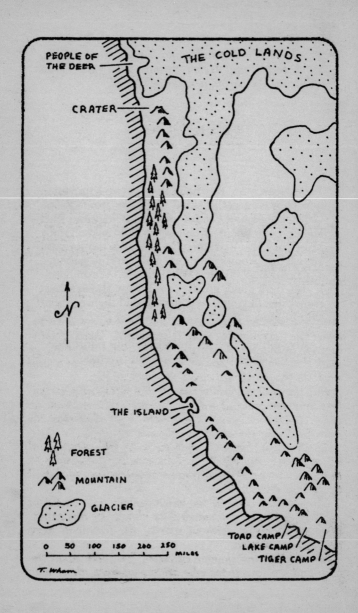

PEOPLE OF THE DEER

THE COLD LANDS

CRATER

THE ISLAND

N

FOREST

MOUNTAIN

GLACIER

TOAD CAMP
LAKE CAMP
TIGER CAMP

0   50   100 150 200 250
                          MILES

T. Wham

PROLOGUE

Out of body travel. The far seeing. Now was the time for such a thing. Mandris, shaman of the Tiger clan, prepared himself to search for his enemies, those who had escaped him for so long. There had been nothing but silence throughout the turning seasons, but still he knew that they lived. Now, he would find them.

He allowed his hands to rest in his lap and took long, slow breaths, drawing them deep into his chest. His breathing slowed, his chest rose and fell but seldom, his heartrate decreased greatly. There was a sense of nothingness, a blackness that was neither friend nor foe, a void that could be turned to one's purposes or could swallow the spirit and cause the body to die.

But the shaman had mastered the dangerous transition long ago and did not linger in the void. Instead, he called forth the great saber tooth tiger that was his power animal, the bearer of his spirit.

The immense creature sprung forth from the top of his head, roaring loudly and shaking itself violently as though glad to be free of the narrow confines of the all too fragile human body.

The shaman allowed the spirit animal its moment of freedom and then commanded its silence, its obeisance. Without speaking, without words, the two who were one, communicated.

"Go forth," the shaman ordered, "go forth upon the land and seek out those who are my enemies, those who

1

*have defeated all attempts to end their lives. Find them
for me and allow me to look upon their faces."*

The tiger snarled once and then turned, already intent upon its mission. Crouching, it sprang into the air
and was gone.

The land sped beneath its broad paws, passing in a
blur of pale green. The spirit that was the tiger noted
the herds of young deer, thick upon the land, yet he did
not stop. He saw the vast herds of wooly bison and the
smaller groups of hairy tuskers and great mammoths.
He lifted his dewlaps in contempt at the sight of the
prowling dire wolves and sharp toothed foxes that lingered on the edges of the large herds, waiting, hoping
to snatch a new borne away from its watchful parent.

Though animals were plentiful, covering the rich,
rolling land like a furry coat, nowhere was there sight
of humans. Then the tiger spirit was over water, trac-
ing the path that the enemy had chosen before Cold
Time had cloaked the land with snow. And still there
was no sign.

The shaman stirred restlessly and nodded once, urging the great spirit animal on, to travel the distance and
scan the land with his greater senses. The tiger continued on, seeking, searching for the men and the saber
tooth lion who were their enemy.

Vast forests of conifers passed beneath him, stretching unbroken as far as the eye could see. Mountains,
capped with sparkling blue ice rose to the east and the
restless waters pounded the rocky shores on the west.

Further and further the spirit cat journeyed and the
shaman felt himself weakening, the vision of the cat
coming to him in short snatches. He was reaching the
end of his strength and knew that he could not continue
much longer. There was a danger here, a danger of
separation between self and spirit. It was possible to
lose the bond, the connection that held the two together. It was a risk that he was unwilling to take,
despite the great hatred that drove him on.

And then he saw it, a brief glimpse, no more. They
were together still, the two men and the lion cub,

now nearly grown. And the woman, too, her belly swollen with child. They were in some snowy land, someplace still locked in the grip of Cold Time. The shaman saw that much and no more before the vision vanished. But it was enough.

The shaman recalled the great cat and reveled in the sense of victory. They were still alive. Somehow, he would find them and this time he would kill them.

CHAPTER ONE

"Emri, we must do something. The children are crying," Hawk said, as he placed his hand on the shoulder of his friend. Emri sat on a large gray boulder, staring vacantly across the jumble of broken ice that lay before him, stretching as far as the eye could see.

"Emri, we must find shelter. Everyone is cold and many are hurt," Hawk said persistently, but Emri continued to sit on the rock, unmoving.

Hawk crouched down and looked up into Emri's eyes. "Emri, you did everything you could to save them. You will fail the living if you brood upon the dead. Come now, help us find shelter from the cold."

The crying of children and the wailing of women began to penetrate the deep despair that Emri had wrapped about himself, despair over his inability to protect the tribe.

"There is nowhere to go," he said in a flat voice. "Look behind us, back where the village was. There's nothing but ice now; no dwellings, no shelter. And there"—he gestured to the east—"there are only mountains with ice and snow on their tops. Even if we could climb them, no man knows what lies beyond. And there"—he pointed west—"there are only the Endless Waters."

"Then we must go that way." Hawk said, pointing due south. "We will find food and shelter and a new life for all of us."

"That way lies the Tiger clan and Mandris, who wishes our death," said Emri. "We cannot take the people into danger."

"There is much land between the Tiger clan and ourselves, and the people will die of cold and hunger long before Mandris finds us if we do not do something now."

"Yes," Emri said heavily, "you are right. We must leave this place. There is nothing for us here anymore."

Rising, he looked around him at the desolate landscape that had given peace and happiness throughout the long dark nights of Cold Time. The sun sparkled and danced on the broken ice that covered the mangled remains of the village; blues and reds and violets and bits of white light dazzled his eyes with their beauty and thrust pain into his heart.

"We must leave," he said forcefully, closing his eyes against the brilliant display, unwilling to admire such treacherous splendor, knowing the magnitude of death it concealed.

"But before we go, we must say the prayers for the dead, to free their spirits from this world and allow them to travel to the next. Come, my good friend, there is much to be done."

Together, Emri and Hawk gathered the stunned survivors. So immersed were they in their own individual grief that they might not have roused for their own sakes, but speeding the spirits of their loved ones to the world of the ancestors could not be ignored.

They gathered in a circle, each of them holding some offering: a bit of sedge dug from beneath the snow, a small stick pried from the ice at the edge of the land, or a fragment of fur and leather cut from their own garments.

Tusk, one of the few young men to escape unharmed, produced a fire-starting kit: two stones and tiny packages of dried powder that would be added to the flame at the appropriate moment.

Tusk crouched and placed a small pinch of dried grass on a broad, flat stone. Next, he struck one stone

against the other, producing a shower of bright sparks.
Again and again he struck the stones together until one
of the sparks fell upon the dried grass and began to
glow. A child, who had been waiting for this exact
moment, began to blow gently, fanning the tiny spark
until it grew bright. Then, the smallest bit of sedge was
added, the stiff dry stalks giving the fragile flame just
the right amount of sustenance. As it grew in size and
appetite, other bits of fuel were added to the flame
until it burned steadily upon the rock.

"Spirits of our ancestors, hear our voices," cried Emri
as he stood in front of the flame. "We ask you to accept
and guide the spirits of those of our tribe who have left
this world and are now making their way toward you.
Open your arms to them. Guide them to the campfires
of loved ones who have gone before them. Help them
find their place so that we may look up into the night
sky and see their campfires and know that they are
safe."

Emri carefully laid a strip cut from his own tunic at
the edge of the fire. As the flame bit into the leather,
he spoke the names of the chief and his mate and that
of Walks Alone and Fawn Woman.

When the words were spoken, he stepped aside and
Hawk took his place, adding a length of his own black
braid and murmuring the name of the shaman whose
apprentice he had become.

One by one the members of the tribe stepped up to
the burning platform and placed their offering in the
flame, uttering the names of their loved ones; even the
tiniest toddler was held up and repeated words whispered into his ear so that even his small voice might
help speed the spirits on their journey to the next
world.

When the last of them had spoken, Emri turned to
face the people who were now his to guide. They were
poorly clothed and there were few tools or weapons
among them, and many were injured. It would be his
responsibility to bring all of them to safety. It was a
difficult if not an impossible task.

Emri straightened at the thought and anger began to build within him; he would not fail, he would not let them down, they would not die.

Emri looked around and saw that one of the young men, one Otuk by name, had managed to grab up a spear before the village collapsed around him. He held out his hand and asked for the spear. Otuk gave it to him reluctantly.

Emri held the base of the spear in the flame until it caught fire, then he handed it back to Otuk. "Guard it well," he said. "This flame will carry the spirit of the life we leave behind as we journey toward the new land." Otuk's chest puffed out and he seemed to grow taller as he held the flaming torch on high. He nodded to Emri, full of gratitude for the honor bestowed on him, all sign of resentment gone from his face.

Hawk and Emri conferred briefly, knowing that the people could not walk far this first day. But it was important that they make a start and remove themselves from the scene of their grief.

"There are no trees," Hawk murmured softly as they took the first steps. "How shall we build shelters?"

"Shelters may be made from things other than trees," said Emri. "We must be watchful and not let anything pass that will be of use to us. Your skills in finding ground foods will be much needed now. You must see to it that the men and boys arm themselves with stones for throwing. We will need all the game we can find."

Dawn appeared at Emri's elbow, holding a fat youngster in the crook of her arm. Its eyes were closed and a wet thumb hung on a sagging lip.

"Her mother is nowhere to be found," said Dawn as she pushed a mass of dark, curly hair back out of her eyes. "I fear that she too has gone to meet the ancestors."

"Isn't she too heavy for you to carry?" asked Emri, staring pointedly at Dawn's own rounded belly. "You should give her to one of the other women."

"I carry her willingly"—Dawn said, wrapping her arms tightly around the fat infant—"and wish that I could do more. If her mother looks down upon us, I would have her see that she is safe."

Remembering the child that Dawn had lost, born before its time during the difficult journey north, Emri could but bend his head in acquiescence, not wishing to cross her on this matter. "If she grows too heavy, I will help you carry her," he said, and was rewarded with a warm smile as Dawn dropped back to walk among the women.

No bit of dry sedge, no fragment of wave-washed wood, no bird track, was too small to avoid their notice as they made their way across the winter-ravaged land.

By mid-afternoon, as the warmest rays of the sun stroked their fatigued bodies, they had gathered several armloads of dried material, including cakes of dung dropped by hairy tuskers and deer, that would feed their fire.

The women had searched the ground carefully and had found six precious eggs, light brown in color and spotted with blue, as well as handfuls of edible if tasteless lichen and withered berries from the past season.

The men had been more fortunate. Even though the season was still early, they had managed to bring down a large brown-and-white bird, one of the first of the vast flights of honkers, as they were called, who would populate this barren land as it grew warmer.

The boys had stoned a variety of smaller birds and several handfuls of rodents who lived in burrows beneath the large boulders that littered the landscape. It was not much food for so many mouths, but it was a start, and the activity kept their minds from their grief.

Long before the shadows fell, it became obvious, even to Emri, that the people could go no farther. Even the exuberant cries of the youngsters had stilled, and the old and the injured lagged behind like a broken wing dragging in the dust.

Emri had scrutinized the snowy landscape since morning, searching for shelter, for any dip in the earth, any fold in the shore that would shield them from the bitter wind. But there had been nothing. Now, as purple shadows lengthened at their sides, dogging their foot-steps, Emri grew desperate. But it was not until one of the infants began to cry, a ragged, insistent sound that grated on Emri's nerves like an accusation, that shelter was found.

Relief washed over him like a balm of warm oil as he spotted three large boulders, each taller than his own head, leaning against one another. Although not ideal, they would create a breakfront against the wind, which had switched direction and was now blowing in from the frozen waters and pouring across the land.

"Ho! Hawk! Tusk! Broken Tooth!" cried Emri as he pointed to the trio of boulders that ordinarily would not have warranted a second glance. Slowly the ragged column turned and made for the rocks, the youngest and the oldest bringing up the rear.

Long faces, gray and drawn with fatigue, stared at Emri as the tribe straggled in, asking nothing, merely waiting to be told what to do next. This was not normal for the People of the Deer, who were usually outgoing and viva-cious, full of curiosity and quick to question that with which they did not agree. But these were not normal times.

"We will stay here for the night," said Emri. At his words, people sank to the ground, just lying where they fell. The ground was still deep with snow, but there was no help for it. There were no ground coverings. They would have to huddle together and hope for the best. The ground did slope away from the rocks slightly so that if the snow melted it would drain, rather than pool beneath them.

Emri and Hawk scraped the snow aside at the base of the center boulder and built a flat platform of stones. They layered the dry materials carefully, trying to cre-ate a fire that would last as long as possible and keeping aside those bits that they would add throughout the night. When it was done, Otuk came forward and lit the fire with his flaming spear. The fire took hold rapidly. Reflecting against the flat surface of the boul-der, it sent waves of heat billowing out toward those who lay supine on the ground.

Roused by the welcome heat, the people began to
stir and sort themselves out into some semblance of
family groups. The birds and rodents were laid out
alongside the fire, and two women, Running Bird and
Opa, brought out small, sharp skinning knives that
hung from thongs about their waists and began to skin
and gut the creatures.

A cooking sack was more difficult to come by. In the
end, one of the young men, called Proud Bear after his
bold, almost arrogant personality, volunteered his own
tunic, slipping it over his head and strutting about in
the cold air as though it were the warmest of days.
Emri noticed several of the young women watching him
beneath downcast lids and knew that the young man's
pride would prevent him from showing even the slightest indication of discomfort, unwilling to appear weak
before his female admirers. Still, it would not do
to lose anyone to the cold, and Emri directed Proud
Bear to sit beside the fire and fashion some sort of
cooking stand out of the few materials they had available to them.

A tripod was built out of Otuk's spear and two shorter
lengths of wood that had been found at the edge of the
frozen waters. These had washed up in warmer days.
Promise of the forests that still lay many days ahead.
The leather shirt was packed with snow, the dressed
meats, and the various lichens and seeds that the women
and children had gathered.

Running Bird, a small, wrinkled woman who had
seen more moons than any other among them, crouched
before the foodsack and stirred it gently with a stick,
careful not to dislodge it from its precarious perch.

It took a long time, but eventually the smell of food
filled their nostrils and they clustered around the fire,
watching it as though it were a precious totem. All eyes
were focused on the cooking sack, and the little ones
were whimpering now for food as much as for their lost
parents.

When at last Running Bird deemed that the food was
done, they were fed each in their turn, starting with

the strongest and fittest, then progressing on to the injured, and lastly, the children.

It was hard on the youngsters, watching others eat before them, but Emri knew that the fate of the small band lay with the few young, strong men and women who would be able to hunt and lead the tribe to safety. If they were weakened through lack of food, their chances for survival were that much slimmer.

Then, even though the Sun God had not yet descended to his own rest beneath the edge of the world, the People of the Deer laid themselves down upon the cold, hard ground and fell asleep instantly.

Dawn nestled beside Emri in the shelter of his arm, the infant asleep once more on her chest, her belly filled with the hot, rich broth. Mosca pressed himself against Emri's back and curled into a tight ball.

"Where will we go, Emri," she asked. "Where will be our home?"

"We will go to the forests, Dawn." Emri had thought of little else throughout the long, hard day. "There is shelter to be found there and game is plentiful."

"I wish we could go home," Dawn said after a long silence. "I wish we could go home."

Emri's mind filled with images of his mother and his younger sisters. He saw the bend of the river that curved around the village and saw the gentle rolling hills and the blue smudge of the mountains on the horizon. His heart hurt within his breast as though he had been struck a fatal blow.

Emri, too, wished that he might go home, but he knew that it was not possible. They were no longer of the Tiger clan but rather, People of the Deer. They would make their home in the forest and please the Gods; all would be well and they would prosper and multiply. Holding that thought to him like a warm talisman, he tucked Dawn's head beneath his chin and allowed himself to sleep.

CHAPTER TWO

In the morning it was found that an old woman had died sometime during the night. No one had heard her cry out, nor were her injuries serious enough to be fatal. Emri was perplexed at the cause of her death and angry that the tribe's numbers had shrunk still further.

"Do not grieve for her," said Running Bird, although her own dark eyes seemed to glitter with unshed tears. "All of her family lie behind us, buried beneath the ice. She had no wish to leave them, and now her spirit will join with theirs."

Her voice broke as she spoke, and Dawn opened her arms and gathered the old woman to her, soothing her as well as the infant, who had begun to whimper at the sound.

Others awakened and gathered around Running Bird and Dawn, doing what little could be done. The ground was still frozen and there was no thought of digging a burial site. Instead, stones were gathered and the body laid in the place where the fire had stood the previous evening. It would be entombed between the three leaning stones.

After much discussion it was decided to strip the body of its clothing. There was some argument as to whether or not spirits wore clothing in the next world, but Running Bird, recovering quickly, decreed that the spirits of her ancestors would share with the newly deceased and that the clothing would best serve the living rather than rot beneath the stones. No one chose to disagree, and the old woman's clothing was soon distributed among those who were most in need.

A shirt was fashioned out of her trousers and given to Proud Bear, who despite being warmed by two young women during the night, was now shivering in the cold light of morning.

There was no food to be had, no fire to cause them to linger, so after covering the small body with a heavy layer of stones and saying the words that would free the spirit from the earth, the small party set out once more.

The day was brilliant, if still extremely cold. The Sun God rose from his night's rest beneath the edge of the world and peered over the tops of the mountains, turning the peaks as red as flame and sending beacons of crimson light streaming through the thin, cold air.

If beauty could fill one's belly, then none would have had cause for complaint. As it was, their bellies were empty and those children, too young to reason with, were crying aloud, begging for food in the only manner available to them. Mosca was none too pleased himself and grunted and moaned in displeasure.

"Is there nothing we can do?" Dawn asked in desperation. She jigged the baby up and down, trying to soothe it, but the child would not be comforted, alternately sucking its whole hand and shrieking its resentment. Her entire face was screwed up in an ugly grimace, and Emri could understand Dawn's distress, for even that short burst of crying caused his head to ache and his chest to tighten in sympathy.

"We have seen no game," said Emri, trying to be heard over the baby's howls. "What can I do if there is no game? I would give up my portion to quiet this one, but I have none!"

"Fish," said Broken Tooth, one of the two men of the Tiger clan who had been sent by Mandris to kill Emri and Hawk. "We must fish."

"We cannot," said Emri, turning to the man, grateful for the interruption so that he might turn away from the screaming child. "The ice is breaking up and it is too dangerous to venture out far enough to fish."

"Look you there, Emri. There is a line of rocks that extends far out into the water up ahead there." Broken Tooth was much used to the squalling of babies, having fathered several himself. "We can fish from the rocks without stepping on the ice."

Emri was more than willing to avail himself of this suggestion, and he directed the tribe down to the shore, where they clustered at the water's edge.

The rocks were black and scored with a multitude of cracks and fissures, but they were free of snow and ice, having been warmed by the morning sun. The People of the Deer sank down on the rocks, grateful for the warmth.

Emri, Broken Tooth, Hawk, and Tusk walked as far out onto the rocks as was possible. Just as Broken Tooth had said, they extended quite a distance, and it was probable that the water was deep enough to attract fish, who would avoid the shallow water at the shoreline. And where there were fish, it was also possible that they would find the black water-beasts who fed upon the fish.

They had no fishhooks and no lines, but Emri and some of the other men quickly fashioned hooks, carving them out of bits of wood hacked from the wood above the charred base of the spear. Lines were cut from the edges of their tunics, and while thick, they were extra sturdy.

There was no bait to lure the fish, so tiny clumps of fur were cut off their outer garments and threaded on the hooks as well as the occasional feather. This had been known to attract the interest of the fish in other instances, and Emri hoped it would work again.

Mosca was much interested in their activities and put his large paw on trailing lines and jumped on the fluttering bits of fur and feather. It became necessary to drive him away with harsh words and pebbles, for the men did not share Emri's love of the big cat when he came between them and their hunting.

Larger stones were used to batter a hole through the ice, exposing the black, frigid water beneath. This water would kill any man unfortunate enough to fall in, the intense cold shocking the spirit right out of him.

The People of the Deer learned to respect and fear these waters at an early age and were always cautious. It only took one mistake, one slip, to kill; there were no second chances.

Holes were made on both sides of the causeway and hooks and lines dropped into the dark waters. The men stayed well back from the openings, stretching their bodies flat against the rocks, making certain that no hint of their shadow was cast on ice or water, for that would reveal their presence and drive away the fish and the black water-beasts.

Now it was but a matter of waiting. The sun grew hot on their backs and the rhythmic slap of water on the edge of the holes all but lulled them to sleep, but their hunger and that of the women and children kept them awake.

A short time later, Tusk gave a brief cry and pulled a long, fat fish from the water, overcoming its struggles by clubbing it on the head with a heavy stone. His face glowed with the success of his efforts, and he hooked his fingers through the gills of the fish and hurried back to shore, handing the fish over to the waiting women.

They caught more fish than the fingers on four hands before the sun had reached the roof of the sky. It seemed that the fish were as hungry as they, and the fur trim on their tunics was showing evidence of their depredations when they gave way to the demands of their own growling stomachs and headed back to shore.

The women gutted the fish, sliced them into large chunks, and placed them in the cooking sack with handfuls of snow, lichen, and moss. The resulting stew was both nourishing and filling.

With their bellies full, and warmed by the heat of the afternoon sun, the people were much heartened and they made good progress before camp was made for the night.

This time there were no sheltering stones, merely a slight dip in the earth, a place where water would run

when Warm Time returned to the land, melting the
snow and ice.

They had found more birds' eggs and two more honkers, as well as a variety of lesser birds and rodents,
brought down with skillful slings. One gangling adolescent named Tall Deer had startled a large rabbit, still
dressed in its winter white, and killed it with a well-
aimed stone. The cooking sack was well-filled, and no
one went to sleep that night with an empty belly.

The cold, however, was a greater danger than hunger. Despite the fire that burned bright throughout the
night, there was no shelter from the wind, which often
carried what heat the fire produced off into the darkness.

The people were not dressed for living outdoors in
the bitter cold. They had been asleep in their dwellings
wrapped in warm furskins at the time of the disaster
that destroyed their village. Only the fact that they
slept fully dressed—additional protection against the
cold that seeped into their dwellings—had enabled them
to survive this long. Walking and moving warmed them
during the day, but at night they suffered.

Even Mosca was troubled by the cold, for he had
grown accustomed to warming himself by the fires that
had burned constantly within the dwelling and disliked
being cold and wet. At night he squalled unhappily and
butted Emri and Hawk with the top of his head before
tunneling under their bodies, seeking whatever warmth
they had to share.

Several children had developed deep, racking coughs
and running noses when the camp wakened on the
morning of the third day, and Dawn and the other
women wore long faces as they discussed what might be
done. The few medicinal plants that might be available
to them were still hidden beneath the snow, and they
could do nothing but worry and hope that the children
would get better.

There were no more deaths, for which Emri was
grateful, but still, he knew all too well that the well-
being of the tribe was a fragile thing that could easily be
destroyed by a single event.

Such a thing nearly occurred on the morning of the fourth day. The camp was wakened by a series of shrill screams accompanied by deep, guttural roars. Scrambling to their feet, reaching for weapons that were not there, they saw an enormous white bear pawing at a woman who lay screaming on the ground. Though the bear's normal diet was water-beasts, he had no objection to eating man.

With only the one spear among them, they could not attack the bear directly. They would have been fearful of doing so in any case, for the bear was nearly two man-heights in length and possessed long curved claws, sharper than any knife, and powerful jaws, lined with teeth like jagged spear points.

Mosca hissed and yowled, the fur on his back and spine standing straight up. He clawed at the bear, from a very safe distance, and spat at his ancient enemy. The bear ignored the cat, still pawing curiously at the woman.

Emri seized a rock and threw it at the bear with all his might. The rock bounced off the bear's shoulder and he looked up, annoyed. Others followed Emri's lead and bombarded the bear with a barrage of stones. Still others banged stones together.

The bear stood up on its hind legs and pawed the air, roaring angrily. The men and even the women and children threw more and more rocks at the huge carnivore. Proud Bear, living up to his name, seized the spear out of Otuk's hands and held it in the tiny remains of the fire.

Ignoring Otuk's cries of alarm and knowing well that one spear could only anger such a deadly enemy, Proud Bear took the blazing spear, ran toward the white bear, and flung it full force at the huge creature's exposed abdomen.

The bear grunted as the spear penetrated its belly, swatting at the shaft and roaring loudly at the resulting pain. But now the flame could be seen crawling on the thick pelt.

The bear seemed confused, uncertain as to what was happening, but as his fur began to smolder, he dropped down onto all fours. As the weight of the bear came

parallel to the ground, the base of the spear's shaft
struck the ground, driving it in deeper.

The bear roared in pain and rage and hesitated for a
long moment. Its great jaws gaping wide, it stared at
the people who had somehow caused this unexpected
agony and tried to decide whether to attack.

But the people seized upon its indecision and increased the pace of their attack, pelting the bear with
stones. Mosca grew more bold and hissed and screeched
and yowled, though he took care to remain out of the
bear's reach.

The bear, coughing and growling, stood its ground
for a long heartbeat and then turned and ran, the spear
dragging along the ground between its legs.

Ragged cheers broke out briefly, and then everyone
rushed to the side of the woman who had been attacked. She lay huddled on the ground, unmoving, her
hands pressed to her face. Emri feared the worst until
it was found that she had suffered no more than a
clawed arm and a ripped tunic. She was more frightened than injured and for a long time could do little
more than sit and tremble and cry hysterically.

When it finally occurred to her that she was still alive
and the focus of everyone's attention, her entire attitude changed. Suddenly it seemed that she had never
been afraid and had screamed only so that the people
might be alerted, so confident was she in their ability to
kill the bear.

Emri turned away, a smile twitching at his lips. He
was glad that they had driven the bear away, for it was
a fearsome enemy and one that was hunted only by
large numbers of well-armed men. However, he was
extremely disturbed by the loss of their single spear.

He himself still possessed the red-and-black-streaked
obsidian knife, the knife that he and Hawk had fashioned so long ago which never left his side, not even
when he slept. The women also possessed the two
skinning knives. Three knives then were the only weapons among them all.

Bears were not the only predators that roamed this

barren wilderness. There were also large dire wolves and their slightly smaller but no less dangerous relatives the long-legged coyotes. Both could easily kill a man.

Emri did not speak of his fears, unwilling to shatter the high spirits that filled the people, but as his eyes met those of Hawk, Tusk, Broken Tooth, and Otuk, he knew that they too shared his concern.

CHAPTER THREE

The blood of the bear left a bright trail for them to follow, dripping and splashing at irregular intervals on the snow. The base of the spear cut a deep groove in the snow between the prints of its large paws.

Emri was not at all interested in following the bear, for a wounded bear was even more dangerous than a healthy bear. But the tracks were paralleling the shore, going in the same direction that they were traveling. There was nothing to be done but continue on and hope that it would change course.

Mosca alone was interested in the bloody trail. He forged ahead of them, his stubby tail quivering excitedly as he sniffed and inhaled through slightly parted jaws, drawing the salty essence of the blood across the sensitive olfactory glands situated on the roof of his mouth. Often he lapped the blood off the snow.

All day they followed the bloody trail, noticing more and more often that the bear appeared to stagger, his back legs going out from under him, leaving gouges in the snow where he pushed himself to his feet.

Brown birds with sharp beaks and hard eyes, those who often drifted above the water during Warm Time, disturbing the calm with their shrill, harsh voices, came to peck at the bloody snow along with the larger white birds. The fact that their flesh was stringy and tough did not protect them from the stones of the people, and several of their number were brought down.

A feeling of cautious excitement crept over the group as it began to seem that the bear had been more badly injured than they had first thought. It also appeared that the spear was still firmly lodged in the creature, for other than small bits of chewed wood, and the ongoing groove in the snow, it was not found. It seemed likely that the barbed point had accomplished its mission and was lodged deep in the bear's flesh.

The land had begun to rise, slowly at first and then more steeply, dropping off on the far side to the icy shore below. It was strenuous going for the travelers. Evidently it was no less difficult for the bear; for signs of its uneven progress were more and more evident.

Then they came to a great disturbance in the snow, and from the tracks they were able to piece together what had happened. The bear had attempted to climb a rocky outcrop on their left, but his claws had slipped and he had fallen a long distance, rolling over and over until he fetched up against an upright boulder. Here there was much blood and even more chewed wood.

They moved more carefully now. Even the children and Mosca were quiet, sensing that something momentous was about to happen. But by nightfall there was still no sign of the bear.

They found shelter that evening beneath a rocky overhang, a place where the earth had fallen away from a tilted strata of rock, leaving a deep cleft beneath it large enough to hold them all comfortably.

Some of the people were hesitant to stop in such a place, fearing that the overhang might crash down upon them in their sleep, much as the mountain of ice had done to their village. But Running Bird pressed through the crowd and made her way to the deepest point of the shelter, where the roof sloped down to the ground, and began to arrange stones in a circle, preparing a firepit.

"Come on, come on," she cried, looking up, her wrinkled face expressing surprise at seeing them still standing outside. "What are you waiting for? This old belly is hungry and wants to be fed. If you are not hungry, well, I will eat your share too!"

Emri choked back a bark of laughter as the rest of the people surged into the shelter, released from their fear by no more than a bit of good-natured teasing. He looked at Running Bird with new eyes, appreciating for the first time just how clever she was. He would do well to listen to her in the future.

Fire made all the difference that night. It chased away the dark shadows and reflected brightly off the back wall and rough overhang.

"This would be a good place to stay until we are better rested and our wounds have healed," said Tusk, who approached Emri with Otuk at his side.

"We ourselves are not tired, nor do we wish to stop," Otuk said hastily, lest he appear to be afraid. "But the women and children and old ones . . ."

Emri saw the wisdom of their words but feared stopping. Once they settled, it might be difficult to get them going again.

As though to bear out this thoughts, Proud Bear approached and said, "This would be a good place to stay. We have shelter here and protection from the wind, and already we have found more game than we had in the old village."

The other men murmured their agreement. Several of the women lifted their heads and listened to the exchange, and from the look in their eyes Emri could see that it had not been entirely the men's idea. A cold chill of alarm ran down his spine. He knew that he must stop this thinking immediately or face continuing argument on all sides.

"This is not a thing to be talked about over stomachs that growl with hunger. Nor a thing that should be decided quickly by a few when it will affect the many. Let us eat and talk about it later," he replied, seeing approval in Hawk's eyes. The men grumbled but could offer no reason to do other than Emri suggested.

The meal was prepared and duly eaten, and as Mosca crunched what bones had not been given to the infants to suck upon, the people gathered themselves around the fire and waited for Emri to speak.

"As you know, Hawk, Dawn, Broken Tooth, and I are not from this land. We journeyed here from far away," Emri began.

"Our land too has its Cold Time, but it stays less long and is not so bitter. There is much game there, game of many different kinds, and foods that grow thick on the ground and on the trees and may be had for the gathering. No one needs go hungry.

"It was the wish of your chief and your shaman that I lead you out of this land of cold and snow and guide you back to where the deer roam so that you may call yourselves in truth the People of the Deer.

"It is said that your stones told of our coming. Never have I known such stones that can speak of what is to come, but I have had visions of my own and know that such things are possible. If it is to be, I will not argue with the Gods but offer willingly to guide you to a better place."

There was a brief silence as the people thought about what Emri had said, and then, in their manner, they all began to speak at once.

The clamor of voices rose to such a din that Mosca raised his head from his bones and growled, but no one but Emri and Hawk paid heed.

"I do not wish to go to a land that I do not know," said Otuk, avoiding Emri's eyes, and others cried out their agreement. "How do we know that such things are true? How do we know that there are as many animals as you say and foods that lie upon the ground waiting to be eaten? Such things are hard to believe."

"It is true," Emri said quietly, and Hawk, Dawn, and Broken Tooth nodded in agreement.

"Then if it is so, why are you here?" asked one of the women, who cradled two children to her breast and looked at Hawk with angry eyes. "Why would you leave a land like that to come here where there is little but cold and hunger?"

"You know our story," Emri said patiently. "We were forced to flee our land, driven out by the hatred of our shaman. I came here because I had always dreamed of

seeing the Cold Lands with my own eyes. I did not know
that it would be such a cruel land and so hard to live."

"Cruel it may be, but it is *our* land," said Proud
Bear, rising from the middle of the group and walking
forward to face Emri, standing no more than four paces
distant in an almost confrontational stance.

"Our Gods smile on our courage and our bravery and
direct our spears to the hearts of the beasts. So long as
we are brave, they will not fail us. Are we cowards that
we should give up our lands and follow one who is
lacking in both years and wisdom into an unknown
world? I say that we should stay here in our own land,
among the things we know, rather than take this one's
word and travel into the unknown."

There was a sharp intake of breath, and all eyes
turned to Emri to see how he would reply, how he
would deal with this sudden assault on his leadership.

Emri himself was taken aback, not having seen the
challenge coming. He cursed his shortsightedness, for
now in hindsight it seemed totally logical that some
members of the tribe would not care to leave that
which was familiar for something that was entirely for-
eign. He did not even contemplate answering the charges
leveled by Proud Bear, for they were not rational. How
could any of them think kindly on Gods who had seen
fit to slay their entire tribe, sparing only the few survivors who gathered beneath the overhang. Emri knew
that it was not logic speaking, nor lack of courage, but
fear of the unknown.

What did surprise him was that Proud Bear had
delivered the ultimatum. Emri would have counted
him among the most forward-thinking of all the tribe,
one who could be counted on to assist him.

He searched for the words to convince Proud Bear
and the others that leaving the Cold Lands was the
right thing to do. Emri knew that they would have to
be powerful words or he would lose their respect and
allegiance, and they would cease to follow him.

The silence grew longer as he sought the proper
words, but he could think of nothing that would serve

to convince them. How could he prove that the land beyond was all that he said it was? There was no proof other than the seeing. The tension grew as the people stared at him, and even Running Bird watched to see what he would say.

"Why do we not ask the stones what to do?" Hawk said smoothly, shattering the tension with his unexpected words. All eyes, including Emri's, turned to Hawk.

Hawk reached into his tunic and pulled out two pouches that hung from leather thongs around his neck. He slipped them over his head and held them out on the palm of his hand for all to see.

"But how did you get them? Speaker always . . ." Otuk began, his words trailing off into silence.

"Speaker always wore the bags around his neck," Hawk replied, finishing the sentence. "He gave them to me the night before the mountain fell, the night before he died."

"Why?" asked the woman with the two children, her voice only slightly less strident. "Why did he give them to you?"

"I asked him that same question," said Hawk, staring at the pouches but seeing the night as it had happened. "He would only say that it was time. The next morning he was dead."

He lifted stricken eyes, remembering the man who had guided him in learning the ways of the spirits and the Gods, the man who had come to mean much to him during the long dark nights of Cold Time. The man whose loss he would mourn for long seasons to come.

"Do you wish me to read the stones?" he asked simply. With only slight murmurs of conversation, they nodded their assent.

Emri watched with concern as the people settled themselves around Hawk, careful not to jostle his arm or crowd in upon him. They were not yet convinced, but there was a new respect in them for this young stranger who had been entrusted with the tribe's most sacred objects.

Emri was not jealous of Hawk; their friendship was too deep and firm to be shaken. But he had been weak at a time when he needed to be strong, and Hawk had been forced to intervene. If they overcame this challenge successfully, it would be due to Hawk's efforts and not his own.

Dawn moved to his side as though guessing his thoughts and slipped her hand into his. For once the child was asleep, her head resting on Dawn's breast, chubby legs straddling her hip. Dawn smiled up at Emri, her dark brown eyes warm and loving in the firelight, and Emri felt the burden on his heart lighten.

They stood at the edge of the circle of people and watched as Hawk smoothed out a patch of damp earth next to the fire and carefully drew a circle two handspans in width. Next he loosened the leather drawstrings of one of the pouches, the heavier of the two, and held it out on the palm of his hand.

"This sack holds the symbols of many of the things that come into our lives: birth, death, game, water, snow, ice, fortune, disaster, strangers, friends, and the wishes of the Gods.

"This sack"—he said, lifting the smaller of the two pouches—"contains the helpers, those things that will further define the message of the Gods: a feather, a bit of greenery, a piece of dried food from a time of plenty, a bit of dry bone from a time of hunger, a piece of horn from a deer, a scrap of fur from a hairy tusker.

"All these and more are the helpers," Hawk said, more for effect than from the need to explain, for there were none among them who needed to be told how the stones worked. The stones governed every major decision the tribe made, as well as foretelling the future. Every member of the tribe knew that the stones spoke with the voice of the Gods and must be obeyed.

"The stones were given to the People of the Deer by the Gods," said Hawk. "The stones are all knowing, but it is our duty to use them correctly, adding new things from time to time if it becomes necessary, for the world changes as the Gods see fit and we must change with it. Nothing stays the same."

The people nodded and muttered among themselves in agreement, for was this not true? Had their world not changed? Collapsed around them, destroying all they had known? Their eyes shone bright with admiration for they were much impressed with Hawk's wisdom.

"We must place two new stones in the bag," said Hawk as he scanned the ground before him. "One stone will signify this land, the old land. Its presence will tell us that the Gods wish for us to stay here."

So saying, he picked up a smooth white stone from the ground and held it up so that all might see.

"We must also have a stone that signifies the new land, and should it appear, it will mean that the Gods wish for us to leave this place forever."

There was a deep silence at these words, but no voice spoke out in opposition, and no one challenged his interpretation of the Gods' wishes.

He picked up a stone from the ground and held it on high to be greeted by sharp gasps from his attentive audience. The stone was dark brown and heavily streaked with lines of sparkling crystal. It was a beautiful stone, unlike anything Emri had seen in this harsh and barren land. In fact, it looked very much like rocks they had found in the great rain forests on their journey north.

Emri looked at Hawk suspiciously, but Hawk stared resolutely at the people and avoided Emri's eyes. For the first time Emri began to wonder if the reading of the stones could be manipulated to suit one's own needs and purposes.

Hawk placed both stones, the white and the brown, in the first sack and placed the second sack on the ground beside him.

Next, he shook the sack thoroughly, jumbling the items within. Then he tossed his hand up, catching the bottom of the sack at the last instant. This action caused a number of items to tumble from the mouth of the sack and fall to the ground, while others remained in the sack itself.

Of those objects that fell to the ground, some fell inside the circle, while others landed outside the line. Those objects that fell outside the line, Hawk picked up and returned to the pouch.

Without looking overly much at the objects inside the circle, Hawk followed the same procedure with the sack that contained the items deemed helpers, those whose purpose was to define and further clarify the items from the first sack.

Although Hawk's manner was cool and detached, the circle was all but obscured from view as the people leaned in over it, commenting aloud on those things that had fallen inside the circle, interpreting freely while comments buzzed through the air like a hive of angry stingers disturbed on a hot day in Warm Time.

Hawk allowed them their comments. Then as silence fell and all eyes turned to him, he crouched beside the circle and studied it carefully.

Only Emri stood upright, alone and isolated as he watched the actions that would decide their future being played out on the stone floor. Even Dawn had left his side and now leaned over Running Bird, anxious to see what had fallen.

Separated by more than his posture, Emri looked at the gathering of people and wondered at his own caring, the fact that this ragged remnant of a tribe should matter so much to him, considering their fickle behavior.

Even Hawk seemed different. With a shock Emri seemed to view him for the first time, and his features were as those of a stranger. Hawk was no longer the young fearful boy he had been when they first met. In the seasons that had passed, Hawk had become a man, no longer dependent on Emri, capable of making his own way in the world and deciding his own future. Emri knew that he should feel happy, but instead, he was saddened and filled with a sense of loss.

"There is much game," said Running Bird, drawing Emri's attention back to the present. "Look, there is the feather and the horn of the deer and the bison fur and the seeds and the dried berry. The Gods will fill our bellies."

"There is death, too," said the woman with the two children. "See, there is the black stone. We will all die if we go to the new land. The Gods are telling us to stay here where we belong!"

"If that is the Gods' wish, then why did the brown stone land within the circle and the white stone fall far outside the lines?" Hawk asked calmly. "Our path is clear. The Gods are telling us to go to the new land."

There was a moment of silence as all eyes rested on Hawk, and he pointed out the signs one after the other.

"And the death stone?" asked that same woman, determined to be heard.

"Death must come to us all," Hawk said softly. "But who is to know what the death stone speaks of? There are animals in the circle as well as men. It could be their death the stone foretells. But even if it is our own, death comes in its own time and there is no way to avoid it. When the Gods wish for us to join the spirits, it does not matter if we go willingly or squalling, the outcome will be the same.

"Here, however, our path is clear. The Gods are telling us to go to the new land. If you wish to disagree, do not speak to me, but send your words directly to the Gods. Perhaps they will listen."

There was little the people could say, for it was clear, even to the most fearful, that Hawk had spoken honestly. There was no other way to interpret the stones. Everything that was familiar to them, everything that signified their old land, had clearly fallen outside the circle. The Gods had shown them their will.

"We will follow you to the new lands," Otuk said, standing up and meeting Emri's gaze full on. Though there were murmurs from some of the others, none spoke out against him.

Having made the momentous decision, or rather, having it made for them, the people turned almost festive. The men relaxed in front of the fire and played with the children as the women filled the cooking sack a second time and set it over the flames. Only Emri's heart was heavy and filled with sadness.

He turned away when Hawk approached, a wide grin lighting his slender features, and strode out into the cold night. Darkness suited his mood far more than the cheerful firelight. He felt Dawn and Hawk's eyes on his back and knew his manner to be rude and abrupt, but his chest ached with pain and it was more than he could bear.

"Emri!" cried Hawk, and he followed his friend out into the chill night. "Emri, do not turn away. We have come too far and endured too much for you to turn away from me," he said softly, following close on Emri's heels. "Have I done something to offend you?"

Emri stopped and looked up at the dark dome of the sky. The campfires of the ancestors glittered brightly above him and he wondered if his father were viewing his actions, seeing his shame.

"You have done *something*—which is more than I can say," Emri said bitterly, clenching his fists so tightly that the nails dug into the flesh of his palm. "It is *I* who have done nothing."

"What are you saying, Emri?" Hawk's voice was filled with confusion. "We would not be here, now, were it not for you. You have done everything."

"No, my friend, I have done nothing. I could not save the people. I could not make them leave the cave of ice before it collapsed; I could not make them go. And even this small group, I do not lead them. They have followed me thus far because they were overwhelmed with sadness and their minds were in turmoil.

"It was Broken Tooth who thought of a way to fish when we were hungry. It was Proud Bear who threw the spear and drove the bear away. It was Running Bird who got them to go into the shelter. It is you who has convinced them to continue on. I pray that my father's spirit does not see me; he would not be proud."

"Emri, you blame yourself wrongly and find offense where none should be taken," Hawk said softly, drawing his friend farther away from the shelter so that their words would not be overheard.

They stopped in the lee of the rocks, where the full brunt of the wind could not reach them. Hawk turned to Emri and said, "Are we not brother to the lion?"

"Yes," Emri said dully, unable to see what that had to do with the matter at hand.

"Think for a time on the manner in which the leader of the lions governs his family," said Hawk. "Does he personally kill all the game needed to feed the pride? Does he himself settle all disputes? Does he interfere in the daily existence of the clan?

"No, my friend. He depends on the best hunters to feed the family. He allows the arguments to be settled between the parties involved, and he gives the daily running of the clan over to the women. Each does what he or she is best at; each has his role to play. The leader is just that. Whether the leader of lions or of men, there is no difference."

"But Hawk, I did not lead. I just stood there and let them overwhelm me. The words did not come. I did not know what to say. If you had not acted, they would never have agreed to leave this place. I have failed. I am not fit to be a leader."

"No, Emri. You are wrong. I did not speak to save you, but because it was fitting that I do so. The stones were needed to give us direction, to tell us the wishes of the Gods. That is why I spoke. You are still the leader and where you lead, I will follow."

"*Aowww!*" cried Mosca, startling them both, for neither man realized that the cub had followed them.

"Ho!" cried Hawk. "This one agrees. Are we not all brother to the lion?"

"*Aowww!*" complained Mosca, shivering in the cold wind.

Emri smiled. "You are right, my brother, and your words hold wisdom. Let us return to the warmth of fire and friends."

Mosca followed close at their heels as Emri and Hawk made their way back to the shelter.

CHAPTER FOUR

The weather turned bitter before dawn. The wind switched direction and hurtled down on them from the north, sweeping all the damp cold of the ice fields before it.

The mouth of the shelter faced south, but still, the wind gained access from the east. Freak gusts made occasional frontal assaults, threatening to extinguish the flames and choking them all with smoke.

Had they been farther south, it would have been short work to weave a latticework of saplings to block off the opening, but there were no trees as yet. In a desperate attempt to protect themselves from the cruel wind, they tried to seal off the opening by erecting a wall of rocks and boulders. This was somewhat effective, shutting out the worst of the weather, but the wind still whistled through the cracks. It soon became apparent, even to the most stubborn among them, that the overhang would never serve as a permanent shelter.

Quarrels broke out and tempers flared over the next several days, aggravated by a shortage of food and firewood and the closeness of quarters. The children seemed to cry endlessly and Mosca paced back and forth restlessly, moaning his displeasure.

Everyone was pleased when the sun emerged on the morning of the third day. They spilled out of the shelter like stones from Hawk's upturned sack, eager to be on their way.

There were no indications that the people were in

any way reluctant to follow Emri. In the glory of the new day, he lifted his face to the brilliant blue sky that stretched above him and smiled.

He confidently chose a path between the jumbled boulders and rugged outcrops, always taking the easiest path to aid the passage of the women, children, and old ones.

As they crested a great hump of windswept land that rose high above the ice-choked shoreline, they nearly stumbled over a huge mass of birds writhing on the ground before them. Wasting no time, they hurled their stones and felled more than the fingers on two hands before the birds took to the air with outraged cries and a loud flapping of wings.

Much to their surprise they discovered the white bear lying dead on the ground. The birds had pecked out its eyes and turned its nose, lips, and tongue to bloody gruel, but the body, protected by the heavy yellowish white pelt and thick hide, was nearly intact.

The area around the wound had also attracted their sharp beaks, and the putrid stench that issued from the gaping hole was enough to cause the people to cover their mouths and turn aside.

No smell would have kept them from taking the pelt, valuable for the warmth that it would bring on even the coldest of nights. But, other than the great canines and the curved claws, that was all they would take from the bear. The flesh was tainted with the scent of sickness and the fat—what little there was—was a peculiar shade of green and the women wanted none of it.

The spear point was recovered by the men after the pelt was peeled off the great carcass. It was found deep in the lower abdomen, its cruel barbs still buried in a loop of intestine. It was here that the death had its origin. The toxic fluids had leaked out of the perforated tube and spread throughout the abdomen, poisoning the bear's entire system until it died.

Proud Bear was much praised. He basked in the admiration of the two young women Leaping Fawn and Sunshine, who had slept by his side since the journey

began, even when the fire was warm enough to do the
job. Watching them rub themselves against the body of
the young hunter, Emri knew that the rites of joining
had best be said soon, or there would be trouble.

No sooner had they turned their backs on the stink-
ing carcass than the birds returned, more eager than
ever now that the hide had been removed. Their stones
brought down more birds, which were scarcely even
noted by the raucous throng as they fought for purchase
on the slippery corpse. More might have been killed,
for they were easy prey, but their stringy flesh and
fishy taste kept them safe as the tribe continued their
journey.

Cold nights and warm days became the pattern. Frost
and ice and sometimes even snow coated the ground
each night and melted in the warm, bright days that
followed. Usually they were able to find some form of
shelter, but not always.

Still, their cooking bags were never empty and their
accumulation of pelts and featherskins was growing,
allowing each of them to fill out their meager ward-
robes and add warmth and ornament to their bodies.

They had met no other large carnivores, although
they had been paced through two days and a night by a
pack of dire wolves so thin that every rib was outlined
beneath their shaggy coats. A barrage of stones had kept
them at bay during the day and the fire had held them
off at night. They vanished one morning and were not
seen again, perhaps having decided to search for easier,
more defenseless prey.

They saw their first bush one morning. Though its
low, outspread branches scarcely rose above the crust
of snow, it was cause for elation. None of the women
and children had ever seen such a thing, their only
knowledge of plant life being ground-hugging sedges,
tough lichens, the moss that grew on the sunny sides of
boulders and the long green strands of vegetation that
sometimes floated up onto the shore. They had foraged
for tree limbs and other bits of wood that had floated

through the vagaries of current onto their cold shores, but never had they seen a tree or a bush with their own eyes.

It was an unremarkable little bit of vegetation, its branches numbering no more than the people among them, and no leaves had yet dared to brave the frigid weather, but the women and children stood around it in a circle and spoke of it with awe, pointing out each of its remarkable properties to each other at length and with much repetition.

Emri was only able to persuade them to move by telling them that it was but the first of many to come, promising them others of infinite variety. Afraid of missing something even more astounding and looking at him as though he were a great and powerful shaman who had single-handedly produced the bush out of thin air, they hurried after Emri with bright eyes.

"This land is beginning to look familiar," Dawn said late that afternoon. "See that low-lying bog over there. I think that it was the second such. It was near the first that we found a large patch of berries. If the Gods will it, perhaps we will find them still."

Her eye was good and her remembrance of the land unerring. She was able to guide them to the tangle of thorny bushes, though they were situated in a low crease of the land and still covered by a hard skin of ice and a blanket of snow.

The snow and ice were a blessing in disguise, for they had protected the berries. Although much withered, they had frozen solid on the thorny canes. When plucked free, they melted with an incredible burst of sweet flavor upon the tongue.

To a people all but starved of any but the barest necessities of life, it was an incredible luxury. They quartered the berry patch, scouring even the ground itself for the sweet treasure. Only when they were certain that there were no more to be found would they leave.

It was as though the berries were an omen. The land

opened itself to them, loosing a flood of bounties that their numbed minds had scarcely imagined, much less hoped for.

Emri, Hawk, Dawn, and Broken Tooth were the guides to this rapturous new land, pointing out each new wonder and explaining how it was used.

The seasons had turned once more, and the land was born anew. With it came a rush of life so sweet as to cause an ache of joy in one's heart.

The wind was warm and came from the south, soughing and sighing in heavy waves above the land. It touched the land lightly, as though by caress alone it could waken the life that had vanished during Cold Time.

Grasses and sedges poked up through the remnants of vanishing snowdrifts and turned from brown to pale green almost before their wondering eyes. Tiny bushes sprouted fragile leaves with delicate veins. Birds appeared, not the white and brown birds that wheeled above the waters shrieking out their strident cries, but small graceful birds tinted blue and rose and yellow, who sang and trilled in melodious ripples as they darted over the greening plains. These they did not kill. To have eaten them would have been a sacrilege. Nor was it necessary to add the birds to the cooking sacks, for animal life had returned as well. Rabbits had popped from the earth as though by magic. They were everywhere, studding the green grasses like white boulders as they fed on the tender vegetation. Still dressed in their winter pelts of white, they were highly visible targets.

One evening as they were looking for a campsite, there was a loud outcry from the children, who had been allowed to run ahead. The adults hurried to catch up, thinking that the children might have stumbled on some dangerous animal. They found the youngsters leaping up and down with excitement and pelting something on the ground with stones.

It was a large pricker-back and the children had been

wise to stand aside. While it was little threat in itself, it was covered from head to toe with prickers, each longer than the length of a man's hand. These prickers were barbed in some mysterious way, and once they lodged in one's skin, it was often necessary to cut them out.

The pricker-back circled in turn, trying to keep its attackers in view. It blinked its large round eyes and looked at them in pain and confusion. It had long claws, but they were only used for digging and clawing at roots, and its broad teeth were of no use against man.

A well-aimed stone felled the pricker-back. The women flipped it over and slit its throat so swiftly that Emri could scarcely believe that they had never seen one before.

Dawn tried to warn them about the prickers, but many of the women were pricked before they had learned the lesson for themselves. By that time the children had joined in, despite the women's warnings, and they began to chase each other round and round, armed with a handful of the barbed darts plucked from the dead animal.

It was obvious that they would go no farther that day, for the children's high spirits had become infectious. Proud Bear pricked Leaping Fawn on her rump and she gave a loud shriek and dropped her bundle. Recovering from the shock, she armed herself with a switch torn from a bush and began chasing Proud Bear around and around, much to the amusement of the children. This seemed to loose something in them all. Soon, nearly everyone had joined the game, pelting friends and companions with pebbles, prickers, twigs, bits of grass, and whatever else came to hand.

Emri was standing beside Running Bird, watching Dawn and Hawk chase each other as the child gamboled behind. He was smiling to himself, thinking that it was good to see them laugh again, when something struck him hard against the back of his knees. So strong was the blow that he toppled face forward onto the damp ground, throwing up his arms only at the last moment. No sooner had he hit the ground than a great weight fell upon his back and head, forcing his face into the earth. Dimly he heard a great growling and felt his tunic jerked and pulled roughly against his throat. Mosca!

He flung himself over on his back, taking the cat by surprise and throwing him to the ground. Before the cat could recover, Emri hurled himself at the cub, screaming loudly and waving his hands above his head. Mosca stared at him with wide eyes, unmoving until it was too late. Emri fell upon him and crushed him against the ground, holding all four paws in one hand aided by the full weight of his body so that the cat could not use them.

"Gotcha this time, little one," he cackled. "You always get me, but this time, I've got you! Now we'll see how you like it!" And despite the cat's ferocious growls and frenetic struggles, Emri teased the cat until it was nearly wild, sprinkling its head and snapping jaws with handfuls of grass and dangling his fingers just out of reach.

When finally he loosed the cat, Mosca sprang to his feet and a great chase ensued. Soon everyone had joined in, and they raced round and round in circles until they collapsed on the ground gasping for breath, exhausted but happier than they had been for a long, long time.

The shaman had thought on the problem and realized that the distance was too great. His powers were not strong enough to allow him to send the tiger spirit against his enemies. Further glimpses had given him the knowledge that the enemy was on the move, traveling back toward the land that had been their home. There were others with them as well, but that did not matter. Nothing mattered except the fact that soon they would be within his reach.

His hatred was like a live thing that dwelled inside his belly. A brief glimpse of the enemy's suffering warmed him with a heat far greater than one built with sticks and fire. The sound of their laughter struck deep to heart and gut, bringing pain as real as that caused by the point of a spear. And knowledge of the friendship and love that bound the four together was the most painful of all.

The shaman watched over them as they journeyed south, drawing closer and closer. Soon, they would be within his grasp. Soon they would be his.

CHAPTER FIVE

It was Running Bird who saw the smoke first. She wakened them all with her loud cries. The smoke rose straight as the shaft of a spear into the clear blue morning sky.

It was thicker than any column of smoke that Emri had ever seen, and he and the other men drew together to discuss it.

"Is it the fire of a large village?" Otuk asked Emri, thinking that since he had traveled so far he must surely know. "If so, it must be a very large camp."

"Such a village would have many, many men. And many women as well," Proud Bear added, and Emri wondered which of the two interested him the most.

"There would be safety in joining such a tribe," said Tusk. "Their spears would be many and the game would fall before them like snow on the wind."

"There would also be much hunger with many empty bellies to fill when Cold Time comes and the animals are gone from the land," said Otuk.

"Perhaps their hearts would not be gladdened to see us," Hawk murmured thoughtfully, recalling his own tribe's difficulties with the Tiger clan. "Maybe it would be best to avoid them. What do you think, Emri?"

All eyes turned to Emri. For a moment he felt his throat tighten, but then he caught Hawk's eye and the moment passed.

"The smoke is still many days distant. I do not know what it is. There is too much smoke to be but one village. Perhaps it is a gathering of clans—or it may not be people at all. It may be only a fire such as those set by the spears of the Gods during a storm. Let us journey in that direction. If it is man, we will see signs long before we reach the boundaries of their village. If it is not man, then we will find out what it is."

There was much nodding of heads and murmurs of agreement at his words. Even the women approved, which Emri had begun to learn was a greater indication of merit than the voices of the men. One unhappy woman could upset the best of plans.

The land continued to unfold before them, greening perceptibly. Fat earth diggers emerged from their burrows, sleepy and bemused, skin hanging from their frames like that of wrinkled old men.

Flowers, tiny little things with pointed petals that opened only after the sun had warmed them, crouched in the grass and lifted their golden centers to the sun. Brown and black bears had emerged from hidden dens, the females with tiny fat cubs trailing at their heels, and the immense males, solitary and fierce.

The bears were carefully avoided, for they were more dangerous now than at any other time of the year other than the rutting season. Much as they might wish it, it seemed unlikely that the Gods would see fit to give them a second bear.

Foxes, still whitely clad in their Cold Time garb, flitted about like tiny spirits. All but invisible until they moved, they pounced on mice and other small creatures hidden in the thick grasses and leaped high in the air for flying insects, their pointed snouts snapping.

The insects were one of the biggest problems—even more of a worry than food. They had hatched in vast numbers with the onset of warm weather. They swarmed through the air in such great numbers that at times they appeared as dark clouds vibrating above the ground. They bit; they stung; they raised welts that itched and hurt. They crawled into every open orifice, making life a misery that bordered on madness.

The women sought out the plants whose juice would

protect them from the biting, stinging plague, but there were too few plants to do much good. Mud was another effective remedy that Hawk's tribe had used, but the earth was composed of a gritty, crumbled rocklike substance that failed to adhere to their skin. Smoke was also of use, but they had no dwellings to huddle inside and the smoke just blew away on the open lands. In the end, there was no solution but to continue on.

"Let us return to the edge of the water," Emri said at last, unable to stand the crying of the children or the sight of their swollen, irritated flesh. "The winds off the water will blow the insects away."

"But that way will take us away from the smoke!" said Otuk. "We will lose the people!"

"We will lose *our* people if we continue on this path," replied Emri. "The insects will not last forever. We will continue on when they are gone."

Dawn's grateful glance told him that he had made the right decision, and there were no other voices raised against him.

So accustomed were they to living beside the water that it seemed as though they had met an old friend upon returning to the shore. They found a deep bay, a cul-de-sac, lined with gentle cliffs, tall enough to protect them from the worst of the winds and possessing a broad beach piled high with silvery driftwood.

Emri and Hawk showed the people how to construct a dwelling out of the wood, driving the longest pieces into the sand and using them as supports to intertwine with shorter lengths. Sedges and long grasses filled in the remaining spaces. Soon they had a dwelling large enough to hold them all and protect them from both insects and weather.

A good-size stream entered the bay through a narrow opening in the cliffs and provided them with fresh drinking water. The waters of the bay itself were still choked with ice, but it was soft and floated heavily, sinking lower and lower with every rising dawn.

Fishing was good. On the morning of the third day the men were fortunate enough to corner a water-beast as it sunned itself on the rocks and killed it with a barrage of stones. The sleek pelt, as well as the fat-layered flesh, was welcomed with loud cries from the women, and the cooking sacks hung full and heavy above the smoky fires.

The people slowly put their lives back in order with the easy flow of days so much like those they had known before the mountain of ice destroyed their village.

The days passed quickly, each slightly warmer and longer than the one before. The people grew as sleek as water-beasts, their bellies filled and their bodies clothed with the furs of their kills.

Tools were made—scrapers and flensers and sharp-pointed hooks and awls from a variety of stones, shells, and wood—but no matter how hard they searched, they were unable to find the proper type of stone for the making of spear points.

Life was good along the edges of the pleasant bay, yet Emri knew in his heart that it would not do to linger here. Cold Time would come again and finding them still here would trap them in this hostile land. It would be hard to make the people leave, but the longer it was delayed, the harder it would become.

Even as he pondered how to persuade the people to leave, Proud Bear was marking off the spot where he intended to build his own dwelling. A dwelling for himself and the two young women.

In tribes of many women and few men, it was not uncommon for a man to lie with more than one woman. But in tribes such as theirs, where there were not enough women, it was frowned upon. Already Emri had watched Tusk's face darken with resentment as he looked at Proud Bear, who had once been his best friend. And Proud Bear himself was boastful, making no effort to conceal his prowess with his women.

Proud Bear had not actually gone so far as to openly challenge Emri's leadership, but Emri knew that it lurked always at the back of the man's mind. Should Emri oppose him on the issue of the women or the dwelling, or anything else for that matter, the matter might well come to a head.

Emri was younger than Proud Bear by several Warm Times. He had traveled farther and seen much, but so far as the tribe knew, he was not as proven a hunter as Proud Bear. Nor had he distinguished himself in any way other than being chosen by their old leader, based upon nothing more than a prophecy. As yet he had not even organized a large kill. This, as everyone knew, was the true basis by which one judged the ability of a chief.

Emri felt the eyes of the tribe on him as Proud Bear stepped off the perimeter of his new dwelling. Emri approached and watched silently as the man carefully marked where each support pole would stand. He said nothing, merely looking on with his hands clasped behind his back.

For a time Proud Bear pretended that he did not see Emri. Then, when it became impossible to pretend any longer, he looked up with an expression of surprise drawn across his face.

"Ho, Emri, I see you," said Proud Bear. "Have you come to help me build my dwelling?"

This was dangerously close to an insult, but Emri did not rise to the bait. Instead he said in a pleasant tone, "I can if you wish the help. Actually I was but wondering who will live in this fine dwelling when we are gone. Perhaps the water-beasts will like it."

"Gone? I am not going anywhere," Proud Bear said with a frown, his dark eyes glinting dangerously. "This is my new dwelling where I will live with my women. No water-beasts will make it their home!"

"That is too bad. I had hoped to have your strong spear at my side. Well, we will have to do the best we can without you." Emri turned and began to walk away. Those people who had been listening to the exchange drew even closer, while pretending not to listen.

"Where is it you are going?" Proud Bear asked casually, as he strolled along next to Emri as though they were the best of friends.

"Hunting. It is time for a hunt and I had hoped that

you would go too. There are not many arms as good as yours with a spear. And now that you have made a new shaft to fit the spearhead, well . . . I know how much it will bother you to have another use it. It's too bad, really, but of course the spear must go with the tribe."

Emri turned and made as if to leave again, but Proud Bear clasped his arm and held him tight, all pretense gone.

"What kind of hunt? More rabbits and water-beasts?"

"No," replied Emri, without commenting on Proud Bear's touch, which was against all tribal etiquette. For a man to lay hands on another, unbidden, was to invite conflict. "I had thought that we would hunt for deer."

"Deer!" exclaimed Proud Bear, his eyes growing bright and electrifying the onlookers with that magical word—for the deer was the totem of their tribe.

"Yes," Emri said casually. "It is deer weather. They will be on the move and it is time that we were too."

"Where would you look for them?"

"In the hills where the smoke was rising. They will be searching out the new grass. If the Gods are with us, we will find them."

"We will find them," Proud Bear said confidently. "And they will fall under my spear like fire before rain."

"Your spear?" Emri asked in a puzzled tone. "Does this mean that you are coming with us? What about your dwelling? Who will build it if you go with us?"

"Pah! Let the water-beasts build it. A man cannot concern himself with such things when the deer are waiting!"

Emri smiled to himself. As he listened with interest as Proud Bear expounded upon where and how they might find the deer, Emri wished that all his problems might be solved so easily.

The entire tribe, with the exception of Proud Bear's women, was excited by the news of the impending hunt. Hawk was somewhat bemused by the suddenness of the project, for Emri had not mentioned it to him in any of their frequent conversations. He was mollified by Emri's explanation and laughed at his solution.

"That one," he said with a laugh, "will always be led by hunting or women. It is all he cares about. But do not look for his women to be happy."

Hawk had not needed his stones to accurately predict the women's reaction. They were most annoyed at the loss of their own dwelling and Emri took care to stay out of their path.

Dawn sat cross-legged on the sandy beach and watched contentedly as Mosca pawed lazily at the fat toddler, who shrieked with glee every time the cat's paw came anywhere close.

"It seems happy these days," Emri said as he sank down beside her. "There is enough food for its belly and that is all they think of at that age."

"She is a girl, not an it," Dawn said with mock anger. "Do you not see the curls and the dimples in her cheeks and the eyes that sparkle so brightly? No boy looks like that!"

Emri looked at the fat toddler, who fell more often than she walked, and smiled to see her happiness. He remembered the drawn face screaming with hunger such a short time before.

"It . . . she, wears far too many clothes for anyone but its mother to know what it is," he replied, "but I will take your word for it."

"I have named her Birdsong for she twitters and chirps all the day long. None of the women remember what name her mother gave her," said Dawn.

"Birdsong, it suits her," said Emri. Growing serious, he laid his palm upon Dawn's distended belly and rubbed it lightly, hoping to feel the kick of the infant within.

"And this one," he said quietly. "What of it? Will it be a boy or a girl?"

"It will be a boy. So that his father may teach him all he knows about bravery and wisdom and living his life with honor."

"I will care for it no matter what it is, boy or girl,"

said Emri. "And it will learn as much from its mother as from me about bravery and honor."

An easy silence fell upon them, yet Dawn knew from a lifetime of observing Emri that something remained unsaid. She did not speak, knowing that he would tell her in his own time. Finally, after Mosca and the child had collapsed in a heap and gone to sleep, Emri picked up a snail shell and examined it closely as though he had never seen such a thing before. Dawn knew that he was about to speak.

"Should I take the entire tribe on the hunt or should I leave some people here and return?" he asked casually.

"Some people?" Dawn asked with raised eyebrows. "Some people who just might be carrying a child?"

"Well, yes," Emri said uncomfortably, wondering how she always knew exactly what he was thinking. "But also those old ones who might find the journey difficult. And little ones too."

"Emri, you need us all, young and old, if there is to be a hunt. And you know it. You need the old ones with their knowledge and the little ones to help drive the beasts and make noise. Most of all, you need everyone to carry. There will be no time to return for anyone. We will be of no use to you here."

"But, what if . . ."

"Nothing will happen, Emri," Dawn said gently, knowing that he was remembering the child that had been lost during the violent crossing of another bay. "The Gods will watch over me and all will be well."

Emri looked down at his hands, large and square and capable, yet totally useless during the birth of a child. He nodded, hoping that she was right.

CHAPTER SIX

It was with great sadness the tribe left their camp on the edge of the peaceful bay, so pleasant had been their stay, yet they looked ahead with even greater excitement.

They traveled more swiftly now that they had a direction and a purpose. The smaller children, those who could not keep up, were carried on the women's hips or bound across their chests and backs with lengths of furskins. Their few possessions and stores of smoked fish, meat, and birds were also packed in pouches of rabbit skin and carried by the women.

The men and Mosca ranged ahead of the women, searching the gently rippling landscape for the first sight of deer or any other large game. The adolescents, two boys and a girl, were allowed to travel with the men so long as they remained silent.

The feeling was festive but controlled, for much rode on the hunt. One good kill would feed them for a long time and could be smoked and dried and stored against the coming Cold Time. If the Gods smiled on them and helped them with the hunt, they would be able to replace all that they had lost and more.

The land rose and fell in gentle folds, concealing little. If there was game, they would see it.

Behind them, to the west, lay the Endless Waters. To the north were the Cold Lands, still locked in their mantle of blue-white ice. Ahead of them to the east lay the great mountain ranges capped with ice and snow.

To the south lay the land that held all the wonders that Emri had promised.

They set a course that would take them southeast, into the foothills of the mountains, where the game would hopefully gather and they might find stone for spear points and wood for spear shafts and throwing sticks and clubs.

Much to their surprise, the plume of smoke still rose high into the air, a great column, thicker than any they had ever seen. If it was indeed a gathering of people, it was larger than any village they had known and possessed more firewood than could be imagined. Their course would take them near the column of smoke and allow them to see for themselves who or what had caused it.

They saw no game the first day other than rabbits, whose coats were now as brown as the tall bracken that covered the hills. Fleet of foot, they were difficult to catch, even for Mosca, whose energy was quickly depleted in short, fast spurts.

On the second day the sharp eyes of one of the adolescents, a tall, thin girl named Shell, spotted a trio of figures that grew larger as the day drew to a close.

Their hearts beat with excitement as they whispered among themselves wondering what the creatures might be. Stags, bison, great sloths, animals from Emri's knowledge, not their own, were guessed. It was not until the soft purple shadows of evening lengthened across the rolling hills that they had drawn close enough to see that the creatures were hairy tuskers. There was a large female, a small calf, and an immense male whose twisted tusks projected far beyond his questing trunk and were so heavy as to bow his head down.

Alarm coursed through Emri's body as he recognized the huge animals. He stopped immediately and a wave of sickness washed over him. The rest of the men stopped as well. The death of their village was vivid in their minds as they remembered the carnage that had ensued when the village was overrun by a herd of tuskers shortly before the mountain of ice fell.

Emri's memories were of another family of tuskers—
the newborn infant killed by the pride of cave lions that
had allowed Hawk and him to share their quarters that
first Cold Time the two had spent on their own. The
memories of the lions were as real and as painful as was
the loss of many of the People of the Deer. None of
them had any desire to hunt the tuskers. Nor was it
possible. They still possessed only the single spear, and
tuskers required far more weapons and a great many
people if there was to be even a hope of success.

The men hid themselves in a low pocket of land and
made an early camp as they waited for the remainder of
the tribe to join them. They were silent as they went
about their chores. There was none of the easy, good-
natured chatter that usually accompanied their meals as
they made do with dried meat and the eggs and ground
foods that the women had gathered during the day.

As they had traveled, Hawk had begun accumulating
smooth flat rocks and bits of plants and earth that might
be used for the making of likenesses. Now, while the
sun still shone, shedding its welcome warmth, he took
out his materials and drew the likeness of a deer upon
the flat surface of a rock.

A small child was the first to notice, and he sat
quietly at Hawk's feet and watched intently as the
figure took shape, growing more and more lifelike with
every motion of the burnt stick. When he was finished
with the first likeness, Hawk laid it aside and began a
second.

Emri sat beside Hawk and watched his friend's fingers move, no less entranced than the child by the
magic in the tiny charred stick.

A doe, her sides bulging and heavy with calf, joined
the first drawing—that of a buck with widespread
antlers—as Hawk picked up a third stone and continued drawing. Five more deer, sleek and fat, took their
places behind the stag before Hawk took up yet another stone and with quick, sure motions drew an accu-
rate likeness of Proud Bear with spear held on high.

A sharp intake of breath caused Emri to turn. Unheard and unnoticed, most of the tribe had gathered behind them and were watching Hawk with openmouthed amazement.

So rapt was Hawk's attention that he was not even aware of the crowd who hung on his every move. Finishing the likeness of Proud Bear, he picked up one final stone, the largest of all. After examining his supply of materials, he chose one that left a smooth white mark and began again.

This last drawing showed Proud Bear plunging his spear deep into the heart of the stag while another deer lay dying at his feet. The drawing done, Hawk placed the stone among the others and then hung his head as though too exhausted to move.

The others, though, were caught up in an excitement too great to stifle. Loud voices broke out, comments on the likenesses of the deer and that of the man. Their bright voices washed over Hawk like the cackle of honkers and he looked up, startled by their presence.

"What do you do now?" they asked him, their eyes bright with newborn admiration.

"Do? What do you mean?" he asked in surprise.

"Do we pray to the Gods for the success of the hunt? What shall we use for an offering?"

Eager hands reached for the drawings, touching them with respect as though they were precious gifts from the Gods themselves.

Emri knew that Hawk did drawings such as these often, but he seldom had an audience other than Emri himself. The Toads had beaten Hawk and threatened him with harm if he continued, thinking the likenesses would draw the attention of evil spirits.

The making of likenesses was a private thing for Hawk and one he would not willingly share. He reached out and tried to take the stones back, but the people would not let them go. The likenesses were carried back to the fire so that everyone might see.

Proud Bear was extremely taken with the likeness of himself and would not put it down. He rushed from one person to the next, drawing their attention to the least detail.

At last it was decided that the likenesses would act as totems. An offering would be burned before them in hopes that the Gods were listening and would answer their prayers and send them the deer they prayed for.

At first Hawk would have nothing to do with the ceremony and sulked on the edge of the camp, his shoulders rigid with anger. Emri came up and stood beside him. He said nothing, merely lending his presence.

Dawn was less subtle, approaching Hawk directly and standing in front of him where she could not be ignored.

"I don't see what you're so upset about," she said, adjusting the child on her hip. "It can't hurt anything to let them make their offering. It might even make them feel better. And if the Gods hear them and send us the deer, your likenesses will have done us a great good."

"They were not meant to be totems," Hawk said stubbornly, his face flushed with anger. "They are mine."

"Pah!" Dawn spat, angry at Hawk for the first time that Emri could recall. Her dark eyes seemed to spark and she leaned forward, her face a mere handspan from Hawk's. "Do you think of no one but yourself?" she asked angrily. "What harm can it do to share this thing with them? Are they so special, these lines, that you must keep them hidden away where only you can see them? Well, keep them, then, we do not need them. We will make our offerings without them. If the Gods wish to hear us, they will do so with or without your help!" So saying, she transferred the child to her other hip with an angry thump and strode away.

Emri and Hawk looked at each other in amazement. Never had Dawn shown such anger! Both of them were taken aback.

"Do . . . do you think that she is right?" Hawk asked Emri. "Am I acting wrongly? The likenesses are nothing but lines made for my own pleasure. I never meant . . . I did not think . . ."

"It does not matter what you meant or what you think," Emri replied slowly. "It is the effect they have had upon the people. It is *their* reaction that we must think about. I think that Dawn is right. Though the people have made them into more than you intended, if it will make them feel better why should you deny them? Our way has been hard. If these likenesses give them reason for hope, I say let them have it."

"Even though you and I both know that it is false hope?" asked Hawk. "They are but simple likenesses and cannot speak to the Gods."

"Are you so sure? Do you remember the time in the cave of the lions when you made a likeness of the Tiger and I spoke with its spirit?"

"That was different, Emri. You used the seeds of the dream weed and entered the spirit world to speak to the Tiger Totem. This is different."

"The intent is the same. We cannot be certain that the Gods will not hear. Either way, it cannot do any harm and may well do some good."

"I will allow it then, because you wish it," said Hawk, "but my heart does not agree."

Emri put his arm around Hawk's narrow shoulders, and together they joined the people.

The ceremony itself was simple. Proud Bear and Otuk had propped the stones up all in a row so that the likenesses seemed to tell the story of the hunt.

Next, a small fire was lit in front of the stones. One by one people passed in front of it and placed whatever small token in the flames that they thought would find favor with the Gods. Some gave bits of food; others bits of deerskin cut from their own garments; one woman offered her good luck charm, a knob of crystalline quartz; and one little girl added a small yellow flower. Their prayers were murmured silently and to themselves.

Seized by the moment, Proud Bear began to shuffle in place before the fire. The ruddy glow of the flames swept across the broad flat planes of his face and the dark, glittering eyes, casting dark shadows beneath his

high, angular cheekbones, giving him an almost savage
appearance.

Soon he began to sway and murmur beneath his
breath. Louder and louder the murmurs, more intense
the movement. His feet began to move and he shuffled
forward, eyes all but closed as he passed before the fire.

Then Otuk followed his lead, head thrown back, arms
outspread, chanting low beneath his breath.

One by one the others followed, until all the men
save Hawk and Emri had joined in, circling round and
round the fire, chanting the words to the ancient song
of the hunt, the song of the deer.

Running Bird, Bright Water, Leaping Fawn, Sunshine, and all the other women began to chant as well,
a soft repetitive melody that countered that of the men's
and underscored the words with guttural sounds of
their own.

Otuk had moved into the lead. He crouched low and
held his hands, fingers outspread, in front of his head so
that the firelight cast his shadow upon the rise of the
ground and gave him the look of an antlered stag.

Those behind him crouched low as well and hop-
skipped in a peculiar tight mincing step that was similar
to that of deer walking. They followed Otuk, chanting
still beneath their breath.

> *We are the deer, fat and sleek and full*
> *of grass.*
> *We are the deer, we return to the land*
> *that is ours.*
> *We are the deer, our eyes are bright, our*
> *spirits strong.*
> *We are the deer, fleet of foot and quick*
> *to scent the enemy.*
> *We are the deer. We are the deer.*

Proud Bear had fallen back and taken on the role of
himself, the proud and crafty hunter. He followed the
deer round and round the circle of the fire, chanting
the song of the hunter:

I am the hunter, bold and strong.
I see the deer, my brother.
His eyes are bright, his feet are fast,
  his spirit strong within him.
But I am the hunter bold and strong
  and my spear it carries death.
Die, my brother, die, for my people weep
  with hunger.
Your eyes will see, your feet will fly,
  your spirit still will soar,
Among the spirits where we will meet once more.

And the women chanted:

  We are the people; our eyes are bright,
    our spirits strong.
  We are the people; our spears are swift,
    our knives are keen.
  Our brother dies that we might live.
  We are the People of the Deer.

Over and over the men danced, circling the fire,
repeating their chant until even Emri and Hawk were
mesmerized by the scene and the harsh melody. When
Proud Bear moved up behind Otuk-the-stag and drove
his imaginary spear deep into his body, they were all
but overcome by the bitter triumph.

One by one the other men/deer were slain and fell
to the ground in poses of death. Slowly, softly, the
women's chant tapered away, leaving a strange, empty
silence in its wake.

Dawn stood among the women, her eyes large and
luminous, still caught up in the magic of the dance and
the words of the chant. She had said the words halt-
ingly at first, then stronger and with conviction as they
grew more familiar.

Emri envied her as he watched her face flush with
radiance, so firm in her belief that the Gods would hear
their words. He wished that he could believe so easily.
He did not think that the Gods would be offended by

their actions, but lately he had come to wonder if they were even listening. His lapse of faith had begun when the mountain of ice collapsed on those who had journeyed inside its belly in order to speak more closely to the Gods.

Emri could not understand how the Gods would cause or allow such a thing to happen. The People of the Deer had been respectful to their Gods and had never failed to honor them, yet they had been nearly completely exterminated. His own father had been loyal and respectful to the totem of their clan, the tiger. Yet the Gods had permitted Mandris to kill Emri's father and take control of both the clan and the totem. Despite all his teachings and his deep-seated faith, Emri was shaken by such doings and in his darkest moments had even wondered if the Gods were indeed all-powerful. It was a disturbing thought.

Hawk looked at Emri, and as their eyes met, Emri knew that his friend understood much more than was ever said. They had both said the words of the chant as they stood on the sidelines, unwilling to break openly with the beliefs of the others. Yet they held their own thoughts firm in their hearts, knowing that what was true for the tribe was not necessarily true for them.

CHAPTER SEVEN

The hunt began in earnest
early the next morning. Confident that their prayers
had reached the ears of the Gods, they left the stones in
place with further offerings of bits of meat held back
from the morning meal.

Once again the men and the three adolescents traveled ahead of the women and old ones. The hairy
tuskers had passed in the night and were now behind
them. This was ascertained by Tusk, who had been sent
to seek out the animals' whereabouts.

The day was barely begun, the sun having just crested
the peaks of the mountains, when they found their first
sign of deer—a small accumulation of round pellets,
smaller than a closed fist.

The men crouched over the dung, as excited as though
a hairy tusker had fallen dead at their feet. Proud Bear
picked up one of the pellets and after feeling it with
sensitive fingers, broke it open and crumbled it between his fingertips. Broken Tooth and several of the
others did the same.

"It is fresh," said Proud Bear, and the others nodded
in agreement, for the pellets were moist and crumbled
reluctantly, clinging together even when broken.

Mosca nosed among the fragments, wuffling softly,
inhaling deeply and blowing out gently. His eyes glazed
in the manner that Emri had come to recognize as
Mosca took in information that they could not hope to
know. Straightening, the cat stretched his head high,

then stood up on his haunches and sniffed the air intently. Returning to all fours, he set off at a rapid pace, heading east, directly toward the mountains.

Emri looked at Hawk and wondered whether the cat had scented the deer and was in pursuit, or if he was merely following some interest of his own.

The tracks seemed to lead in a more southerly direction, but Mosca seemed so intent on the path that he was following that they quickly decided to trust to the cat's instincts.

Emri was concerned, for he, better than anyone, knew that Mosca frequently took off to chase down a rabbit or seek out some other small prey, but never had he seen the cat sit up and scent the air in such a manner. He could but hope that Mosca's and the tribe's goals were the same.

They followed Mosca throughout the morning and saw nothing more than rabbits, earth diggers, and large numbers of birds nesting on the ground and circling across the empty sky. Then, just as they were beginning to doubt their wisdom in following the cat, they encountered a thick welter of hoof marks, cut deep in the earth, that had trampled the vegetation, releasing its sharp scent into the cold air.

"He has found the deer for us!" whispered Otuk. "Look, you, see how the tracks come up from the south. The deer circled around. Had we followed them, we would have lost much time and would perhaps have lost them."

"We have not found them yet," growled Proud Bear, unhappy, Emri thought, at having his prowess diminished by the lion cub. But despite his words, it was apparent to all that the deer were close. The marks in the earth were still clearly defined and free of moisture, and dung heaps were still steaming in the cold air.

They had entered the foothills of the mountains and the land was broken and rough. Large boulders and great rocks were strewn across the land as though a God had thrown them from the heights above. There were many places for the deer to hide in the sudden dips and abrupt folds of the land, and they followed the tracks closely, knowing that much depended on the success of the hunt.

All but forgotten was the thick column of smoke that still rose steadily into the sky, now quite close, possibly beyond the first set of ridges that rose before them.

Emri found it strange that the deer would seek out such a place, for the grass was sparse and the sedge had all but disappeared.

Now Mosca began a low, moaning "*unnnh, unnnh, unnnhh*" that came from deep in his chest and was more of a guttural cough than a cry. His head wove back and forth, mouth open, inhaling deeply, tasting the air. Then he fell into a low crouch and began slinking forward, his attention fixed on a tumble of boulders that lay ahead.

The men tightened their grip on their weapons—clubs and driftwood sticks with stones bound to the ends by leather strips. Proud Bear was in the lead, wielding the spear. Hawk carried only a long staff of smooth wood that was not really suited as a weapon, and Emri held a length of wood with the red-and-black obsidian knife attached to the end.

As they drew near the rocks, Mosca set aside all pretense of stealth and rushed forward bawling loudly. The men rushed after him, not knowing what was happening as the cat vanished between the rocks. Then there came the sound of thundering hooves and frightened bleating. All of a sudden, out from behind the rocks a group of deer burst forth, their eyes rolling in terror. The cat was a screaming ball of fury at their heels, a wild flurry of claws, fangs, and high-pitched screams.

Even as the men ran forward, Mosca leaped on the neck of a doe heavy with calf. Wrapping his long forearms around her neck, he sank his great curved canines into her throat. The doe stopped short. Digging her feet into the stony earth, she threw up her head in a frantic attempt to shake the cat loose and screamed a cry so terribly human that Emri felt its pain and fear to the depth of his soul.

The blood spurted out in great gouts and fell across the clinging cat and onto the hard ground below. Weakening, the doe sank to her knees, panting hard. Her mouth opened and closed, mewling piteously, her eyes glazed, and she toppled onto her side. The cat still held tight, growling savagely through blood-filled jaws.

Emri had but a heartbeat to take in the cat's actions, for the deer were upon them now, hooves beating a frantic tattoo as they flung themselves headlong down the slope, hoping to escape their attackers.

The men cried aloud and hurled themselves into the midst of the deer, clubs swinging, spear plunging, knife slashing. The stink of hot blood filled the air along with anguished shrieks, harsh panting, deep grunts, and exultant cries of victory.

When it was over, five deer raced away—the sound of their clattering hooves receding in the distance—but four of their kind lay dead or dying on the ground, as well as the fifth animal slain by the cat.

The men whooped and hollered and screamed aloud for joy, then slowly sank to their knees and collapsed alongside their victims, momentarily exhausted both mentally and physically by the vast outlay of energy.

"You have done it, Emri. You have brought us back to the deer," Otuk said as he pushed himself upright and stroked the fat sides of the doe beside him. "Speaker and Taug were right in their choice," he continued, referring to the former chief and shaman of the tribe. "You and Hawk have led us well this day."

Hawk and Emri exchanged amused smiles. "I have done little enough this day except be one of you," said Emri. "The credit must go to Mosca. It was he we followed."

"The three are as one," said Broken Tooth. "For whatever reasons the Gods saw fit to give you the cat and then send you to us. They did so with a reason. Otuk speaks with truth."

More might have been said, but Emri was uncomfortable with the conversation and climbed to his feet, saying, "We must give thanks for this gift of the deer."

The men leapt to their feet. The girl, Shell, was sent to collect a handful of sweet grass and sedge with which they might build the fire and say the words of thankfulness.

When Shell returned with the coarse grass and dry sedge, Emri twisted it into a tight bundle and set it afire, using a fire coal kept for safekeeping in a clamshell hung from Hawk's belt.

Emri held the smoking bundle of grass aloft and circled slowly. "Thank you, sister deer, for the gift of your lives. Your flesh will give us strength and help us through this difficult time. Your fur will clothe us and keep us warm. Your hearts will give us courage and your blood will give us strength. Travel to the next world and know that you live on in us. May your spirits go in peace."

Having said the words, Emri fanned the smoking grass over the bodies of the deer, even the one held in the grip of the snarling cat. All watched intently to make certain that the smoke rose straight into the sky, carrying their message to the spirit world, rather than drifting away aimlessly.

It was clear that Mosca did not like Emri's intrusion. Considering his hunger, Emri was not surprised. He was surprised, however, at the cat's hostility. Returning, Emri knelt down and attempted to speak to the cat, to soothe him. But Mosca growled at his approach and moved so that he lay atop the deer, covering it with his body and snarling in a most convincing manner.

Mosca's teeth and jaws dripped with blood, and his entire muzzle and throat were drenched in the gore. Looking at the cat—ears laid flat against his head, eyes closed to mere slits, harsh growls rumbling through his chest—Emri hardly recognized the cub that he had reared from its earliest days and loved like a brother. He was disturbed at this open show of distrust and wondered what would happen if he actually attempted to take the deer away from the cat.

He stood his ground and murmured soft words, hop-

ing to calm the cat, but Mosca, distrustful of Emri's
actions, gripped the deer in his powerful jaws and
dragged it away, behind a large boulder, never once
removing his amber eyes from Emri's face.

Emri watched him go without moving and wondered
if it were the end of their friendship. Would the day
come when the cat would actually turn on him? Emri
was shaken at the thought and turned away sadly, wondering if things would ever be the same.

The small interchange had gone unnoticed by the
others. When Emri finished saying the prayers, the
men had fallen upon the deer and begun butchering
them. Emri had little liking for this portion of the hunt,
and with so many willing hands, and the women soon to
follow, he and Hawk walked apart to talk among
themselves.

"I wonder what the deer were doing in such a place,"
Emri said, looking about. There were no grasses and no
sedges and not even moss or lichen upon the rocks to
attract the animals.

"Let us look and see what they were doing," said
Hawk. "Perhaps there is some pool of sweet water
hidden among the rocks that draws them from their
path. Look at the tracks. This is no casual happening;
the path between the rocks has been cut deep by the
passage of many hooves. This is a place that deer come
often."

Their curiosity roused, they followed the hard-beaten
path between two immense boulders and through a
narrow cut lined with great stones, emerging in a circular clearing ringed completely with walls of stone that
rose higher than their heads. The clearing was perhaps
six man-lengths in all directions. It was obvious at first
glance that the structure was man-made.

Excitement filled them as they examined the curious
pen, eliminating all question that the thing had been
built by man. As though to settle their doubts, they
found neat piles of white and yellow crystals placed at
the far end of the enclosure.

Hawk and Emri looked at each other, knowing that

the crystals, whatever they were, could not have come to this place without the help of man.

Emri touched his finger to the pile of white crystals, sniffed it cautiously, and then touched it to the tip of his tongue. Salt! And the waters were two days distant! The salt obviously had been placed in the pen with the intention of drawing the deer.

Placement of the salt would greatly increase one's chances of having a steady supply of deer on hand and would all but eliminate the need to travel great distances to hunt. It was an ingenious arrangement. The yellow crystals were tasted in turn and while unfamiliar to the two men were obviously enjoyed by the deer.

"I wonder who did this," Emri murmured in a low tone, eyeing the walls and wondering if the builders were anywhere near.

"It must be the people of the smoke," replied Hawk. "How could it be any other?"

"Do you think they are friendly? Perhaps they will be angered that we have taken their deer."

"If they were hunting, they would be here," said Hawk. "I see no one. The deer belong to no man, not even those who build such clever things as this. The deer belong to the Gods and only the Gods may give them or take them away."

"Bold words, Hawk. I hope the people of the smoke will agree with you."

They looked around the enclosure, examining it more closely, searching for some clue as to the identity of the builders, but there was nothing to be seen. On the far side, the side nearest the base of the mountain that rose in a broken jumble of pale gray stone, they discovered a faint trail that had not been made by deer. It traveled straight toward the mountain beyond and then disappeared behind a great fall of rocks that they did not attempt to investigate.

"Shall we tell the people?" asked Emri. "I do not like the feel of this place. There is a sense of wrongness about it that makes me uneasy."

"I share your feelings." Hawk looked around slowly,

allowing his eyes to pass over the entire area. "It feels as though we are being watched? Do you sense that too?"

"Like spears against my skin," Emri replied casually. "I think we should leave this place." He began to walk slowly back in the direction from which they had come.

The feeling of being watched was with them even after they had passed through the narrow place and hurried down the slope. Never had it felt so good to be among people.

Everything was as they had left it. The men were deeply immersed in skinning the carcasses and cutting the meat into pieces small enough to be smoked.

The absence of wood presented a problem that they had not considered. Grass and sedge, while flammable, burned too quickly and would not do for the long, slow fires required to smoke meat so that it would not spoil. As the men debated, Shell ran up to announce in her high, sweet voice that the women and old ones could be seen in the distance.

During the commotion, Hawk turned to Emri and said, "Were the spirits playing tricks on us, or were we really being watched?"

"It felt as though we were being watched, but now I am not certain. Still, there is the column of smoke and the pen was certainly built by man. It would be wise to believe that we are not alone in this place and keep a guard in case the watchers are hostile as well as real. It may not be necessary, but it will do no harm."

"Agreed," said Hawk, and together they went to greet the women.

CHAPTER EIGHT

Their bellies were full, heavy with meat roasted over the flames and eggs and the flesh of birds obtained by the women. A hot brew made of flower heads and sweet grasses soothed the rumblings of their bellies and warmed them against the chill of night.

Hawk and Emri had told of the finding of the deer trap, and everyone, even the smallest child, had to be taken to see the place. Accompanied by so many, the place seemed to lose its feeling of evil. Emri and Hawk exchanged embarrassed glances, wondering if they had but imagined the feeling of being watched.

Still, it was decided that it would be best to keep guard throughout the night in the event that the builders of the pen were not friendly. They also decided to follow the path in the morning and find out where it led. People clever enough to build such a pen might be well worth joining. The thought of other people was so exciting that many members of the tribe remained awake far into the night, wondering aloud what such a people might be like.

Tusk was chosen to keep watch through the first part of the night, until the campfire of his ancestors was clearly visible above the hump of the mountain. At that point he would waken Proud Bear, who, against the wishes of his women, had volunteered to keep watch throughout the last half of the night.

Of Mosca there was no sign. He had appeared toward

dusk, carrying a deer haunch in his jaws, and settled down close to Emri, as though in apology for his surly behavior. The children gathered close around him, ignoring Emri's words of warning. They had teased the cat by darting in and pretending to grab at the meat, then ran shrieking when he pawed at them, claws extended. Mosca had no sense of humor when it came to food and under the cover of darkness, carried his meat away once more.

Despite the vague worry over the unknown people, and concern about Mosca, Emri felt good. The people were fed, there was food enough for the immediate future, and their steps would now turn toward home. He smiled at Dawn and rested his chin atop her head as they sat in a circle around the fire with the people who were fast becoming friends, family, clan.

Birdsong had fallen asleep sucking a sweet marrow bone, her face glistening greasily in the firelight, dark curls framing her face. Emri took her from Dawn, wrapped her in a furskin of rabbit, and laid her down beside them. Drawing Dawn to him, they lay down next to the child and nestled together under their own small furskin, watching the sparks shoot into the dark sky. Emri pillowed Dawn's head with his arm and rested his other hand outstretched on her belly. He went to sleep with a smile, feeling the child move beneath his palm.

He wakened stiff and alert with a feeling that something was wrong. The dark night sky had given way to the cold, pale misty-gray of early dawn. The fire had burned out, only a faint whisper of smoke rising to betray its former presence. All around him people slept, heavier than normal because of the large meal.

Emri blinked himself fully alert, all of his senses tingling. He was quite certain that something was wrong; the hair on the back of his arms and on the nape of his neck was standing up, and his scalp was prickling sharply. He strained to hear, hoping to catch some hint of what it was.

He heard Tusk's deep rumbling snores and Running

Bird's whispery whistle as the air escaped her lips. A child murmured sleepily and a bird answered querulously, a three-toned cry ending on a questioning note.

Emri was almost lulled back into slumber, thinking that he had made a mistake. Surely they were safe if the birds, those nervous natural sentries, were not alarmed. Then it came to him in a rush that the bird that answered the child's cry was one that did not waken in early morning, rising only after the sun had risen and warmed its nest.

He stiffened with alarm, knowing the sound to be some watchword, some signal between people not his own. Slowly, so as not to be seen, his hand reached for the knife at his waist. But before he completed the motion, he felt a sharp prick at the center of his back. He halted abruptly.

Another jab came, this one more demanding. He felt it slicing through the tough skin of his tunic and breaking the skin, then felt the warm flow of blood trickling down his ribs. Was it a warning or a demand? He wanted to turn his head to see who was doing this, but he knew instinctively that it would only earn him further pain, or perhaps even death.

The jab came a third time. This time it was accompanied by a harsh grunt, a command. The meaning was clear: he was to rise and do so immediately.

Emri separated himself from Dawn, sleeping still, and rose slowly. He turned with his hands held wide and away from both his body and the knife, to avoid giving his captor cause for further violence.

In fact, violence was the first thing Emri had thought of, but Dawn was at risk—as were the child and everyone else. It would be best to learn all he could of the spear wielder and then assess the situation anew, if he were allowed to live that long.

Another jab, this time on the side. Following the thrust of the spear, he turned around slowly to face his attacker.

It was a man, far far older than Emri. The skin sagged from cheekbone and chin; his eyebrows were

furred thick and white above sharp black eyes; and his
nose was a high, thin, humped arch like the beak of a
hawk. His hair was white as snow and hung about his
face loose and unkempt. His body was but skin and
bone and the corded remnants of once powerful muscle. He wore only a small loincloth, not even the mer-
est of covering on his feet.

Emri was cold, even dressed from neck to toe in
furskins. He wondered how the old man could survive
in the great cold of this land, dressed so poorly.

The man's great age was as apparent as it was unusual. Emri could not recall having seen many old
ones, whether male or female, who had approached this
point in life. He would have guessed that the man had
seen more Cold Times than all the fingers on two hands
opened four times, although such a great age seemed
unlikely.

It was also apparent that the old one found him to be
of equal interest, for he studied Emri as carefully as
Emri studied him.

What he saw must not have been to his liking. He
did not lower his spear—which was made of some stout
wood and tipped with a long, sharp stone point—but
jabbed at Emri's chest and uttered a soft, sibilant stream
of words that sounded as though he were asking a
question. But the words were in no tongue that Emri
had ever heard, and he did not understand anything
that was said.

The man thrust the spear at Emri once again, his
black eyes bright with anger, and he repeated his question. Emri could do nothing but shrug and reply in his
own tongue, hoping that some words would be understood.

The old man looked at him for a time, studying his
face closely to see if some trick was being played on
him. Satisfied that it was not, he warbled another bird
cry. The sounds dripped fluidly from his lips so accu-
rate in tone that Emri felt appreciation as much as he
felt fear for whomever the cry was summoning.

Silently, so silently that he did not even hear the

passage of steps, a second figure appeared and stood beside the old one. This one was not so old, no more than Emri's age of twenty-three Warm Times. While he was large, well-muscled, and in good health, there was a peculiar dullness in his eyes that was an odd contrast to the brightness of the old one's. There was also a third figure—that of a young boy no more than nine or ten Warm Times. He shrank back from the old one. From his frightened demeanor and emaciated frame, Emri could see that the boy was an unwilling accomplice.

The old one spoke softly in the unknown tongue, and the younger man raised his own spear and pointed it at Emri's throat. Despite the dullness of his eyes, there was little doubt in Emri's mind that the man knew how to use the weapon and would not hesitate to do so if Emri made even the smallest gesture.

When the old one was certain that his comrade was in position, he reached down. Before Emri could react, the old one seized both Dawn and Birdsong by the hair and yanked them upright.

Dawn, flushed and foggy with sleep, cried out and slapped at the old one, not knowing who or what had hurt her. But the old one was as nimble as he was strong and avoided her easily, holding her at arm's length where she could not reach him.

Birdsong, too young to understand anything at all except the pain, shrieked loudly, bringing the entire camp to its feet within a matter of heartbeats.

There was a loud outcry and then silence as each in their turn noticed the old one and the spear pointed at Emri's throat. There was some muttered conversation among them, and Emri could all but picture Proud Bear suggesting that they rush the strangers.

Words came to his lips, but Emri bit them back, not trusting the spear holder's reactions. He prayed to the spirits that reason would prevail and that the others would not listen to Proud Bear.

As shock and sleep passed from her, Dawn realized what was happening and ceased her struggles. The old man, still not showing the least sign of exertion, had given her the screaming child and transferred his grip so that his wiry arm now crossed her throat. The other hand held a knife fashioned out of deer horn, pressed against her side next to her heart.

Tears glistened in Dawn's eyes but she did not attempt to free herself. She snuggled the screaming child as best she was able, murmuring to it softly.

Emri felt the blood pounding in his head and the pressure building in his ears. He clenched his teeth in an effort to keep the rage from reaching dangerous proportions. Dawn was safe as yet, but should the old one's knife-hand make any further move toward her . . .

"Who are you and what do you want?" cried a voice that Emri recognized as Hawk's.

This was evidently what the old one was waiting for. Speaking rapidly to the younger man, Emri was told through gestures and jabs to turn around so that he faced the tribe. The spear wielder remained behind him, and the point of the spear came to rest between his shoulder blades. The old one advanced so that he stood alongside Emri, yet far enough away so that Emri could not reach him.

He spoke out in a loud, strong voice, heavy with guttural rolling sounds, a statement that clearly demanded an answer. But no one spoke. The old one spoke again, this time more insistently, and pressed the point of the knife against Dawn's ribs.

With this new threat Emri forgot his fear of the man behind him and lunged toward the old one. Instantly the butt of the spear clubbed him hard on the side of the head. As he fell to the ground, stunned, the man thrust the spear into Emri's back with such force that the tip penetrated his flesh. The shock and the pain were so great that Emri made no further attempt to move.

There was an audible gasp as the tribe watched the attack on their chief, helpless to intervene.

The old man called out again and jerked savagely against Dawn's throat, causing her to gag and choke.

Then, hesitantly, as though feeling her way through an unfamiliar path in the dark, Running Bird spoke the same strange guttural sounds.

The words were few, but a look of satisfaction spread across the old one's face and he nodded to himself as though he had known all along that they could speak his tongue and had refused to do so out of sheer obstinancy.

He called Running Bird to him with a jerk of his head. She crept forward out of the safety of the crowd and approached the old one on trembling legs.

The words came fast and harsh and were answered slowly and fearfully in a voice that could scarcely be heard, far from the loud, raucous tones that the old woman normally used. It was impossible to follow them and their meaning did not become clear with the hearing. Emri could but hope that Running Bird would consider her words and speak with wisdom.

At last the flow stopped and Running Bird turned to face Emri, her face drawn and pale, looking far older and more frail than ever before.

"He says that we are to take the deer, every last bit of it, and go with them," she said in a small voice. "He says we must do so or he will kill all three of you. We must go now." Then, not even allowing Emri to reply, she began to walk toward the carcasses of the deer.

One after the other, without waiting to be told, the people followed, packing the deer in their own skins and loading them on the backs of the strongest men. They shushed the crying of the children and then hurried forward, obeying the old man's gestures. Eyes averted, they passed Emri, who lay sprawled on the ground with blood staining his tunic and seeping onto the earth in slow, steady drips.

They went with heads held high, showing no sign of fear, and Emri took strength from their strength. Hawk paused in front of him as though to speak or make some gesture, but a sharp word from the old one urged him on after the others, following the thin, frightened youngster who led the way.

Only after the last of them had passed did the spear

holder prod Emri to his feet and push him toward the
path. From the whimpers of Birdsong, Emri knew that
Dawn and the old one followed.

They passed through the place of tumbled boulders,
and Emri wondered briefly where Mosca was, realizing
for the first time that the cat had not returned during
the night to sleep against his back, as was his habit. A
part of him wished that the cat would appear and create
some diversion that might allow him to overcome the
man with the spear. Even as he formed the thought, he
cast it from his mind, knowing that he would not do
anything that would put Dawn at risk.

They passed without seeing any sign of the cat other
than a trail of blood and faint scrapings where the body
of the deer had been dragged along the ground. They
entered the narrow defile and finally came to the circle
of rocks. A sharp remark from the old one directed
Emri onto the trail that led up onto the shoulder of the
mountain itself.

The trail was steep and hard to climb with few hand-
holds to ease the way, but there was no stopping. If
they paused, the old one threatened them in his strange
tongue. Far above them, the boy could be seen, making his way along the faint trail, guiding those who
followed.

As they climbed, the spear always at his back, Emri
cursed beneath his breath and wondered at the fates
that would allow two men—one ancient, the other lacking a full degree of wits—and a small boy to hold a far
greater number of people—superior in strength and
weapons—hostage. He wondered what reason the Gods
could have for such an action and tried to imagine what
awaited them at their final destination.

This he was not to discover for some time, for the old
one directed their steps higher and higher until they
came to a place where the mountain split in two, forming the base of two separate peaks.

The peak on their left was short, ending abruptly in a
ragged line almost as though the top half had been
broken off by some immense hand.

Emri realized that this was the source of much of the loose stone that lay shattered on the slopes and the ground below. It was from this peak that the great column of smoke rose into the sky. Viewed from this distance, the column of smoke seemed even larger. The peak on their right disappeared into the clouds, unbroken.

The old man stopped only momentarily, more in deference to the needs of his captives than for himself. Emri could see that he was barely winded and did not even seem aware of the cold, which was even greater here than at the lower levels.

Before the women and children had recovered their breath, they were climbing again. Much to Emri's surprise, it was to the peak on the left.

Now the going was easier, and for this Emri was grateful. His wound was paining him and the blood continued to flow, saturating his tunic and pants and pooling inside his furskin boots.

The pain in his head grew worse, coming and going and making him dizzy as well as filling his throat with the taste of sickness. He concentrated on walking steadily, focusing on one rock and then another, denying the bright spots that danced before his eyes and threatened to overwhelm him.

The climb was endless but somehow easier, and he realized that it was because of the same incident that had destroyed the top of the mountain. The rock was rough and unstable underfoot, in sharp contrast to the smooth surface that had formed the base. It seemed as though some great force had attempted to destroy the mountain, pounding it repeatedly with terrible blows.

The gray rock was riven with cracks, some small, others of considerable size. Whole chunks of rock were missing from the surface layer as though torn away by giant fingers. These occasional craters and fractured rock surfaces provided them with hand- and foot-holds and they climbed more swiftly than before still following the nimble figure of the boy child who scampered along the trail with the ease of a mountain goat.

As they came within range of the top of the moun-

tain, Emri was able to see that they were following a
clear-cut trail, one that rose to the very summit. He
wondered, not for the first time, where they could be
going and what they would find when they reached
there.

Ahead he began to hear the murmur of voices and
saw Otuk and Tusk and several of the women pointing
down at the path and speaking excitedly. When he
reached that point he understood their concern. Here
wisps of smoke rose from cracks in the rock and curled
around his ankles. The smoke had a curious smell to it,
like that of broken eggs that had lain too long in the
sun. And even more disturbing, Emri realized that the
stone itself was warm.

The great pillar of smoke rose into the sky, so vast
that whole forests would need to be burned to create
such a tower of clouds. Emri could not imagine what
the old one was burning to create such smoke. Now he
began to hear a faint hissing like that of rain falling into
a campfire.

A small cloud of smoke detached itself from the ground
and floated toward them, wispy and thin. The smell of
rotting eggs grew more intense as the cloud enveloped
him, and then suddenly his eyes began to burn and
sting. His breath rasped in his throat and he doubled
over, clutching his ribs, trying to breathe. For a heartbeat, even the angry jab of the spear was not enough to
drive him on.

When finally he straightened, drawing deep breaths
of fresh air into his aching lungs, it was to see the last of
his people vanishing over the ragged lip of the mountain. Then they were gone.

CHAPTER NINE

$\mathbf{A}$nxious to know where the people had gone, Emri hurried forward, needing no urging from the spear at his back. They reached the ragged line of rock that marked the crest of the mountain, and despite himself, Emri stopped, stunned by the view spread before him.

Not only had the top of the mountain vanished, but the heart of the mountain as well. It was as though the Gods had reached down and ripped off the peak and then hollowed out the center with their hands. What was left was the most barren, desolate landscape Emri could imagine.

Dark gray was the predominant color, flowing down from the ragged rim in drifts of broken rock and finely ground particles of porous stone and stretching across to the far edge. Had it been but one smooth, unbroken expanse, it would have been terrible enough, but it was not.

Wisps of smoke emerged from the cracks in the rock and rose into the air where they hung motionless like low-lying clouds. Here and there the rocks gaped and glowed with an eerie incandescence. A constant rumble seemed to shake the ground. Now and then there was a curious burping sound and a puff of smoke would emerge from the ground and float leisurely upward.

But dominating the entire panorama was the column of smoke, centered in the middle of the crater. Far, far larger than Emri had judged, it rose high into the air

and hung, towering above them like some pillar of the
Gods, dwarfing them with its immensity.

Emri was so overwhelmed by the sight of this huge
monolith that he descended into the crater at the first
prick of the spear. The soft, gritty particles closed round
his feet and he sank with each step to the depth of his
ankles, pulling his feet free before he could continue.

They lurched and staggered down into the pit, his
captor no less ungainly than he on the unstable, shifting
surface. Emri might easily have tried to grab the spear
and wrench it out of the man's hands. He could have
overcome the man with the aid of the slippery footing,
but the people had vanished from sight and there were
still Dawn and the child to consider.

The farther they descended, the closer they came to
the great billowing cloud, the louder the sound. At first
it had seemed but a gentle hiss, but now, nearer the
base, it was a roar so loud that Emri could no longer
hear the terrified screams of the child behind him. As
they came under the cover of the cloud itself, they
were enveloped in a fine warm mist that coated their
bodies and made it difficult to breathe. Emri covered
his nose with his hand and struggled on.

The point of the spear directed him onto a rocky
ledge whose edges were lost in the foggy smoke. It was
impossible to see what lay beyond the ledge. Only now
was he able to realize the incredible force behind the
tower of smoke as it burst forth from the earth and shot
into the sky.

Emri was certain that if he were stupid enough to put
his hand into the column, it would disappear or melt,
for he suddenly understood that it was not smoke but
steam that rose from the crater.

The noise had increased as well and had become so
loud that he lost all sense of his own body. He saw his
feet rise and fall; saw his hands and arms move; looked
down upon his body; but it was as though they belonged to someone else, so great was the sense of
disembodiment.

Then, just as he thought that he could bear the heat

and sound no longer, his captor directed him away from the ledge. They began to climb once more, away from the terrible column of smoke.

Now they began to see smaller craters pockmarking the gray surface. Some of the holes were empty, holding only wisps of smoke. Others held mud, steaming hot and colored strangely with streaks of red and blue and yellow. Still others were filled with water, as clear as any Emri had ever seen.

Emri peered into one such pool as he passed. The sides of the rock were ringed with bright colors, one atop the other, and peculiar, delicate formations crusted the edges as though the water had leaped out, draped itself on rocks, and then frozen into stone. Emri had never seen anything like it and, despite the dangerous situation, wished that he might stop and examine the pools more closely.

The smell of rotten eggs had grown stronger as they passed among the smoking craters. Now and then sharp, stinging, acrid smells assaulted them, burning their eyes, noses, and throats.

Emri's legs were aching from the strain of walking up the slope with the soft, thick grains tugging at his every step. Suddenly the man behind him, all but forgotten except for the jab of his spear, grunted and shoved him forward.

A veil of mist hung before Emri like a furskin hung from a doorway. The force of the shove threw him into the curtain of mist. He held his breath as he stumbled forward, wondering if he had been brought this far only to die in a cloud of poisonous air.

But once on the other side, he knew that he had been wrong. His people were huddled together in a tight mass on the edge of another of the pools of water.

Trembling with fatigue and stress, Emri stumbled over to join them. Barely feeling the blow that landed on his shoulder, he collapsed wearily beside Hawk. Heartbeats later, Dawn and the child were thrown down beside him.

Dawn's face was pale and tear marks streaked her

cheeks. She looked at Emri and tried to smile, but her
lips trembled. She bit her lower lip and shook her head
as she bent to comfort Birdsong, whose voice was hoarse
and reedy from continuous crying. Birdsong burrowed
against Dawn's chest and wept in hiccuping sobs, her
distress slowly diminishing as Dawn rocked her back
and forth and murmured to her softly.

Emri could do nothing but place his arm around
Dawn's shoulders, feeling his wound break open and
bleed afresh. His head spun dizzily and he lowered his
head and breathed deeply. Now was not the time to
grow weak. Now was a time for strength if he were to
save himself and his people.

"What is this place?" he asked in a low tone, but
Hawk merely shook his head, unable to answer. Emri
raised his head and looked around him, taking in the
details of their immediate surroundings.

They were seated on a broad ledge of flat rock that
surrounded the pool of water. Yet this one was different
from others they had seen. It was large, more than
twenty man-lengths across in all directions, and deep as
well.

The water was so clear that one could look down into
the pool, past the concentric rings of color—gradations
of white, yellow, red, and blue—and still not see the
bottom. The sloping sides were littered with vast quantities of bones covered in various degrees by the strange
accretions that gave them the appearance of stone. A
fine layer of sediment blanketed the lower levels of
stone.

Emri stared at the thick layer of bones and an ominous feeling came over him. His grip tightened on
Dawn's shoulder as he turned to look for the old one
and his helpers.

The two men and the child were standing on the far
side of the tribe, undoing the furskins that contained
the deer meat. Beyond them the stone ledge nosed into
the side of the crater before it was completely buried
by the soft, drifting gray sand. A dwelling had been
built at this farthest point, a simple dwelling of stones

big enough to hold the two men and no more. Without being told, Emri knew that the child, while with the two older men, was not part of them. It was obvious from the way he cowered every time the old man spoke to him, that the child was terrified of the old one. Briefly, Emri wondered where the child slept, and how he had come to be there.

Emri could not imagine why anyone would choose to live in such a terrible place and what they did for the most basic of needs. Surely they did not descend the mountain for their every need, yet there was nothing in this desolate place that would sustain a man for long.

He became aware of a murmuring around him, all but indistinguishable from the low rumbling that never ceased. It was the people, talking among themselves.

He felt soft fingers on his back and turned his head slightly to see Running Bird pressing close against him, her eyes clouded with concern.

"Are you all right? Are you hurt? Do you bleed still?" she asked fearfully, and Emri felt the depth of her concern. He was strangely touched and hurried to assure her that he was merely tired and in no great pain. "I am strong, mother," he replied with a heartiness that he did not feel. "It will take more than an old one and a fool with a spear to defeat me. Do not forget that I am brother to the lion."

Running Bird smiled, her wrinkled old face lighting with unconcealed joy, and she turned aside and relayed his words to those clustered behind her.

"Running Bird, who is this old one and what does he want with us?" asked Emri. "What did he say to you and with what strange sounds? How is it you speak his tongue?"

"I have not always been part of the People of the Deer," said Running Bird. "I was born to the clan of the White Bear and these sounds are of that tongue. I have not heard it for many, many Warm Times, and it had all but passed from my mind. It made me think of my mother and the times before I joined the People of

the Deer as a mate. When I left my clan my mother
said to me—"

"Running Bird, please, tell me what the old one
said," Emri said patiently. "Then tell me of your mother's words later."

"Forgive me," sniffled Running Bird. "I am but a
useless old woman who has lived too long."

Emri could see the tears pooling in her eyes. He bit
back a sigh and stroked the old woman's face gently.

"Never useless, mother of mothers. We could not do
without the wisdom of your years to guide us. No one
else among us has such knowledge. Only you know the
words of this old one and know how to speak to him.
Please share his words with me now, so that I might
think on them."

Running Bird quickly lost her doleful look, and leaning forward with barely restrained excitement, she said,
"He says that we have offended the God. I asked him
which Gods he meant and he said *the* God—as though
there were not more Gods than could be numbered on
the hands of all the men among us, but only one single
God, which everyone knows is not true. There is the
God of the sky, and the God of the earth, and the God
of the waters, and—"

"Yes, yes, I know and I agree with you," Emri inter-
rupted hastily, as Running Bird began listing all the
Gods. "But did he say what he wanted with us?"

"No. Just that we would have to answer to the God
for our offense. He said that we would be judged."

Emri closed his eyes and took a deep breath to
steady himself. It did not matter what the old one
thought, or which God he sought to appease. Emri
knew that if he were to allow the old man to judge
them, it would be no judgment at all, but a pronounce-
ment of guilt. He could not allow that to happen.

He had half-risen to his feet, no plan as yet formulated, when the old one and his dull-eyed, vigilant
companion returned and stood before them. The younger man placed the tip of his spear at Emri's throat and
Emri sank back on his heels, willing to wait and hear

what was to be said. But spear or no spear, he was determined that none of his people would be harmed.

The old one gestured for Running Bird to stand beside him, and then, clearly expecting her to translate his words, he began to speak in slow, measured tones.

"You have come onto the land that belongs to the God. It is his home. You did not come with respect in your hearts to worship. You came to kill and use the God's offerings for your own petty purposes. The God speaks of his anger and will punish the land and all upon it unless an offering is made in his honor." The old man spoke in loud, ringing tones and his dark eyes sparked with an anger of his own. "The anger of the God must be appeased!" And with a sudden, abrupt gesture, he raised his hand and pointed to the pool of water.

Their attention was drawn to the boy, who perched precariously on a rock that extended out over the pool for nearly a full man-length. He had dragged one of the deer out onto the rock with him. With the raising of the old man's hand, he picked up several of the chunks of meat.

The old man began to chant, the words spilling from his lips so swiftly that Running Bird did not even attempt to translate their meaning. He reached the end suddenly. The boy cast the meat into the pool as far as he was able, throwing it far enough from him so that none of the resulting splashes touched him.

Not until the meat entered the water did Emri realize just how hot it was. He had seen the vapor curling upon the clear surface and felt the heat warming the rocky ledge beneath him but had never considered the temperature of the water. But as the meat struck the water, it sizzled briefly and then dropped through the clear depths, trailing a thick line of bubbles.

Emri watched in horror as the flesh of the deer changed from red to brown to gray to white in swift progression. Landing on the sloping side, it fell away from the bone and finally disappeared completely. The small bits that remained slowly drifted to the bottom

where they merged with the other bits of sediment,
remains of other offerings to the grim God.

Emri's mind was numb with the horror of what he
had witnessed. As the boy completed his task, not
ceasing until every last bit of the deer was gone, Emri
had no words in him to express his distress. He was not
alone, for the entire tribe had been similarly affected.
There was but one thought on their minds: If the water
could peel the flesh from the bones of a deer and cook
it till it dissolved, what would it do to a man?

As the thought took hold of them, they were similarly
affected with a kind of mindless hysteria that brought
them to their feet and filled them with the need to run,
to be anywhere but here with this terrible old man and
his unforgiving God.

As they rose, the old man spoke out once more in his
imperious voice. Again Running Bird translated, tears
running down her wrinkled cheeks, staring at the old
one much as a bird stares spellbound at a snake.

"Do not think to run," she translated. "There is
nowhere to go. There are pools everywhere, in places
that you cannot see, lying hidden below the surface of
the sands. They will not hold the weight of a man. If
you step on one, you will fall through and die."

Emri looked back the way he had come and thought
that it would be a simple enough matter to follow his
own footsteps, retracing the path until he was clear of
the evil place. But the old one noticed the direction of
his gaze and smiled.

"Nor can you find the way out by following the trail
in, for the sand is soft and holds no impression longer
than a heartbeat. There is no escape. Your old life is
gone. Now you belong to the God."

CHAPTER TEN

They lived on the ledge at the side of the crater for three long days. The young boy brought them the few bits of food the old man would allow, mostly the least desirable scraps of the deer. This meat was not cooked or smoked, but raw and slippery to the touch and gamy in taste. Their water, one skin for all of them, was foul in taste and several of them became sick.

The children cried constantly and tempers grew short as the feeling of frustration rose. They were not guarded in any way; the old man depending on his words to keep them in place.

They attempted to speak to the boy as he brought them their food and water, but the child was too afraid to reply. His big dark eyes spoke eloquently of his unhappiness. Emri felt as though the boy wished to speak to them, but each time he cast a look in the direction of the old man and scurried away in fear. His small, emaciated frame bore the marks of the old man's beatings, and they often saw the old one strike the child for no apparent reason. The boy was not sheltered in the stone hut but slept outside in a nest dug in the warm gray grit. Emri felt as though the child would be an ally, could they but give him the courage.

Each day another deer was sacrificed to the God, always in the same manner with the old one chanting his words on the edge of the pool.

They talked among themselves, discussing what would

happen when the old man ran out of deer. Would he begin sacrificing them one at a time? As terrible as it seemed, Emri could think of no other reason why they had been brought to the place. He was determined to find a way out, despite the old man's warnings. They had thought of rushing the hut at night and overwhelming the two men, but they eventually discarded the plan fearing that the boy would still refuse to help them.

Before dawn of the third day, Tusk, chosen for his speed and lightness of foot, crept away from the small group huddled at the edge of the pool. Following the trail as best they were able to remember, he hoped to reach the far edge of the crater in safety. If he was successful, they would follow in his carefully noted footsteps.

The old one and his younger companion never emerged before the sun rose over the snowcapped peaks to the east. The boy rose whenever hunger or thirst dictated.

Tusk was making good progress, staying along the line of ledges as much as possible. Motioning for the others to follow, Emri and the rest of the tribe advanced to the farthest point of the pool's edge.

Emri had just stepped out onto the first of the soft, gray, drifting material when he heard a subdued commotion behind him. Worried that something might go wrong at this point, he turned around and saw the boy, eyes wide with fright, being passed along from one set of hands to the next until he was standing next to him.

"Don't go. Stop him. He will die!" the boy said in a rush, his words tumbling out so fast he all but stammered. "Quick! Call him back!" he begged. "That is not the right way; he will die!"

The boy was shivering and tears glistened in his eyes. Emri was suddenly sure that he was telling the truth. He turned swiftly and called to Tusk, stopping the man in midstep. He waved him back.

Tusk frowned and shook his head, turning slightly and placing his foot to one side of the path he had chosen. Immediately he fell sideways, the soft, gray drifts falling away beneath his weight. His arms shot out and waved in circles as he tried to gain his balance. Still he slid, and there was a collective gasp of breath as they watched, helpless. But at the very last he managed to throw his weight to the side of the path. His body half submerged in the treacherous drifts, he hung there, unable to gain further purchase and pull himself free.

Emri could not let Tusk die. If he were to be saved, someone would have to help him. Emri turned to the boy, held the small, pointed chin in his hand, and said softly, "Help me."

"I'm afraid," the boy whispered, as tears ran down his face. "I will die like the others."

"No, you won't," Emri said. "You were able to guide the tribe here. You can do it if you try." Still the boy cried, and Emri realized just how young he was, certainly no more than eight Warm Times. But there was no one else. "Please," he said. "We need your help."

"I cannot," the boy cried. "The old one will give me to the God!" Before Emri could say any more, the boy turned and ran away. Looking after him, Emri saw the old one standing beside his dwelling, watching all that transpired, a look of satisfaction on his cold face.

The look, more than anything else, decided Emri. His eyes met those of the old one, and then he turned and deliberately set foot on the shifting gray sands. Dawn cried his name aloud and would have followed him had Leaping Fawn not grabbed her arms and held her back. Birdsong began to scream.

Emri did not look back but concentrated on his every step, visualizing where Tusk had stepped and placing his feet in the exact same places. It seemed to take forever, but at last he approached the ledge that Tusk gripped with numbed fingers.

Not trusting the footing, Emri lay down upon the ledge and gripping it firmly with legs and hand, extended his hand to Tusk. But Tusk's fingers shook with fatigue and he gasped, "I cannot let go, one hand will not hold me. I am tired Emri. I cannot hold on; my fingers are slipping!"

Emri edged forward, feeling his own grip growing more tenuous as the ledge narrowed. Now there was no support for his upper body and only his legs and thighs gripped the sharp-edged rock that cut into his flesh. But it was far enough to reach Tusk.

Emri gripped Tusk's wrists and began wriggling backward, feeling the rock slice his skin with every move. Tusk let go his hold on the outcrop and seized Emri's wrists, forming a double bond and placing his full weight on Emri.

Tusk kicked out with his legs, seeking some firm ground so that he might aid Emri's efforts, but as he did so, the ground beneath him collapsed completely, sliding away and falling into what appeared to be a great crevasse.

The entire weight of his body now hung from Emri's wrists. Emri felt himself being pulled toward the crevasse and he jerked back instinctively, but he could not use his hands, for Tusk still gripped them with all his might. Emri clenched his thighs around the ledge and groaned with the effort. The rock was nearly level and provided little to cling to. The muscles stood out in his arms, neck, back, and thighs as he used whatever means possible to lever himself and the helpless Tusk back onto firm ground.

At last it was done. Both men lay on the narrow spit of rock, gasping from the effort and the fright. Even now the crevasse yawned larger, growing by the heartbeat as the porous rock and sand disturbed by their activity, slid into the hole.

The crevasse was but a narrow crack in the floor of the crater. Rocks disturbed by the periodic tremors tumbled into the crack, damming it lightly. Sand and fine granular dust then blew on top of the rocks and eventually concealed the crevasse from sight until another tremor dislodged the rocks and opened the crevasse again. The sequence repeated itself over and over.

The two men got to their feet shakily. Turning, they

saw the entire tribe huddled at the farthest point of the
ledge, as though by their very presence alone they
could somehow lend their aid.

But they were not alone. The old one and his younger companion stood beside the pool, smiling as though
they had won some victory from the ordeal. And well
they might have, Emri reflected wearily, for he did not
know if he would have the courage to attempt the
crossing a second time. Some other manner of escape
would have to be found.

The deer were gone, sacrificed to the God of the
pool. That afternoon the assistant passed among them
and handed out dried meat and the one skin of water
they were allowed.

Emri watched him closely, but as the man made no
overt gesture of hostility, it began to seem as though
there were no meaning to his presence. They had not
seen the young boy since the morning. Perhaps he was
being punished for his part in the morning's episode.

Then, just as he had finished handing out the last of
the meat and turned to go, Sunshine stepped in front of
the man. She smiled at him in a winsome manner,
holding her long black braid between her fingers and
rolling it suggestively.

Emri did not hear what she said, but suddenly the
man's hand shot out and grabbed the woman by the
wrist. She screamed, but it had no effect.

Before they realized what was happening, the man
picked the woman up under one arm and carried her
back to the old one. She kicked and screamed and beat
him with her hands, but he took no more notice of her
blows than a stag might notice a fly crawling on its
back.

Proud Bear rushed forward, unmindful of his own
safety, and would surely have attacked the two men had
Otuk and Broken Tooth not seized him and held him
securely.

Emri thrust his way through the tribe and placing

himself in front of Proud Bear, called out to the old one.

"Let the woman go," he cried. "She has done nothing. Let her go." Running Bird appeared at his side and translated quickly, adding perhaps a plea of her own.

The old one smiled. "The woman has offered herself to the God," he said, ignoring her frantic efforts to free herself. Following some unseen movement, the assistant carried the screaming woman out onto the stone spit that hung over the pool. Her terrified screams echoed throughout the crater, cutting through the constant hiss of the column of steam and the low, dull rumble.

"Wait!" cried Emri, advancing toward both of the men. "Do not do this. Give the God deer, not people."

"There are no more deer," said the old man, turning toward them once more, his face an ugly grimace. "They come no more. Once there were many, many deer. Now they are gone and the God is angry. He shows his displeasure more and more and demands daily sacrifices to appease his anger.

"He would destroy everything with his great anger if I did not appease him. If I fail to honor him, all will vanish. Birds, deer, water, sun, earth, everything! Everything will die!" Running Bird translated hurriedly, attempting to keep up with the old one's rush of words.

Emri realized now that the old one walked a different path than they, his mind twisted in some strange manner. It would not do to talk to him in a normal way. He would require careful handling.

"Why do you say this?" Emri asked in a quiet, respectful tone. "Tell me, for I am very interested in your God and would know more of him and his ways."

The old one looked at Emri suspiciously. Then, as Emri's face did not betray any hidden smiles or doubting looks, the old man began to speak.

"Once this was a fertile valley covered with grass and flowers. There was water from the rains and snows. Deer came, and other animals as well. My tribe lived here for many lifetimes and life was good.

"Then the people began to forget the old ways. They ate and slept and pleasured their women and forgot to honor the gods. I was young then, too young to take a woman to my furskin, but I remember well all that happened.

"There were those who spoke out in favor of the old ways, tried to make the people listen, but they did not.

"The God began to speak then, muttering low as we slept, then growing louder and more bold until he spoke all the day and all the night.

"The women and children were afraid and wanted to leave this place that had been our home. But the men would not go. They made fun of the women and children and laughed at them.

"Then one night the earth beneath us split apart. Fire and smoke and flaming rocks burst forth out of the ground and fell back upon us, destroying the village, the people, and all the world that I had known. Everyone, everyone, was dead except for me.

"The rocks continued to fall and I was afraid to move. I stayed in that place for three days and three nights, praying to the God, praising his might and his power. I promised that if he would spare me, I would live my life honoring his name.

"On the morning of the fourth day, the God was silent. The fire and stones no longer shot from the earth, but the world I had known was gone, covered by this gray earth where nothing grows, and the air was strange and foul.

"I have lived my life honoring the God as I promised. I praise him daily and sacrifice the deer in his name. But the deer come here no more and it grows harder and harder for me to descend the mountain. This one helps as best he can"—he gestured to the younger man—"but often there are no deer at all and the God goes hungry.

"He grows angry over the lack of honor and speaks his displeasure more and more often, as you have heard. Now, the great cloud forms. This is surely an omen of his anger and I must do what I can to appease him. This

time, he will not be content with this small valley but
will destroy the entire world.

"You must understand that I do what I do for the
good of all." And then, while they all still hung on his
words, thinking there was more, he lifted a finger and
his assistant flung Sunshine into the pool of water.

The woman shrieked and her cry seemed to linger in
the air even after she entered the water, cutting off her
cry in mid-voice.

They watched horror-stricken, shocked beyond thought
or movement, frozen still as stones, as the woman plum-
meted through the crystal-clear water, bouncing gently
from one ridge to the next. They watched as her skin
turned dark and then burst apart and began to peel
away from her flesh. A strange, almost human shape,
still encased in clothing yet no longer human, the body
finally reached the bottom.

Proud Bear hurled himself forward, screaming, his
arms taut, his fingers reaching. No matter what the
cost, he was ready to seize the old one and fling him
into the pool after the woman. The others hurried to
hold him. Though they wrapped their arms around
every part of his body, still he struggled. Finally they
wrestled him to the ground and held him there until he
subsided into groaning sobs.

There were others who cried as well, including Leaping Fawn. Emri was dry-eyed as he held himself in
tight control. He could not allow himself the luxury of
emotion, for he knew that once it was freed, it would
be difficult if not impossible to control. Instead he
stepped forward and spoke out, calling to the old man
again, shaking Running Bird's shoulder to enlist her
aid.

"Old one," he called out respectfully. "I understand
that you are acting in accordance with the God's wishes
and would not harm us were it not necessary."

Running Bird stared up at him, mouth agape, wondering at his calm words. Emri did not take his eyes off
the old one, but pinched Running Bird sharply, urging
her to translate his words.

"It is true," said the old one. "The God much prefers deer—as do I, for without them I too go hungry."

"I know where there is another deer," said Emri.

"We took all that you had," said the old one. "Do not think to trick me."

"I would not do so. I only wish to help you honor the God. I do not want to see the world end. I speak with truth."

The old one cocked his head to one side and waited for Emri to continue.

"We killed a fifth deer," Emri said, "but we were unable to slaughter it before darkness fell. We hid it in the rocks to keep it from the predators until the light of day. It should be there still."

"It is a trick," said the old one.

"It is no trick. I will tell this one exactly how to find it."

Emri and the old one looked into each other's eyes until the old one blinked and looked away. "Maybe you speak the truth," he said. "Even if there is no deer, he will still be back by morning in time for the day's prayers."

His mind now made up, the old one turned back to Emri and said, "Tell us where to find this deer. And do not think to overcome me. The boy will not help you and you will never find the way out on your own."

Emri did as he was instructed. Using Running Bird, he told the man exactly where to find the deer . . . Mosca's deer . . . and watched in silence with an absence of guilt, knowing that he was sending the man to his death.

CHAPTER ELEVEN

They waited all that day for the return of the old man's helper, but by nightfall he had still not arrived. The old one retired into his hut and did not emerge. Emri wondered if the old one were perhaps afraid of them, for he would be easy to kill without the younger man at his side. His only protection was their inability to find the way out of the crater.

The day was long and without further incident. The people talked softly among themselves, occasionally touching Proud Bear and Leaping Fawn to show respect for their loss. Proud Bear said little, averting his head and nodding when spoken to.

"Emri, we cannot allow this old one to kill us one by one," Dawn said. Birdsong clung to Dawn's neck and stared at Emri with big eyes, her thumb jammed in her mouth.

"He will not have any more of us," Emri replied stolidly. "Had I but realized—"

"None of us realized," said Dawn. "Do not berate yourself. It was too late to stop him. But what will happen now? Do you think that Mosca . . . ?"

"If he is good enough to find the deer, Mosca will take care of him for us. I only pray that he does not injure or kill the cub in turn."

Discussing the possible scenarios concerning Mosca and the old one's assistant filled much of the day and allowed the tribe to think of something other than Proud Bear's woman. Even though he was not expected back before morning—if at all—they watched anxiously to see what would happen.

The boy appeared slightly after dusk, creeping along through the shadows until he reached Emri's side. Emri saw that his small, thin body was covered with bruises and welts, evidence that the old one had beaten him for his part in the morning's events.

"Take me with you," he said in a tiny whisper. "I am not from this place. I am afraid. Maybe if we go far away, the God will not know where to find us and will not kill us."

"Do you know the way out of this place?" Emri asked. "Can you show us?"

"Not at night," the boy whimpered. "The sands shift and things change all the time. It is hard even during the day, but I think I can do it if you will promise to take me with you."

"I would not leave you here! Who are you? How do you come to be here? Where are your people?"

"I am called Brunk. But the old one never calls me anything at all. Still I remember. I have no people anymore. The old one killed them just as he will kill you if you do not leave. He let me live so that I would help him and because I was too small to be of danger to him. But I will kill him now, if I can, before the other returns."

"The other will not return," Emri said, impressed by the child's ferocity. Quietly Emri told the child about Mosca and sending the other to take his deer.

"I hope he hurts him bad and then eats him while he is still alive," the boy said, and Emri wondered what the two men had done to the child to earn such hatred.

"Sleep," said Emri. "We will go with the morning's light. The old one will not be able to stop us with you to show us the way."

"No," said Brunk with a small smile, "he won't."

The sun crested the peaks and found the people awake and waiting. Word of the boy's help had spread quickly, and they smiled at him and touched him to show their happiness. He smiled shyly in return and ducked his head as though uncertain how to act among people who did not want to beat him or treat him cruelly.

The old one had not yet appeared when the boy decreed that it was light enough to leave. They rose excitedly and formed themselves into a line. Men were interspersed with women and children so that they might help each other if the need arose, and also, although the thought was not expressed, so that no one group would be lost if a crevasse opened beneath them.

The boy was several paces out on the gray sands when the old one appeared in the doorway of his stone hut. He realized what was happening and ran toward them, screaming.

"Do not go! You cannot leave! I will not let you. The God will kill us all! Stop!" He ran among them, striking them with his staff and attempting to drive them back. But they avoided his blows and all but ignored him as they continued on, following the boy, who had not looked back.

"You! You know the God! You know his power!" the old man raged as he pushed his way through the people and began striking the boy about the head and shoulders. "How can you betray me?"

"Stop hitting me!" cried Brunk as he turned around and grabbed the old man's staff. "Always you are hitting me, hitting me! I hate you and I hate your God. I am going and you cannot stop me. If the God wishes to kill me, then let him do so. It cannot hurt me worse than all your blows. At least then it will be over!"

The old man and the boy struggled back and forth, staggering in the soft sand, each attempting to gain possession of the staff. Small as the boy was, the old one was not much larger. Their strength was nearly equal. The old man was perhaps stronger, but his endurance was far shorter than that of the boy, who had the added force of his hatred.

The old one felt the ledge against his foot. He swung

the staff so that the boy was forced up onto the harder ground as well. Here the boy was pushed back repeatedly until he stood on the edge of the steaming pool. The women cried aloud and several covered their eyes.

Emri had not interfered in the fight for it appeared that the boy could hold his own, but as the fight moved to the ledge and the old one seemed to gain the upper hand, he moved swiftly to intervene. If they lost the boy, they would never escape.

"No!" cried Brunk as Emri moved in to help him. "Go away. I will do this myself!" He pulled the old one toward him, a move that was unexpected and threw the old man off balance. As the man stumbled toward Brunk, the boy swung the staff with all his might, catching the old man across the chest, knocking the breath out of him and throwing him to the side.

As he stood there, chest heaving, trying to catch his breath, Brunk stuck him again, this time with the base of the staff in the center of his stomach. He followed through, pushing with the staff, pushing the old one before him, stumbling backward, backward, until the old one was falling more than walking, unable to catch his balance.

People scattered, moving out of the way quickly as the two antagonists rushed past. Women screamed. Then it happened, as it had to. The old one felt himself at the edge of the pool, cast a terrified look behind him, swung his arms in wide arcs, and then toppled into the pool.

A woman continued to scream although everyone else had fallen silent. It was like a bad vision that came in the night, but this was a vision that would not vanish with the morning's light.

The old one fell through the clear water, arms outspread, mouth stretched in grimace of pain or humor at the final joke of being sacrificed himself to the God whom he had worshiped all his life. He came to rest on the bottom of the pool, not far from the sad remains of Proud Bear's woman.

Slowly they became aware of the sound of crying.

They turned away from the pool and looked at the boy. Stripped of his anger, he now appeared to be no more than he was, a small, frightened child who had just killed his first man.

Immediately he was surrounded by the men and women who were closest to him. The women spoke gently and tried to soothe him. The men clapped him on the back and touched his arms, telling him what a good job he had done. Emri knelt beside him and spoke, calling him by name and telling him how brave he had been.

"I couldn't do it anymore," Brunk said, hiccuping as he spoke, tears still pouring down his thin cheeks. "I just couldn't let him hit me anymore."

After a time his tears ceased. Bolstered by the praise and admiration of the tribe, he moved to the end of the ledge once more, stepping determinedly out onto the gray, shifting sands.

The way was treacherous and often they sat in utter silence, waiting for the boy to decide which way to go. Some crevasses were readily apparent, others were more deceptive, being buried by drifting dunes of the loose material. These were found by probing each step of the way with the old one's staff. In this way they traversed the hidden dangers and came to the edge of the crater before the Sun God had reached his highest point.

Always at the back of their minds was the fear that the old one's God would seek to avenge his death and their lack of honor. But no flaming rocks shot into the sky, and the plume of steam remained constant. The low rumbling sounded louder in their vulnerable state, but even it did not change.

In the end, as they hurried down the side of the mountain nearly overcome with relief at having escaped, it was decided that the God had accepted the old one as the supreme sacrifice and was content.

They did not stop to rest at the fork of the peaks but continued on, more eager than words could tell, to feel the solid, flat earth beneath their feet once more.

They came to the place where the deer had come and paused only to stamp upon the salt and the other crystals, scattering them and grinding them into the earth. They passed through the narrow place and then came to the place of tumbled boulders. Here they paused and looked about as though expecting to see Mosca or the old one's helper. But there was no sign, bloody or otherwise.

They rushed on, heedless of the fact that Emri had remained behind, anxious to put as much distance between themselves and the mountain as possible.

Dawn, Birdsong, and Hawk remained with Emri.

"Do you think he still lives?" Dawn asked fearfully, eyeing the boulders with trepidation.

"No, he cannot," replied Emri with a confidence he did not feel. "Mosca would not allow him to take the deer away."

"Maybe he surprised Mosca. He had a spear, Emri."

"Our brother would not be taken by surprise," Hawk assured her. "His hearing is keen and his eyes sharp. We will find him unharmed."

They entered the rock-strewn gully, picking their way between the boulders. Emri and Hawk took the lead, Dawn and the child trailing behind.

Emri began to call Mosca by name, trilling softly as he had done when the cat was but a tiny cub. They advanced slowly, following the scuffed trail where the deer's body had dragged along the ground, now more than four days old.

Emri was still calling when he heard a low, rumbling. He looked up to see Mosca lying atop a boulder, sunning himself, his eyes all but closed in contented slits, his head resting on his paws.

"Ho! Mosca old friend, we see you," Emri said with a broad smile, feeling the tension drain out of his shoulders. "We see that you are well."

The cat rose to his feet leisurely, then lowered the front half of his body and stretched his paws out on the boulder, claws extended to their greatest length. His

jaws opened in a long yawn. Emri noted that the fur at
the base of the cat's claws was clotted with blood.

Mosca, his sides bulging hugely, leaped down from
the rock and padded beside them as they walked farther into the rocky defile.

They found the meager remains of the deer—the
skull, hooves, and bits of bone and fur—scattered on
the ground between two large rock outcrops. The man
lay outstretched beside it, his throat ripped out and his
body torn and mutilated.

Emri did not look at him long and wasted little time
saying the words that would send his spirit to the land
of the ancestors. He would not have done so at all—so
great was his dislike of the man—but he did not want to
meet his spirit again in this world.

The spear and the man's knife lay apart, unbroken.
There was no blood on either blade, and Emri picked
them up and handed them to Hawk, grateful that they
had not been damaged. Now their weapons had doubled, and their chances for survival increased.

They stepped over the man, not troubling to cover
his body with boulders, not caring whether his flesh
was eaten and his bones scattered. He was dead and
their concern was with the living.

CHAPTER TWELVE

Emri, Hawk, and Dawn gathered what little remained of the deer, for even such pitiful remnants would be useful in feeding the people if they were unsuccessful in finding game.

They found the tribe just beyond the old camp. The people had not gone far, their hunger being too great and the cries of the children too loud.

They had come upon a small clump of low-lying bushes that would bear a large crop of tasty berries in the peak of Warm Time. These they had eaten, though they were still hard and sour and lay uneasily in their bellies. Unfulfilled, yet exhausted mentally and physically, they had gone no farther. Instead they probed the soil and grass for insects and seed heads, eating anything that came to hand.

Their hunger had so debilitated them as to make them appear little more than animals as they crawled through the grass on hands and knees. During their days on the mountain, they had sucked and chewed on their uncured skins for what little nourishment they could give, but it had not been enough. This hunger was worse than the one that occurred following the death of the village, for that had lasted no more than a day. This hunger had lasted more than four. Had it happened during Warm Time it would not have been so serious, for people ate as much as they were able when food was plentiful and their bodies took on a layer of fat. But Cold Time had just ended and their bodies were thin and had no reserves of fat to call upon.

Emri knew that he had to find food quickly or begin
to lose his people. They were in no condition to defend
themselves and would fall prey to the first pack of
predators that came along.

He looked about him, trying to see some sign of
prey—earth diggers or birds or rabbits—but the land
appeared empty with only grass and low-lying bushes
and a scattering of boulders at the base of the mountain. A flash of movement caught his eye and he turned
in time to see a small brown blur dart beneath a boulder. A smile crossed his face.

He chose Hawk, Broken Tooth, and Otuk to accompany him. They left the people, instructing them to
build a fire and fill a cooking sack with water. They
plied him with questions, but Emri would say no more,
promising only to return with food. Seeing that he was
serious, they began gathering material for the fire. Their
spirits seemed to rise rapidly with the promise of food,
and Emri hoped that he would not fail them.

Emri felt the exhaustion in his legs, as well as cramps
in his thighs and belly, and his ears rang with a constant
high-pitched tone. When he turned his head or moved
quickly, he became dizzy and light-headed. He knew
that his own reserves of strength were dwindling quickly.

The rocks had appeared closer than they really were,
and it took longer than Emri had expected before they
reached them. His legs were trembling and he felt sick
to his stomach, but he was cheered to see that he had
not been mistaken.

Throughout the thin grass and all along the edges of
the rocks were numerous piles of small, round, hard
pellets. Emri picked up a handful and passed them to
Hawk, who nodded his head in happy agreement and
showed them in turn to Otuk and Broken Tooth.

This was no time for subtlety, no time for snares or
lures or traps. It was a time for strength and direct
action.

They moved to the nearest of the boulders, which
was fortunately the smallest as well. While Otuk and
Broken Tooth positioned themselves behind the boul-

der on the up side of the slope, Hawk and Emri stood on either side. There was a soft rumble and Emri looked down to discover Mosca, who had evidently decided that their actions were of more interest than the women and children they had left behind.

Emri was about to speak sharply to Mosca and send him away when he remembered how the cat had learned to kill rabbits during his first Cold Time. Perhaps that lesson would serve them as well in this instance. He pushed the cat into place beside him and then showed him the pellets.

Mosca looked up at him with sleepy, hooded eyes and Emri suddenly felt foolish. With his greater scenting powers, the cat would surely know the whereabouts of the prey they sought.

Broken Tooth and Otuk began rocking the boulder back and forth. An alarmed chittering broke out, accompanied by the sound of rustling leaves. As the boulder began to move, showing more and more of the ground beneath it, the chittering turned to loud piercing whistles.

Otuk and Broken Tooth chanted in unison as they rocked the boulder. The rock teetered on edge and fell, rolling over and over until it collapsed on its side in the grass. But no one was watching the stone, for in leaving its berth it had exposed their quarry.

Round, fat brown bodies exploded in all directions as the creatures scurried out of their nests and sought a place to hide. Mosca darted into action even more swiftly than Hawk or Emri. He swung one heavy paw, scooped up one of the terrified creatures, took it in his jaws and snapped its neck. No sooner was this done than he dropped the animal and went on to another. Hawk and Emri jabbed at the animals with their spears, skewering some and missing others. When it was done, they had killed more of the creatures than the fingers on two hands.

They laid them out in a line and examined them. The golden brown pelted adult animals were longer than a man's hand with short stubby tails and tiny fat legs.

Their bodies were heavy with fat, even after Cold Time, for they were always at work gathering seeds and grasses and flowers to eat when snow and ice buried the land.

The nests were also examined with care, for they would still contain dried seeds, grains, tubers, and lichens that would now fill the people's bellies instead.

They were able to turn five boulders in all—the others being too heavy to move—and killed more of the fat creatures than all their fingers twice counted, as well as two handfuls of newborns. They also gathered large quantities of the dried foods gleaned from the nests.

Their legs were wobbling with strain and their last reserves of energy were all but depleted as they entered the small camp and dropped their booty at the feet of the waiting women.

So great was their hunger it was all the people could do to wait until the animals were skinned, gutted, cut into pieces, and put in the sack of boiling water. The children were crying aloud, and the rich aromas that emanated from the cooking sack caused their bellies to cramp in spasms. The women held the children close and told them that their bellies would soon be full while their own bodies ached with hunger as well.

The sack was removed from the fire long before the meat was well-cooked—the flesh was still bright pink in color—but they could wait no longer. The cooking sack was set upon another tripod made of green sticks broken from the bushes and spread wide to allow easy access.

Women and children crowded round the sack and tried to hide their discomfort, waiting for the men to eat their fill. The men ate quickly, dipping their long shells inside the sack, gulping down the welcome food, unmindful of the bubbling liquid that burned their fingers and scalded their mouths and throats.

When the men had finished, the women and children were allowed to take their share, and soon even their bellies were filled.

Others of the creatures were skinned and gutted, rolled in a ball, and then buried in the coals of the fire.

Here the outer layer of flesh would sear, sealing in all the juices and rich flavors, and allow the creatures to bake in their own fat.

They ate until they could hold no more, then rolled the little black balls of meat from the coals and built up the fire a second time.

The cooking sack was returned to the fire and replenished with more meat and dried materials. It would be allowed to remain undisturbed until morning so that the contents would cook down into a thick, rich gruel that would be eaten for first meal.

Mosca alone was unhungry and turned up his nose at the entrails that he would normally have delighted in.

The boy Brunk ate the most, dipping his hand into the cooking sack again and again until his belly rivaled Dawn's in size. He received much teasing about his condition. He flushed a deep red and hung his head, wondering if he had taken more than his share, but soon realized that the comments were meant in good humor and carried no feeling of hostility. The women realized that the boy had grown up strangely with little love or caring and went out of their way to make him feel a part of the tribe.

Everyone realized that they would not have escaped from the mountain had it not been for his help. So before they slept, Emri praised the boy's bravery, extended their thanks, stated that they would be the stronger for having one so brave among them, and asked him to join the tribe. Brunk accepted shyly.

It was intended that a guard should be kept so that they should not be caught unawares as they had been before. Proud Bear had admitted with shamed face that he had fallen asleep near dawn, thus allowing the tribe to be captured. But the heavy meal coupled with extreme exhaustion caused Tusk to fall asleep almost immediately despite his intentions and he slept through the night until dawn. Fortunately, there was no threat of danger and they slept in safety.

CHAPTER THIRTEEN

It was as though they had pleased the Gods in some way, for from that day on, things seemed to flow in their favor. Game presented itself to their spears and slings and the weather grew steadily better. The days grew longer and warmer. The land opened itself before them like an unending gift, exhibiting wondrously colored flowers and birds that they had never seen before, seeming to grow more beautiful daily.

Emri, Dawn, Hawk, and Broken Tooth took the greatest of pleasure in showing the tribe new things. They were delighted with the most simple of things, such as birch trees with their startling white bark that could be peeled off in great sheets and worked into handsome containers. They fashioned silly hats for the children that made them shriek with laughter. They also made small replicas of the floater that had carried them so far. These were put into the multitude of streams that they camped beside. The children played and it was good to hear their laughter ringing through the camp.

They made good progress with the constant supply of food. Soon they reached the land where birches grew in large stands, accompanied by alders, larches, willows, and a variety of other unidentified trees. They marveled over each and every new thing, scarcely believing the trees themselves, and wondering aloud that they could grow so tall without falling over.

Now they entered the outer edge of the hardwood

104

forest. Each tree rose tall and separate, surrounded by
large expanses of grassland filled with a wide variety of
animal life.

Slowly the land began to change. The mountains
withdrew from the coast. Though still paralleling their
path inland, the mountains left behind great folds in the
land covered with lush grasses and the first of the great
stands of evergreens.

Seeing this land again, pointing out the spot where
they had found the dead bear and where Mosca had
been chased by a live one, was like coming home to
Hawk and Dawn and Emri. They told the people these
tales, and Broken Tooth regaled them with the story of
the chase, following on their heels, intent on their death.

As they entered the great evergreen forest, inhaled
the rich fragrance, and felt the awe that the huge trees
inspired, Emri brought up the subject that had plagued
them all since the first days of their voyage: Where
would they settle, where would they make their new
home? As yet, they had seen no sign of people other
than the men on the mountain. They had hoped to join
another tribe, yet Emri and Hawk knew that they had
seen no others on their voyage north. This, Broken
Tooth confirmed. Dawn was strangely silent.

As they sat around the fire talking, the flames throwing bright sheets of light against the roughly grained
trunks of the trees, the huge nodding ferns casting
strange shadows of their own, they discussed the possibilities of building a home in this beautiful forest.

Otuk and Tusk were much in favor, as were several
of the women, who were delighted with the great abundance of ground foods that Hawk and Dawn had led
them to discover. Also a point in its favor was the
closeness of the coast. The movement of the waves was
a constant murmur in their ears, providing a reassuring
familiarity to them in this land of strangeness. It could
always be counted on to provide them with food and
other materials necessary for their way of life.

Oddly, it was Running Bird who presented the first
argument against staying in the forest.

"Where are the deer?" she asked, looking Emri full in the face. "You have promised to bring us back to the deer. Yet I have seen no deer or any sign of them aside from those we slew at the foot of the mountain."

"Mother of mothers, it is true that I gave my word to lead you back to the deer," Emri said, somewhat flustered and glancing at Hawk for reassurance. "There are deer in this place. We saw them with our own eyes and killed a stag not far from this place before we journeyed to your village."

"That was then, this is now," Running Bird said firmly. "We are the People of the Deer. Not part of the time, but *all* of the time. People of the Deer must have deer or we will no longer exist."

Emri stared at her, wondering what he could say that would convince her of the illogic of her argument, but no adequate words came to mind. Even worse, others were beginning to nod their heads in agreement!

"But mother, there are squirrels and pricker-backs and rabbits and birds, nuts and ground foods in plenty," he argued.

"Shall we then be People of the Birds or People of the Rabbits," Running Bird asked implacably, and Emri knew that he had lost.

"Where shall we go then, mother?" he asked.

"Where the deer may be found all of the time."

Emri could do naught but defer to her, knowing that it would do him no good to argue.

"Is there such a place, Emri?" Proud Bear asked wistfully. Emri was jolted from his thoughts by the man's question, for Proud Bear had fallen into a deep sadness following the death of Sunshine and now bore little resemblance to the arrogant, boastful fellow he had been before her death. Proud Bear had drawn inside himself, perhaps brooding on his failure to save the woman, and while he still functioned, his face was empty and without expression. He seldom spoke. His remaining woman, Leaping Fawn, had done all that she was able to bring him out of his strange silence, but even she was all but ignored.

"Tell us about the place that you come from, the place where your people live," Proud Bear urged. "Tell us about the animals."

"There are deer," Emri said, clearing his throat roughly, uneasy at the man's strange manner. Proud Bear had not been one of those he liked best, but it unnerved him to see the man acting so. He wished that Proud Bear could return to normal. Even his overbearing, superior attitude would be better than this lethargy. "There are deer all the time, even in Cold Time—which is not so cold as it was in your land. There is snow in the mountains, but never on the plains where our tribe dwells.

"There are deer and hairy tuskers and antelope and their larger brothers, who wear great wooden horns on their heads, larger in all directions than even a man with arms and legs outspread. So heavy are these horns that a man must have help carrying them if the spirits guide his spear truely.

"There are pricker-backs and squirrels and rabbits and bears and great hulking ones with long snuffling noses and coarse hair that eat only leaves and are easily killed. Then there are the squealers with their long sharp tusks, mean eyes, hooves sharp as knives and sweet meat that is worth the danger of the hunt.

"The Endless Waters are not so close, but there are other waters, rivers and streams that flow sweet and clean without the taste of salt. It is a beautiful land," he concluded, and for a time his heart was heavy with sadness. Dawn pressed her forehead against his shoulder and he knew that she too was yearning for home.

"I do not wish to live among these tall trees," cried that same woman who had wanted to live beneath the overhang. "They are too tall and they shut out the sun. I am afraid that they will fall down and kill me! Take us to this wondrous land!"

Other voices shouted out in agreement, and Emri lowered his head to hide the feeling of rage that swept across him. He almost wished that a tree would fall on the woman and still her trouble-making tongue.

"I cannot go home," Emri said quietly. "I would do so if I could, but the shaman, Mandris, has cast me out of the tribe and vowed to kill me should I return."

"We are not afraid of him!" shouted Tusk. "You are not alone anymore; you have a tribe of your own. We would not let him harm you. He would not dare to fight you with us standing at your side!"

There were many such cries, and Hawk and Emri looked at each other with equal parts of astonishment and cautious wonder that such a thing might be possible. Never had they thought of returning, except in their own private visions. Much as it was desired, it had seemed an all but impossible dream.

Dawn looked up at Emri and there were tears in her eyes. "I want to go home," she whispered. "I want to go home."

Proud Bear looked at Emri with eyes that shone with an unnatural brightness. "You could return if you wished to do so," he said quietly in a tone that cut across the boisterous conversation. "You are not afraid of anything, animal or human. We have witnessed your courage. As you have told us yourself, you are brother to the lion. Take us, Emri. Take us to the land that does not die with the coming of Cold Time, take us to the land of sweet water and deer. Take us, Emri, take us home."

Silence fell on the camp, leaving only the snap and crackle of burning wood to be heard and the sleepy murmur of the child in Dawn's arms. Then everyone began speaking at once with the exception of Emri and Hawk, who did not know what to say. How could they explain to the people the black, unreasoning hatred of the shaman who would not be deterred by anyone's presence but would seek Emri's death in spite of them? Any denial from Emri and Hawk would only make it seem as though they did not wish to return to their tribe with the people—which was anything but the truth.

"Maybe . . . maybe I could help," Broken Tooth said tentatively. "I am expected to return. My woman and children await me, as does the shaman. I could go back before you and tell the people how it really was.

"I will tell them that the totem, the great tiger, was sick and dying with the pain and the poison of his broken fang. I will tell them that Mandris fed the tiger painkilling herbs in order to command him and make him do his will.

"I will tell them that Mandris sent the tiger against your father in order to kill him and take his place as chief as well as shaman, and that he wished to rid himself of you before you became a threat. I will tell them that he sent the tiger against you and that you killed it only to save your own life.

"They will listen to me," said Broken Tooth, "and they will believe me. Mandris is feared, but he is not loved. Once they understand, they will welcome you back, for you are your father's son and the true chief of the tribe."

"And what will happen to Mandris?" Emri asked dryly. "He will not stand aside meekly and allow you to take away what he has acquired. Whatever else he may be, his is no coward. He will fight to keep what he has, whether it belongs to him rightly or wrongly."

"You are *our* chief. We will not allow him to harm you," said Otuk. "Our spears will drive him back into the forest where he belongs. Never will we see him again!"

Emri listened to the brave cries echoing around him and rubbed his eyes with the heels of his hands, sighing and wondering if it could really be so easy. Was it possible that he and Hawk had misjudged the man's power? Although it was but one full turning of the seasons since last they met the man, it seemed a far greater length of time. When he thought back on it, he appeared in his own thoughts as little more than a child. It had been a long time since he had felt that young in truth.

Emri looked at Hawk and saw his own indecision mirrored in his friend's eyes. "What do you think?" he asked softly. "Do you think such a thing could be done? Are we strong enough to take him if he will not listen to reason?"

Doubt crept into Hawk's brown eyes and he tilted his
head to one side, considering the issue. "Such a thing
may be possible," he said at last, "if one is willing to
take the risk. But I do not know what will be the
outcome.

"I cannot imagine that one so filled with hate would
allow you to return and take away that which he has
gained. He needs the feeling of power to make him big.
Without power, he is nothing. He will fight to keep his
power."

"Can we beat him?" Emri asked, seeking truth and
an honest assessment rather than enthusiastic rhetoric.

"I don't know. Perhaps," replied Hawk. "If we control the circumstances . . . decide the place of meeting,
make him come to us at a place of our choosing . . .
perhaps then. But he will not fight fairly, no matter
what the setting."

"Then," Emri said with a cold smile, "there is nothing binding us to honor, either."

Excitement ran high as the People of the Deer realized that Emri and Hawk had decided to return to the
land that they had heard so much about, the land of
mild weather and plentiful food, the land where deer
were to be found always.

Talk continued far into the night. For the first time in
a long time, Dawn smiled at Emri and the shadow of
sadness that always lurked behind her eyes was gone.
Happiness seemed to radiate from her, speaking more
loudly than words of her joy at his decision.

As he took her in his arms and wrapped the furskin
around them, waiting for sleep to come, Emri stared up
at the campfires of the ancestors twinkling high above
him in the dark sky and prayed that he had made the
right decision.

CHAPTER FOURTEEN

The days passed swiftly from that point on, for all were eager to reach their final destination.

They were slowed momentarily at a place where the land had broken away from itself and slid into the Endless Waters below.

While searching for a way around the treacherous landfall, they came upon a great outcrop of stone that was suitable for the making of spear points and knives. As much as they wished to hurry, all agreed that weapons were a necessity that could not be dismissed. They set up camp in a nearby grove and immediately set out to gather a supply of stone to work from.

Although Emri and Hawk had fashioned spear points and the knife that Emri wore at his side, it had been a laborious process and neither of them judged themselves proficient at the skill. They had assumed that there would be one who was well skilled in working stones among the People of the Deer. Unfortunately, this was not the case.

"Long Lip was our best stone worker," Otuk said with dismay. "But he was killed by the hairy tuskers. Botha was good too, but he died inside the mountain of ice."

"But Tusk, I thought you told me that you made this spear point," Emri cried, pointing to the ivory point that crowned the only spear that had survived the destruction of the village.

"I did," said Tusk. "But carving bone and stone are two different things. Botha tried to teach me when I was a child and then gave up, saying I might do better if I used my toes. I will gladly try my hand with the stone, but I do not think my skills will have improved much since I sat at Botha's knee."

In the end Emri and Hawk were forced to conclude that any spear making that was done would depend entirely on them.

The rock was finely grained and grayish black in color. The land slippage had exposed wide bands of it in the raw earth, interspersed with chalky deposits and broad swaths of sandstone. The stress of the break had caused the stone to shatter into large rectangular blocks, which, when carefully drawn from the broken face of the newly formed cliff, were more than half a man-height in all directions.

Not realizing at first how large or how heavy the sheets of rock were, several were dropped before they were able to get one safely on top of the cliff.

Emri heaved a deep sigh, looking down at the great rock that lay in front of him, and shook his head, wishing that the Gods had seen fit to spare one of the stone workers.

He bent down to study the stone, running his hand over the smooth dark surface and admiring the tight, almost imperceptible grain. If they succeeded in freeing the points from the rock, they would make excellent weapons.

The first problem was in finding hammerstones, those stones that would actually break the sheet of rock into workable pieces, and then others of various weights that would aid in forming it.

Emri and Hawk, followed by Brunk, the other adolescent boys and Mosca, ranged up and down a nearby creek, searching for rocks that would serve as the valuable hammerstones. The men meanwhile sought to wrestle still another sheet of rock to the top of the cliff.

Emri and Hawk picked up rock after rock, hefting

them up and down, getting the feel of them, until they had found a goodly number that were judged as possibilities. These they carried back to the edge of the cliff where the men waited for them. A second sheet of rock now rested beside the first.

During the course of the first day, they studied the stone, searching out its flaws and imperfections, pointing out places to each other where it might be expected to break whether desired or not. Next they used pieces of the chalky material to rough out those sections that they desired, marking especially the primary strike points. When they were finished, it appeared that a large bird had marched back and forth over the surface of the rock, marking it with strange and bizarre patterns of excrement.

They left the actual cutting of the stone for the morning of the following day, for steady hands and steady nerves were required.

They returned to the camp that the women had established and ate their fill of the meal that had been prepared. Birdsong was walking unsteadily at Dawn's side, her short legs creased with fat that was good to see. Her chubby arms were raised above her curly head as she cried, " 'Ama, 'ama," in plaintive tones, begging to be picked up. But Dawn was carrying a basket of fish—some of which were still alive and wriggling over the bodies of their dead companions toward the edges of the basket—and was unable to comply with the child's request.

Emri called her name. As she turned unsteadily, her bow lips pouting out in the beginnings of a cry, her heavily hooded eyes mere slits in her plump round face, Emri caught her up in his arms and threw her high into the air. She shrieked aloud with equal amounts of fear and excitement. Dawn tossed him a grateful smile and hurried on her way to gut and halve the fish.

Emri continued to play with the child, chasing her through camp, almost allowing her to escape before he caught her again, and then tickling her till she could laugh no more. When she tired of the game, he carried

her back to their furskin, which had grown with the
addition of new furs as they were acquired, cured, and
then stitched onto the ever-expanding patchwork.

Emri laid Birdsong down on the soft gray patch of
rabbit fur, the child's favorite spot, and gave her a
length of tree stem cut from a hardwood sapling earlier
that day. The sweet, sticky sap had oozed from the cuts
and hardened. Birdsong squealed with joy, for sweets
were hard to come by and a favorite among adults and
children alike.

She sucked greedily on the stick, pausing occasionally to look up at Emri and murmur more to herself
than to him, " 'Ama." She fell asleep finally, one hand
still tightly gripping the sapling; the other, also liberally
coated with stickiness, entwined in one of her long
curls. Her little flower-petal lips were slightly parted
and her breath came in soft whispers. Her long, curved
lashes lay thick and delicately on her red cheeks. Emri's
heart ached as he looked at her and he knew with a
rush of sudden insight that he could scarcely love the
child more if she were his own. He had barely known of
her existence only a short time before, and now she had
grown in importance till she claimed a part of his heart.

He looked down at the sleeping child and wondered,
not for the first time, if the spirits of the ancestors had
sent the child to them to ease the loss of their first
born.

That night Hawk sat in front of the blazing fire,
wrapped in a furskin of his own against the chill wind
blowing off the waters below, and drew upon a bit of
flat rock with a piece of chalk.

The people had become accustomed to Hawk's likenesses and were not quite so ready to think them
totems or other symbols of the Gods. Still, they were
special items and his skills were accorded great respect.

"What are you doing, old friend?" Emri asked as he
sat next to Hawk and looked down at the stone. Emri
started back in horror, for there, staring back at him,
thin lip curled in a contemptuous sneer, was the shaman Mandris. "Why do you make a likeness of this

one!" Emri asked, pulling back from the stone. "Will we not see his hated face soon enough? Why do you bring his presence into our camp?"

"He has been much on my mind," Hawk replied, placing the stone down on the ground. "I did not wish to cause you distress. But I thought that if I could image him, some message might come to me."

"And has it?" asked Emri, interested in spite of himself.

"No. I feel nothing but hate. But still, the feeling is with me, some message that I cannot understand. Perhaps I will ask the stones."

"Hawk, do the stones really speak to you?" Emri wanted desperately to know the answer, for if there were really a way to know the future . . .

"I think sometimes they do, yes. Although not in the manner that you mean. The answers are not always clear-cut, easy to understand, but as in the way of life, are often open to interpretation. The stones speak their own language and must be read as carefully as the track of an animal. It is not always easy to understand. I had thought that I would use the smoke weed to aid my understanding." After a moment of deliberation he said, "Yes, there is a message here that I am not receiving. Perhaps the smoke weed will help."

Hawk pulled a thong from around his neck and drew a small sack from beneath his tunic. The sack was made of some soft skin and had taken on the darkened shiny patina of leather of great age. Hawk opened the mouth of the sack carefully and took out yet another bit of leather, this one wrapped around an oval object. Hawk unwrapped it carefully and laid a small cream-colored pipe on the ground in front of him. Then he took a second pouch out of the sack. He untied it and using his thumb and forefinger, removed a pinch of some dried powdery material and placed it in the bowl of the pipe.

He propped the stone with the likeness of Mandris in front of him where he could see it easily. Then he took a tiny twig, lit it in the fire, and touched it to the bowl of the pipe. He inhaled deeply and the scent hung

redolent on the air. Much to Emri's surprise, Hawk
passed the pipe to him. He took it somewhat uncer-
tainly, for he had never smoked a pipe before. He put
the pipe to his lips and inhaled as he had seen Hawk
do. Immediately he choked and gagged and doubled
over in a fit of coughing as his throat and chest were
seized in a band of tightness that drove all of the air out
of his lungs. Tears came to his eyes and still he coughed,
wheezing painfully. When finally he was able to catch
his breath and sit upright, Hawk handed him the pipe
again.

This time he drew on the pipe more cautiously, and
though his throat tightened, he was careful to allow the
smoke no farther than his mouth, where it numbed his
tongue.

Back and forth the pipe went, a tiny tendril of smoke
curling up from the ivory bowl. Emri became intent on
watching this small thread of smoke as it issued from
the pipe only to be swept away by the wind. He found
himself admiring its delicate beauty and wondering where
smoke went, what became of it after it left the fires. He
admired the fire itself, picking out the reds and yellows
and blues, attempting to separate each of the intricate
shades and look into its white-gold heart.

He found to his bemusement that the terrible raw
ache had vanished and that he was now able to draw
the smoke down deep into his chest, and had been
doing so for some time. The smoke had lost its harsh-
ness and now felt both pleasant and deeply satisfying.

He glanced at Hawk as their fingers touched on the
pipe and saw him, it seemed, as though for the first
time. Hawk's eyes, deep brown, nearly black in color,
seemed to penetrate, touching not the skin or the exte-
rior that did not matter, but the inner spirit.

A warm glow began to spread through Emri's chest,
spreading outward in radiant waves from that secret
heart of him until it enveloped him completely. The
glow had encompassed Hawk as well and still the two
men stared into each other's eyes, seeing things that
none other could share.

After a time Hawk turned aside slowly, emptying the pipe and returning it to its ancient wrappings. The pouch followed the pipe, and soon they were tucked away safely beneath Hawk's tunic.

Another set of pouches had appeared in his hands. These Emri recognized as the pouches that held the stones and their helpers, the stones that would point the way and tell what was to be. He allowed his gaze to fall on the likeness of the shaman, his enemy. The shaman's face leapt into prominence: the high sharp cheekbones, the long thin nose, the hard eyes, and the cruel mouth.

Enthralled, Emri stared at the likeness as the face seemed to move, to breathe, seemed almost to speak. With great effort Emri closed his eyes, breaking the connection. Even then he felt the weight of the man's eyes upon him.

He raised his hand and rubbed his face as though to drive away the image. His flesh felt stiff and wooden to the touch, almost as though it belonged to another. His head dropped forward and rested on his chest, and he closed his eyes and allowed himself to drift, like the smoke, away from the horrible likeness, away from the pressure of responsibility, away from the weight of decisions.

It was very difficult to return, to bring himself back, to answer the insistent tug on his arm. He opened his eyes and felt an incredible rush of dizziness as though he had returned from a great distance in that very instant. He blinked and looked into Hawk's eyes. Hawk shook his arm again and said, "It is time to cast the stones."

Hawk had cleared a space before him and drawn a circle on the ground. Now he shook the sack, jumbling its contents. Although that would not deter the Gods from selecting those items which they desired in order to show the poor humans the way, mused Emri.

Hawk tossed the sack into the air, grasping the bottom of it at the last second. A number of rocks and stones of various sizes, shapes, and colors cascaded from the mouth of the sack and tumbled through the air.

It seemed to Emri that they did so with a sense of deliberateness that was not of their own choosing. Certain rocks rose straight up and then fell straight down. Other rocks seemed to fall sideways, certain to land outside the circle. Emri smiled and nodded knowingly with sudden insight, knowing that this was the way it was meant to be, wondering why he had never realized it before.

Without really looking, Hawk scooped up those rocks that had fallen outside the circle and returned them to the sack. Next he shook up the pouch that contained the helpers and continued as before, allowing them to leave the bag and enter the circle or fall outside, whatever the Gods dictated.

When those that had not been chosen had been returned to the sack, Hawk allowed himself to study the inner circle. Slowly Emri lowered his gaze and looked down at the ground too, wondering what he would see.

Although he was not as adept as Hawk at reading the stones, it was obvious, even to him, that something odd had occurred. The circle contained a very strange mixture of stones and helpers. He leaned forward and studied them more carefully.

"Look, you," said Hawk in a gravelly voice. "I have never seen this before. Every single stone and helper that signifies life: plant, animal, bird, water, fish, is here; none have been left out."

"I am there too," mused Emri, spotting the stone that held the likeness of a man and a cat in its folds if one looked carefully.

"And I." Hawk picked out the stone that was formed in the profile of a hawk. "And here is the stone that signifies death." He picked up the round black stone, closing his fist around it. "But whose death does it foretell?"

They looked at each other, seeking an answer, when there was a sharp report from the fire as a log split and broke in half. Then, with no warning or reason, the likeness of the shaman, which had in no way touched the fire or been disturbed by the falling log, toppled over and landed well inside the circle, face up, surrounded by all of the others.

Emri and Hawk looked at each other with shocked eyes, wondering at this omen that the Gods had added to the circle in such a forthright manner. Neither of them spoke, not knowing what to say. For a time they sat there, unmoving, staring down at the circle.

"It is no more than we have always known," Hawk said at last. "Our lives and our fates are tied up with that of the shaman. It does not matter how far we travel, we must eventually return to face him. And we have always known it, I think."

"He knows it too," said Emri with sudden conviction as he stared down at the stone shaman. "He knows that we are coming."

CHAPTER FIFTEEN

Emri wakened with a sense of great calm. He looked up at the sky, still gray and cloaked with the heavy mist that covered the land each day before the coming of the sun. He felt the heaviness that was Mosca, pressed against his back. He felt the soft exhalations of the child on his shoulder and inhaled the warm, woman scent that was Dawn.

He wondered, with the same sense of calm, whether he would be alive to see the child that Dawn was carrying in her belly, and then dismissed the thought, knowing that it was in the hands of the Gods. What would be, would be. There was no sense in struggling against destiny.

Yet it would not do to relinquish all action. The Gods would not respect a man who did not fight for what was his and do his best to live rightly. Despite the coming battle, which he now knew was inevitable, he would continue to lead his life in a proper manner.

This was the day of stone cutting. If the Gods were willing, his aim would be true and the stone would break in the desired shapes. This first cutting was all important, and Emri hoped that the Gods would be with him.

Slipping from beneath the warmth of the furskin and dislodging Mosca in the process, Emri padded over to the face of the cliff and stared out across the restless waters.

A grumbling Mosca joined him, sitting down atop his

foot. The low-lying clouds of mist parted momentarily and allowed him to see a line of the giant gray fish swimming north—those same immense creatures that they had seen swimming south on their journey to the land of ice. They were so very huge, larger than the largest of hairy tuskers, that they stopped his breath with the wonder of them.

As though in response to his admiration, one of the creatures dove beneath the cold gray waters in a single fluid motion, seeming almost to balance on its head, hesitating. Its great, broad, curved tail slapped the water with a resounding boom and only then did it vanish beneath the waves. Then the mists closed above the waters and they were gone. Emri smiled down at the cat and stroked his head, knowing that the Gods had given him a gift, an omen, and he hoped it meant that the day's work would go well.

Leaving Mosca to follow sleepily, Emri returned to camp, now ready to begin the cutting.

Mosca lay beside him, gnawing contentedly on a chunk of meat that he had stolen from the women's supplies as Emri studied the stone, deciding where to make the first strike.

His decision made, he selected one of the heavier hammerstones, a smooth, round stone that had been tumbled over and over across the rough creek bed as it was washed down from the higher elevations. It fit his hand well, filling it amply, yet not so far that his fingers were stretched and might drop the stone at a crucial moment.

He hefted the rock, raising and lowering it until it felt just right in his hand, and then, taking a deep breath, he struck the rock a sharp blow. It broke along the line he had drawn. He smiled, then raised his face to the sky and spoke his thanks to the Gods for guiding his aim.

By the time the sun had burned the last of the fog from the land and the men had risen from their furskins and filled their bellies with hot broth and roasted meat,

Emri had broken a stack of rough squares from the rock. It was from these squares that the blades and points would be shaped.

His back and thighs stiff with sitting in one position for so long, Emri rose from the ground and stretched, glad for the warmth of the rising sun.

He joined the men, took the wooden bowl that had been handed to him, and filled it from the cooking sack, anticipating the rich warmth of the broth in his belly. He was content to keep his silence this morning and did not join in the good-natured conversation that occupied the others. When he had eaten his fill, he returned to the stone.

Now came the difficult part. Emri sat down on the ground, crossing his legs in front of him. He placed a thick piece of bearskin across his left thigh. Next he chose a hammerstone, smaller than the one he had used to free the blanks, yet not the smallest of those he had acquired. Holding the unshaped stone in his left hand, he rested it against the bearskin. Holding the hammerstone in his right hand, he began to strike the stone all along its edges, removing a thin, round flake with every blow. This he did until he had gone around the stone entirely, leaving a rough, wavy edge.

Emri straightened and stretched, feeling the tightness between his shoulder blades. He looked down at his work and was pleased. Were he to leave off at this point, the stone could be used as a hand ax or even as a chopper. Feeling his confidence rise, Emri selected a smaller hammerstone and bent to his work once more.

This stage was more difficult than the previous step. Here, the edge was straightened and the more obvious bumps and ridges removed from the rough form. Using the smaller hammerstone, Emri struck carefully and only after great deliberation. Striking on a severe angle from the center of the piece, he knocked off long, thin flakes of stone.

When this step was completed, Emri heaved a great sigh. Setting the stone aside, he got up and walked around, swinging his arms back and forth to ease the tension. He twisted his head in a circle, feeling the strain in all parts of his body.

"How goes the making of spears?" Hawk asked, joining Emri as he stood on the edge of the creek bed.

"As well as can be expected." Emri grinned at his friend, who had himself shared the frustrations of making points during their first Cold Time together. "The Gods must be guiding my hand, for I have not yet ruined the stone."

"It is but a matter of time," said Hawk, grinning in return. "Patience."

Emri feinted a blow to Hawk's chin as though chiding him for his words and then returned to his work, cheered by the exchange.

As the day wore on, he was joined by the younger children and the men as well. Some had just come to watch and talk. Others, including the two adolescent boys and the youngster Brunk seemed eager to try their own hands at the attempt.

Finally, more to occupy them and thus keep them from disturbing his concentration, Emri set them to striking bits of stone gathered from the creek. This also got them accustomed to the feel of the hammerstones. They set about with great seriousness and in the end had a small pile of chips and many bruised and bleeding fingers to show for their efforts. Most of the men, those whose interest was not strong, wandered away, and Emri was left with the three boys, Tusk, and Hawk.

Hawk, who knew as much about the making of spears as Emri, took the four apprentices in hand, freeing Emri to continue with his work.

He had now reached the fourth stage of the shaping, and for this he used the point of a deer antler, one of many that they had found in the forest. The single tine fit into his hand nicely. Resting the stone against the bearskin, he applied pressure to the tine, pressing it against the edge of the half-formed stone until a flake of stone popped off. This was done all around the stone until it began to take on the shape that it would bear when finished.

Hawk declared a halt. The boys rushed to Emri's side
with a loud clamor, anxious to show him their work.
Emri was pleased to note that Brunk had what appeared to be real talent: the flakes along the edge of his
rock were aligned in neat, precise waves. Tusk, too,
showed aptitude, and Emri was relieved to think that
others might one day share the difficult task.

The sun was beginning its final descent into the
Endless Waters when Emri rose from his position and
tucked the precious point into his pouch.

Those men who had not worked at stone cutting had
not been idle. They had spent the day in the forest with
their slings and snares and had brought back large
numbers of squirrels and rabbits. These had been
skinned, gutted, quartered, and placed in the cooking
sack along with a variety of tender, unfurled fern tips,
fungi, and seeds, resulting in a rich and tasty stew.

Birdsong tottered up to Emri as he approached and
raised her arms to be lifted. She was all but naked
because of the onset of warm weather and to ease in the
training of proper toilet manners. In this matter she
seemed stubbornly determined not to learn.

"Phew! Little one, you smell as bad as a dead fish!"
cried Emri as he grasped her beneath the arms and
held her out in front of him. Before she realized what
was happening, he had carried her over to the creek
bed and plunged her into the frigid water. He held her
there, despite her screams, until he had scrubbed her
thoroughly from head to toe with handfuls of coarse
sand.

She emerged from the creek crying loudly and squirm-
ing in his arms like a wet fish. She refused to be
comforted and held out her arms to Dawn, crying all
the louder as though Emri had beaten her with a stick.

"I told her she smelled worse than a dead fish," Emri
explained as he handed the squalling child to Dawn.
"Now I smell bad and I am wet too."

"She will learn," Dawn said with a smile, tucking
Birdsong's head into her neck and rubbing her back in
small, soothing circles. "These things take time."

"It is all right," said Emri as he took them both in his arms, resting his forehead against Dawn's and rubbing the hard rise of her belly against his stomach. "I can use the practice to use with this one in its turn."

He was back at work as soon as the mists cleared on the morning of the following day, ready for the difficult work that was to come. Here the point of the antler was used again, struck on its base by a hammerstone until a tiny stone flake popped free, further straightening the edge on both sides and creating the desired shape. This final process took Emri the entire morning, but when he was done, he held a spear point in his hands that was adequate if not precisely perfect.

Over the course of the next ten days, Emri and Hawk were able to finish enough spear points for every man in the tribe as well as a variety of knives, choppers, axes, and other cutting tools to be used by the women. There had been a number of mistakes, some of which had ruined the points after much of the work had already been done.

The three boys and Tusk had proved to be able students, Brunk being foremost among them. He proudly wore a very nicely fashioned knife and carried a crude spear point in his pouch, both of his own making. It was hard to recognize the boisterous well-fed youngster as the scrawny, terrified boy they had found on the mountain. Brunk flashed an impish gap-toothed smile at Emri and dashed past, followed by the two other boys. Emri smiled in return, watching them go.

CHAPTER SIXTEEN

As pleasant as the camp at the edge of the cliff had been, they were not unhappy to leave it behind, eager as they were to reach their destination.

Along with the journey itself and the constant gathering of food, the chief goal now was the finding of wood that would serve as shafts for their spears. They were surrounded for the most part by evergreens, which were not suitable for this purpose, being too soft and easily split. Emri knew that the oak hardwoods were the best for spears and it was this that they sought. Some oak trees were found, but they rose straight and tall without branching until they were far above the ground, and their trunks were wider than a man could grasp between his thighs.

The land grew more wild and the trees grew closer together, casting dark shadows on the land below. The morning mists lingered longer and became soft rains that continued throughout the day and night. The rain fell on them in the spaces between the trees and dripped off their branches till the people were wet and cold all of the time. It was all but impossible to build a fire, and several adults and most of the children developed deep, racking coughs and their bodies burned with fever.

It was feared that an evil spirit had found them—perhaps that of the old man of the mountain—for they could attribute the sickness to no other cause.

Hawk was asked to throw the stones or drive the

spirit away with the proper chants. But Hawk was among those taken by the illness, and his head ached at the mere thought of casting the stones and having to think about what they meant. Nor did he know any chants that would drive away evil spirits. All he really wanted to do was lie down and sleep, but Emri would not allow him to do so. He drove them relentlessly, day after day, determined to find an end to the rainfall.

But the rain did not end, continuing on and on as though the Gods intended to drown the world. Fire and warmth were all but forgotten as they walked through the dark, dripping forests by day and slept on the wet ground each night. There was little or no shelter to be found.

One morning the young girl, Shell, failed to waken and could not be roused even when shaken. They clustered around her and called her name and did their best to warm her, but it was to no avail. She died on the morning of the second day without ever having opened her eyes.

Running Bird wailed the loudest, for the girl was the daughter of a daughter and had been much loved. But none of them were untouched by grief. Shell had been bright and clever and always willing to lend a hand with whatever task needed to be done.

Tears stung Emri's eyes as much as his sense of failure stabbed his heart, and he blamed himself for the girl's death.

A deep hole was dug, deep enough to hold the girl and the few belongings she would want with her in the land of the ancestors. The bottom of the pit was lined with fragrant fir branches and she was placed atop them with her hands folded on her chest, holding one of the precious skinning knives. Her hair was neatly braided and garnished with clusters of tiny shells that Emri had gathered from the wave-tossed shore far below.

The words were said that would speed her to the land of her ancestors, and then one by one the people took their turn laying a branch on her body till she

could be seen no more. Emri and Tusk pushed the
earth back into the hole, and Dawn held Running Bird,
who shrieked aloud and called the girl's name, attempting to throw herself into the grave.

Emri finished the onerous chore and then gently took
the old woman from Dawn, hugging the skinny figure
to his chest. "Do not cry," he said. "She is free from
pain now and will soon be among those who loved her
in life and went before her to show the way."

"Me," wailed Running Bird. "They should have taken
me. I am old and of no use. Why did they not take me
instead?" But Emri had no reply.

They took up their journey again with spirits as dark
as the sky above. Mosca disliked the wetness as much
as the people and slunk along from one tree to the next
with moisture dripping off his fur at every step.

They did not stop for meals but ate from their supplies of smoked and dried meats and gathered what
ground foods they could find along the way.

More than half their number were plagued by coughs,
runny noses, sneezing, and fevers. Periodically, one or
more of those afflicted would lag behind and would be
found huddled against the cool, wet bark of a tree.
They were not grateful to be found and would fight and
then beg and plead to be left alone. But Emri knew
that if he honored their wishes, they would never be
seen again this side of the land of the spirits.

More and more of the people became ill, until only
three of them, Emri, Running Bird, and the boy Brunk,
were free of the dread symptoms. People no longer
showed any interest in eating and their bowels had
turned to water. The fever now alternated with chills,
which frightened Emri even more. It became impossible to keep the people moving. Emri knew that they
had to find shelter from the rain or die.

The land was heavily wooded yet some distance from
the mountains where they might have found shelter in
a cave. No dwelling could be built for the trees were all
of an immense size, rising far above their heads before
the branches formed. And the descent to the rocky

shore was far too steep to climb, falling away in sheer cliffs.

Emri felt as though he were reaching the very limit of his abilities. He was physically exhausted and half mad with worry. Worst of all was knowing that he was helpless. He could think of nothing that would be of any help. Not for the first time he lowered his head and murmured a prayer to the spirits, begging them to help him.

All around him people were staggering, barely even able to lift their legs for yet another step. Emri half supported, half carried Dawn and held Birdsong, who was burning with heat, across his shoulder. He trudged on, eyes all but closed, all but overwhelmed by exhaustion and despair. He knew that when they stopped this time, many would not rise.

A branch slapped him in the face and then another, shocking him to wakefulness. He opened his eyes and saw a wide clearing covered with a dense new growth of saplings. None were more than two man-heights above his head or thicker than his wrist. He stood staring at the strange sight, almost unable to realize what he was seeing. Then it came to him with a rush. A forest giant, one of the truly old trees, had died. Whether eaten away by disease or struck down by one of the great bolts that the Gods hurled from the sky, he could not say. But whatever the reason, the tree had fallen, leaving a great circular depression in the earth. Seizing the opportunity for growth, hundreds of tiny saplings had spring up in its place, each of them reaching out for the distant space in the canopy of branches above. Only the strongest sapling of all would reach that space, crowding out all the others.

None of that mattered to Emri; all that mattered was that he had found the means for making a shelter large enough to hold them all. He raised his face to the sky and whispered a prayer of thanks to the Spirits.

"We will stop here," said Emri. One by one the people collapsed on the ground, many of them too weak

to crawl beneath trees and uncaring of the rain that fell
on their numbed bodies.

Emri called Brunk and Running Bird to his side and
explained what was needed. He gave each of them one
of the sharpened ax heads and set them to building the
shelter.

First, Emri paced around the clearing and pointed
out those saplings that would form the outer ring of the
dwelling. These were left intact. All others inside that
circle were cut off at the base and piled in a heap.
When they were done, a crude circle of saplings marched
around the perimeter of the depression.

Emri reached up and grasped the tip of a sapling.
This he held in one hand while grasping the one next to
it as well. He continued until he held seven saplings in
one hand. He bound the tips together tightly with a
long, thin strip of leather, leaving a long end hanging
out. He continued on around the circle of saplings,
binding them until he had completed the circle.

Next he stood in the center of the circle. Running
Bird and Brunk handed him the ends of the leather
strips, which he then pulled toward him, forcing the
saplings to bend inward. When the leather strips could
be drawn no tighter, Brunk tied them off above Emri's
closed fist. The ends of the strips were then braided
tightly to prevent them from coming loose.

When they were done, they had formed a circle of
saplings roughly four man-lengths in diameter. This was
the basis of their dwelling.

Next they took the saplings that had been cut from
the center of the depression and began to weave them in
and out of the uprights. The small branches were not
trimmed off but were left intact and would be further
woven into the whole when the structure was completed.

It took them all of the remainder of that day to finish
the dwelling, sealing off all cracks with moss and branches
until no moisture leaked inside. But long before the
dwelling was completed, they had moved the people
inside, reasoning that half a shelter was better than
none at all.

When at last they were done, it was discovered that the precious fire starting stones had been lost, left behind during one of their many stops. Exhausted as they were, they were forced to set about the heart-breakingly difficult task of building a fire with wet wood.

Emri trimmed away all outer layers of wet wood. Even so it was a difficult task and the resulting fire smoked intensely because of the extreme dampness.

The surface of the ground was rough and uncomfortable, ridged as it was with stumps of the saplings. None of it—neither smoke nor discomfort—seemed to matter, for they were inside, sheltered from the rain with a fire glowing before them.

Furskins were spread close to the fire and wet garments were stripped from shivering, feverish bodies. The cooking sack was filled with water, handfuls of dried meats, and ground foods. This was suspended over the fire, and soon the welcome smell of food began to permeate the dwelling, mixing with the fragrant scents of fresh-cut evergreens and wood smoke.

By the time the broth was ready, Emri and Running Bird had placed those people who were the sickest closest to the fire, where they could be easily tended. Many of the people did not wish to eat, but Running Bird persisted and was able to get some of the hot broth into everyone, no matter how much they protested.

Mosca was more than willing to eat whatever was left and proved difficult to dislodge from the spot he had claimed in front of the fire. Emri was able to settle him next to Dawn and Birdsong. There he stayed, licking the dribbles of broth from the child's face and chin.

Deep rumbles of satisfaction filled his broad chest, and Emri knew that the cat would remain next to the child, licking her and thoroughly warming her with his body heat as they slept.

Emri could do no more. He had cleaned Hawk as best he was able and positioned him on the white bearskin in front of the fire. Hawk would take little broth, turning his head away from the shell and muttering to himself. Emri was very worried, but he could think of nothing else to do. He left his friend with a prayer to the Spirits to watch over Hawk as he slept, begging them not to take his spirit should it appear before them.

Dawn was in little better condition than Hawk or the child. Her cheeks were unnaturally flushed and a deep cough racked her slender frame, but she was awake and conscious of what was going on around her. This Emri found very encouraging.

Emri was exhausted. Brunk had already tumbled into sleep alongside one of his many friends. Running Bird was sitting by the side of a feverish woman, stroking her limbs with a damp furskin and murmuring soft words to soothe her.

Emri eased himself down on the furskin next to Dawn and brushed the heavy dark tangles of curls away from her face, feeling the heat radiate from her skin. She nuzzled his hand with her face, cradling her cheek into the hollow of his palm and taking comfort from his touch.

"We must make spruce tea," she said in a voice that was raspy and harsh. "It is the only thing I know that will help. We will gather some in the morning."

"*I* will gather some in the morning," said Emri. "You will go nowhere until you are well. I need you beside me in this life, not sitting next to the campfires of the ancestors."

Dawn smiled at his words but she did not protest. Even this small exchange seemed to tire her, and soon her eyes closed and she slept.

Emri watched her sleep and became concerned that perhaps it was something other than a normal sleep. He thought that perhaps she had fallen into the final sleep that had claimed Shell. Overcome with worry, he shook her arm and was instantly relieved to see her open her eyes. She asked him what he wanted in a sleepy voice. He only nodded and smiled and she closed her eyes and slept again.

Emri stayed awake all that long night, searching the nearby woods for fallen branches and feeding the fire until the dwelling was warm and dry and heavy with the scent of the evergreens.

When the first light appeared, he gathered the spruce branches, taking only the tender tips. He drew water from one of the many rivulets that coursed along the ground and streamed through the wet forest toward the cliffs where it would fall in thin cascades to the sea below.

The spruce tips were simmered in a second cooking sack. They made a bitter, astringent brew that would find no favor among the sick, but Emri knew that it would do them much good if they would swallow it.

He tended the steaming potion as well as the cooking sack, which he had refilled and set to boiling, until Brunk wakened, then he turned the chore over to the boy. Stretching himself out on the furskin next to Dawn, Emri was asleep within heartbeats.

He wakened slowly, listening to the sounds of a child's laughter. He stared up at the closely knit branches above his head and tried to sort out his thoughts. The child giggled again. Turning his head, Emri saw Birdsong outstretched on the furskin. Mosca was holding her in place with one large paw on her chest and was licking her belly. Birdsong laughed again and struck Mosca on the nose with a tiny fist. Mosca merely blinked, then renewed his licking.

Emri smiled, knowing from personal experience what it felt like to be licked by one of the giant cats. It was a delicate balance between pleasure and discomfort, yet it would do no good to struggle. The cat's paw was as good a restraint as any mother's hand.

Dawn was sleeping still. Emri was pleased to note that her breathing seemed easier and the deep red flush had faded from her cheeks. He rose quietly so as not to waken her.

Hawk, however, seemed worse. Emri stared down at the figure of his friend and frowned with deep concern.

Running Bird called his name, greeted him with a happy smile, and beckoned him to sit beside her. "You have done well," she said. "Most of the people are much improved. People need fire and a dwelling around them. It is not natural to sleep out in the open like animals. Bad spirits can climb inside your body and make you sick—although never would I have thought that so many bad spirits could be found together in one place."

"I do not know about *many* bad spirits, old mother," Emri said. "I think perhaps it is only one, that of the old man on the mountain. We said no words for his passing. His spirit lingers still on this world and knows that we caused his death.

"I think that we must appease this spirit or continue to watch our people sicken and die. His spirit has already claimed one of us. I am determined that it shall have no more."

"What shall we do?" asked Running Bird. "Hawk is too sick to chant or cast the stones, and he told us that he knew no spells to drive away evil spirits."

"We will have to find a way. We must find a spell to drive this evil spirit out. Only then will the people be well."

"Noise," said Running Bird. "Evil spirits do not like noise. This I know to be true. Nor do they like bad smells. More than that, I cannot say."

"Be assured, old mother," said Emri, rising from the furskin, "we will find a way."

Emri stepped over the sleeping, feverish bodies and sat down beside Hawk, hoping to draw some inspiration from him, some idea of how to cast the spell.

But Hawk lay still upon the furskin. His skin was very pale and hot to the touch. Only two bright red spots of color showed high on his cheekbones. His hair was soaked with sweat and lay stringy and lank on the furskin. His chest rose and fell in quick shallow breaths, and there was a moist rattling sound each time he exhaled. He did not open his eyes when Emri called to him. This worried Emri more than anything, for he had still been conscious the night before.

Emri sat for a moment staring at his friend and

thinking. If the evil spirit was indeed causing this illness, he would choose to strike down Emri or Hawk, knowing them to be the leaders of the tribe and holding them responsible for his death.

Emri did not know why the spirit had killed the girl—perhaps she had just been for practice. He rose to his feet, determined that he would not allow the evil spirit to kill Hawk. Somehow he would find a way to drive the evil spirit out of Hawk's body.

CHAPTER SEVENTEEN

The more Emri thought about it, the more he became convinced that it was as he had said. There was no reason for the people to sicken and die unless their own spirits were being attacked by one that was stronger and more evil.

As he watched Hawk struggle for breath, he knew that this was what was happening. Even now as he watched, the old one's spirit was grappling with Hawk's and the old one was winning.

And then, Emri knew what he had to do. Part of him was afraid, but he had journeyed this way before and survived. He would do so again.

His decision made, he rose from the furskin and returned to Running Bird. She had now been joined by Brunk, who sat by the fire blinking the sleep out of his eyes.

"I know now what it is that I must do," Emri said. "I must do battle with the old man's spirit and drive it away or it will surely kill us all."

Running Bird gasped and her eyes grew large as she stared at Emri in disbelief. Brunk was speechless. His mouth fell open and he stared at Emri with awe.

"It will kill you," Running Bird said at last. "It is too dangerous. What will happen to us if you die?" Running Bird began to whimper.

"I will take care of you, old mother," Brunk said softly as he placed his hand on her arm. "But I think that Emri-*thann* will come back."

Emri stared at the boy, deeply touched. The addition of *thann* to one's name was a great honor usually only accorded those who had battled a dangerous beast single-handedly and won, or perhaps a mighty chief with a reputation for both bravely and wisdom.

Emri laid his palm on top of the boy's head and Brunk looked up at him with shining eyes. For him, Emri was already a hero.

"What shall we do?" Running Bird asked, beginning to lose her fear of the coming battle and growing excited.

"Do nothing," said Emri, who was less certain of their role than his. "Continue to feed the fire. Try to make the people eat and get as much spruce tea down them as you can."

Aware of their eyes on him, Emri returned to Hawk, crouched down beside him, and withdrew the pouch that contained the pipe and the smoking herbs. He stared at his friend for a moment, wishing that Hawk could be with him as he had been the first time he ventured into the spirit world. But why not do the thing here next to Hawk? That way his presence and perhaps even his spirit could be felt during the coming ordeal.

Growing ever more certain of his actions and filled with the sense of rightness, Emri passed among the sick and sleeping people. He kneeled to speak to those who were awake, saying words of cheer and urging them to eat and drink, and taking special note of those who seemed more seriously afflicted.

Dawn was still sleeping as he paused by her side. He smoothed her hair back from her brow and ran his fingers alongside her cheek, knowing how much he wished to keep her alive.

Mosca had grown tired of grooming the child and had pushed his way out of the dwelling, no doubt gone hunting. Emri wished him success. Running Bird had given Birdsong a handful of cooked meat and a bone to gnaw. She gurgled happily at Emri and kicked her feet in the air. Emri was glad that she seemed to have escaped the evil spirit. He ruffled her curls and smiled in return.

He returned to Hawk's side and sat in front of the fire opening the pouch, determined to do this thing before the evil spirit further strengthened his grip on the people. The pipe was soon loaded with herbs and Emri included small bits of dried fungus as well.

He lit the pipe with a small taper and sucked smoke deep into his chest, holding it there as long as possible, resisting the desire to cough. Time and again he repeated the action, rubbing the creamy ivory of the pipe between thumb and forefinger, the feel of the smooth surface calming him.

He gazed into the fire and slowly the colors began to change. Reds and blues and yellows were there as well as violet and green and silver. He nodded to them gravely, welcoming their beauty, knowing that it was but the threshold, the doorway through which he must pass.

His movements had become slow, stylized. The pipe, his arm, rising and falling, the smoke curling around his face and rising in lazy spirals, all mingled with the smoke of the fire.

He became aware that he had not moved for some time but had been staring into the fire, unblinking. As before, most of his body felt numb; he could not feel the top of his head at all. He let his eyes roam over the dwelling and it seemed to be full of shadows—writhing, twisting shadows that were not made of smoke.

He opened his eyes wide and looked at the shadows more closely, trying to bring them into focus. The more he looked, the more fuzzy the shadows became, as though they were retreating before his scrutiny, fading away as he drew near. "Ha!" he said aloud. "Your spirit is as weak and cowardly as you were in life, old man. Stand and do battle!"

No sooner had he spoken than the shadows grouped and took shape. Emri could see the figure of a bear, powerful and huge with great long teeth and curved claws, grappling with the figure of a man.

"You cannot have that one!" Emri said firmly. He made as if to rise and strike the bear, but his body would not obey him, remaining on the ground as though it were rooted.

Emri struggled mightily but his body would not rise and the bear snarled at him and turned back to the man on the ground.

Emri slowly realized that he himself could not approach the evil spirit in his human form. The old man's spirit had taken on the shape of a bear, which had evidently been his power animal in life. Emri's power animal was the saber tooth lion, just as Hawk's was the bird whose name he bore.

Concentrating, he called up his power animal, his totem, and felt his spirit slip out of the top of his head, freeing itself of the heavy confines of his body. He reveled in his freedom, his sense of lightness, his sense of power. He padded across the smoke-filled room, looking down on the puny humans sleeping below, their sick stink filling his nostrils, and felt his great cat muscles sliding smoothly beneath his glossy pelt.

The bear seemed unaware of him and was still standing on the chest of the man who proved to be Proud Bear. He hooked his cruel, curved claws into Proud Bear's chest, and his paw seemed to disappear into the very flesh of the man. Over and over the bear probed, as though seeking something that could not be found. It snarled in frustration and slaver dripped from its jaws and drifted away in a swirl of smoke.

Emri-the-cat felt a deep growl growing in his chest, and he dug his powerful hind legs into a heavy cloud of smoke and launched himself at the bear. Two bounds and he was there, leaping onto the bear's back. Over and over they rolled, fetching up against the wall of the dwelling, and Emri saw his body pass through the wall as though it did not exist. Then the bear rolled back in the opposite direction and they came to rest directly above the fire, which Brunk was feeding with small twigs, seemingly unaware of the fight going on a mere handspan above his head.

Emri wrapped his front paws around the bear's thick neck, dug his hind claws into the bear's haunches and attempted to sink his long, curved saber teeth into the bear's throat.

But the bear was too wily for that maneuver. Rolling forward onto his head, the bear somersaulted over, shaking Emri loose. Instantly the bear was on his feet and driving toward Emri, jaws agape, seeking Emri's throat.

Emri-the-cat scrambled to his feet, claws digging into the top of Brunk's head and passing through completely. He avoided the bear's rush and slashed the bear's side with his claws, feeling the skin part beneath them.

The bear stopped short and rose on its hind legs, towering over Emri, the upper half of its body hidden by the roof of the dwelling. Before the bear could advance any farther, Emri drove himself forward, hurling himself into the bear's midsection.

But the bear's belly was banded with muscles that were hard as rock and Emri staggered back, momentarily stunned. He shook his head and then felt himself scooped up, rising in the bear's massive forelimbs.

He struggled, knowing that he did not wish to be brought within range of the bear's fearsome jaws, but the bear was stronger than he. He was but a gnat on the flank of a mountain.

The bear brought him higher. His head and forepaws passed through the roof of the dwelling into the gray mist that lay thick on the ground, and he saw the bear's head above him.

The eyes were silver, glittering with a strange light, like no eyes ever seen this side of the spirit world. But the teeth were long and sharp and deadly and capable of killing in both this world and the next.

The bear raised Emri higher and higher, bringing him within range of the terrible teeth, squeezing him against his chest so that he could not even move his front paws. The bear lowered his head, fixing Emri with his terrible silver eyes.

Emri did the only thing he could. He brought up his hind legs, heavily bound with muscle, and positioned them against the bear's abdomen. As the bear lowered its head, jaws gaping, Emri drove his claws into the bear's belly with all the force he could muster. He felt his claws rip through the pelt and then cut through the many layers of fat. Only at the very last did he feel his claws catch and then tear through the uppermost layer of muscle.

The bear threw back his head and roared in rage and pain. His grip loosened momentarily and Emri fell through the roof and landed lightly at the bear's feet. He noticed with satisfaction that thick yellow fat was oozing out of the torn flesh, and dark blood was already staining the glossy pelt.

Emri did not give the bear time to regroup, but circled behind the animal and leaped upon his back, reaching for the bear's neck even as he landed.

The bear attempted to roll, but Emri was prepared and threw himself clear as the bear landed, and then he was on the bear again before it could rise. Wrapping his short forelimbs around the bear's neck, he bit down, hard; felt his teeth pass through the bear's throat; felt them pierce the great arteries; tasted the instant spurt of hot, salty blood; felt the great bear's body jerk and shudder beneath him and then slowly tremble away into whatever death lies beyond that of the spirit world.

So great was his hatred of the enemy, so great was his feeling of victory, that Emri was reluctant to release the bear. Only when it turned to mist between his jaws and drifted away through the smoke hole did he shake himself and allow his hatred and rage to flow away like the smoke, cleansing him in the process.

Emri-the-cat padded over to his human form and curled itself around the still body, a part of it, yet separate still.

Emri-the-human felt a curious sense of separateness. A small part of him was still locked in his human body.

That part, he knew, must never leave or there would
be nothing left to return to except an empty shell.

But most of himself had merged with or become
Emri-the-cat, his own personal power animal. Using his
cat self, Emri gazed around the room and saw that it
was free of evil spirits. But there were many other
spirits lurking in the room, their forms hidden in the
murky smoke.

Some spirits appeared quite strong and moved about
with vigor. But others, such as the small pale bear cub
now curled atop Proud Bear's chest, were listless and
appeared to be near death. Emri studied the spirits and
defined several that seemed as weak as Proud Bear's.
One of them was Hawk's.

Hawk's power animal lay cradled on his chest, its
proud wings crumpled and ruffled, the plumage dull
and without luster. Its eyes were opaque and did not
blink, and its mouth was agape as though air would not
come.

Emri knew somehow that his person could not rouse
these spirit animals, that only his power animal could
do so.

Emri-the-cat drew his power to him and then forced
it upon the recumbent hawk. The hawk opened and
shut its beak weakly, blinked, and then was still.

Emri withdrew, terrified that he had somehow killed
Hawk's guardian spirit, but then he saw it move feebly.
He allowed his force to flow from him again, more
slowly this time, and permitted it to trickle down to the
hawk in smaller doses. The hawk squirmed as though
uncomfortable. Its wings folded to its sides, extended,
and then braced the body as it rose shakily and stood
breathing heavily through its open beak atop Hawk's
chest. Hawk stirred and mumbled, throwing his arm up
and placing it across his eyes. The spirit hawk bent
down and pecked irritably at Hawk's chest. It blinked
its yellow eyes and glared balefully at Emri-the-cat as
though angry that it had not been allowed to die.

"Not this time, old friend," Emri said silently. The

bird dipped its head as though it had understood. Then it shook itself violently, settling its plumage into a more suitable state, and began to preen, still casting the occasional angry look at Emri.

Emri sat beside the angry bird for a time, sharing his power until he was convinced that the bird would not relapse. The hawk was not grateful. As Emri-the-cat turned to leave, it snapped at his hindquarters, delivering a painful nip to his flank. Hawk-the-spirit was definitely more violent than his human form, Emri thought, as the spirit cat hissed angrily in return.

The bear cub lying atop Proud Bear's chest was another matter completely. Try as he might, no amount of energy would rouse the creature. It lay there, far smaller and shrunken that Emri would have guessed from the man's proud demeanor. For the first time Emri saw that much of the man's arrogant attitude was perhaps a sham, a cover trying to live up to his name.

It was hopeless. Emri could not make the creature move. He could barely see its chest rise and fall, and he knew that Proud Bear was near death. The man would die unless he could think of a way to save him.

Pacing around the man, Emri noticed that the woman, Leaping Fawn, lay next to him. She was awake, although unmoving, and stared at Emri as he paused above her, frowning as though she actually saw him. Her spirit animal was a small, slender deer, so tiny and delicate that Emri wondered if it contained enough power to help.

There was no time for doubt; the creature would have to do. Lying down beside it, Emri explained what was needed. Its huge, all-but-transparent ears flicked back and forth, the blood visible as it pulsed through tiny, fragile veins. Its eyes were great huge pools of shining liquid gold, and they looked into Emri's great cat eyes without fear.

It stood on legs too thin and improbable to support its weight and leaped across to Proud Bear's chest, landing lightly beside the bear cub. It nuzzled the cub, its dark nose snuffling around nose and ear, prodding, poking, its shell-pink tongue flicking the fur around the bear's eyes. Its tiny stub of a tail twitched back and forth rapidly as it ministered to the all-but-lifeless spirit.

The small cub seemed to draw in upon itself as does a child unwilling to waken, and the fawn renewed its efforts. Emri too sent his power to the diminishing life force, lending it his strength to draw upon. The bear cub squirmed and covered his eyes with its paws, resisting their efforts.

But the fawn would not give up. Long after Emri had become discouraged, it continued, never once allowing the bear cub to pull away completely, perhaps knowing that to do so would be to allow it to die.

At last they were rewarded by the sight of the cub climbing to its feet, where it stood swaying on trembling legs, head bowed. Emri felt a rush of power surge through him, knowing that although it was still weak, the spirit would not die.

The fawn turned to him and her great shining eyes blazed with power, more than enough to share with the mate of her choice. Emri bowed his head in recognition of her achievement and then left her to help those who were still in need.

When the day was done, the struggle had been lost only once. Sadly, it was the spirit of Otuk who could not be roused.

As Emri sat on his haunches and watched that brave spirit dissipate into smoke, the grief lay heavy on his heart. The spirit had been willing, but its strength had been too greatly diminished by the time Emri reached it.

Emri returned to his own body, beginning to feel as though he were fraying around the edges. Already it seemed as though he could see through himself. He stepped back into his head just as the edges began to waver and break up.

The hawk looked up at him over its wing and opened its beak to say something spiteful, but then it spiraled together in a whirl of brown- and cream-colored feathers and disappeared.

Emri opened his eyes and saw the fire.

The shaman had been busy for a time organizing a great hunt, the hunt that always followed the passing of Cold Time and replenished the clan's depleted food supplies. Now the air was redolent with the scent of roasting meat and the racks were bowed beneath the weight of smoking joints. The people's bellies were stretched and swollen with food and they were content once more.

Now Mandris was free to tend to his own interests. He climbed the mountain to the cave that had once sheltered the old tiger, the totem of the clan whom Emri had defeated in battle. Settling himself, he called forth his spirit tiger.

This time the transition was rougher, bumpier as though there were some invisible resistance. The shaman remained calm, knowing that such a thing was not uncommon but merely a barrier of some form between the real world and that of the spirits. The turbulence passed and the tiger spirit slipped from his head and appeared before him.

As before, there was no need to tell the tiger what was required of him and he vanished in the blink of an eye.

The shaman barely noticed the land flowing beneath the tiger's paws, so eager was he for the first glimpse of the enemy. He wondered how far they had traveled, how much closer they had come.

He found them in the great forest, and touching their minds learned with shock all that had transpired since last he had viewed them. He was disturbed to learn that they had almost perished at the hands of the mad man on the mountain and had come close to death from starvation and illness.

At one time, he would have been glad to learn of their deaths, no matter what the cause. But it was different now. His hatred had grown so intense that it had become necessary for him to end their lives and destroy their spirits himself. Only then would he be satisfied.

Taking warning from the events that had happened without his notice, he determined to keep a closer watch on the enemy, give warning if it was necessary. For when they next encountered danger or faced death, it would be he whom they saw.

CHAPTER EIGHTEEN

The people mended, growing stronger by the day. By the time their strength had returned so that they might travel, so had the sun.

They traveled slowly at first, stopping often and resting in the warmth of the sun. Still they made progress daily, and although they saw no deer, game was plentiful. In time they passed out of the great rain forest and left the last of the tall, wet ferns behind them. They had entered the vast hardwood forest that stretched along the high ridges, paralleling the coast until it reached the immense bay that had nearly cost Dawn her life.

It was here among the huge oaks, pines, hemlocks, and cedars that they found the hardwood necessary for making hafts for their clubs and spears. These were carefully chosen from the fallen trees and branches that littered the ground. It was important that the wood not be green, for when it dried, it could easily warp, render-ing the weapon useless. Nor could it be too old, weakened by the boring of insects and hidden cracks. It had to be dry, yet retain enough moisture to be supple and give beneath the shock of a blow. It had to be perfect.

Such wood was found with careful searching. One after the other, the stone points were attached to their shafts, bound in place with strips of steaming hot leather and globs of sticky pine resin. The leather would dry and draw tight around the stones, forming a bond that would not be easily broken.

Now they were armed and Emri rested easier knowing that it was so. Only their fire, their numbers, and
easier prey had kept them safe this long.

In time they came to the great bay, the largest single,
natural obstacle that stood between them and their
goal. Broken Tooth lead them to the floater that he and
Walks Alone had hidden on their journey north. It had
been well shielded and had not been harmed by its
months of concealment.

The People of the Deer were not as fearful as Emri
had expected, having made floaters of their own of
another design. They were well familiar with water
travel and indeed, were adept with building and handling the strange craft.

Their crafts were built from materials taken from the
huge gray fish and the monsterous water tuskers, none
of which were available to them here in this warmer
clime. But by working together and studying Broken
Tooth's floater, they were able to build seven more
vessels of slender saplings and the skins of water-men
to carry them to the land of the deer.

They made offerings of meat and groundfoods to the
God of the Waters, promising him further gifts if he
allowed them safe passage. Also, they prayed to the
spirits of their ancestors begging them to watch over
them.

Then, choosing their moment well, a bright, calm
morning when the waters lay heavy and still and the
skies were clear with no sign of storms, they crossed
the wide bay.

This time, confident of their skills and surrounded by
friends on all sides, the crossing was far less frightening
and was accomplished in one long day. When at last
they stood on the far side, they gave the God his due
and said their thanks to the spirits of their ancestors.

They rested that night, with the sounds of the waves,
the barking grunts of the noisy water-men, and the cries
of the white water birds echoing in their ears, knowing
that they were nearly home.

Hawk wakened in the moment before dawn and listened to the sound of the waves lapping on the rocks. It was a peaceful sound, and as he drifted between sleep and waking, his mind unguarded, it seemed to him that there was a feeling of danger in the air.

He came awake instantly and cast about him, attempting to learn the nature of the danger. In some unexplained way, he knew that it was no man or beast that threatened him, but some vague, half-formed feeling, almost as though an unseen enemy were lying somewhere out of sight, watching him.

The thought was enough to bring him upright. Totally awake and peering into the early-morning mists, he hoped to catch a glimpse or find a hint of the danger.

He leaped to his feet and grabbed a smoldering brand from the fire and waved it all around him, hoping that it would drive the invisible foe away.

Emri came awake and after watching Hawk for a short time, realized that something was seriously wrong. Throwing his furskin aside, Emri got to his feet and moved to Hawk's side.

"What is wrong?" he asked in a whisper.

"I don't know," replied Hawk in a low tone. "It feels as though I am being watched. Can you not feel it? It is here still."

Emri looked at the low-hanging clouds that surrounded the camp, blotting out the landscape, and he felt a cold chill come over his body. A low rumbling growl sounded, and looking down, he saw Mosca standing beside him. The cat's ears were plastered flat against his skull and his lips were drawn back from his fangs. He hissed and stepped backward, pressing closer to Emri's legs. His amber eyes were focused at a spot of swirling mist above their heads.

Emri and Hawk followed the cat's gaze. Acting swiftly, Hawk thrust the glowing brand up into the spot of mist. It crackled and sputtered and the mist seemed to draw back, almost flinching away from the flames like a live creature rather than a mindless bit of cloud.

The mist disintegrated, broke up into tiny wisps and

drifted away. As it vanished, so did their feeling of dread.

"What was it?" asked Emri as he looked around him, wondering if he had imagined the strange happening, yet knowing that it had been real.

"Something was watching us," Hawk replied, his limbs beginning to tremble.

"Was it an evil spirit?" asked Emri, fearful of another sickness.

"No, it did not have that feeling. This was different somehow. I do not think this was the spirit of a dead one; it felt too alive, too real. I almost felt that I could reach out and touch it."

"Maybe it's Mandris," Hawk said slowly. "Do you think that he has the ability to send his spirit this far in search of us?"

"My father often spoke of spirit time," Emri said thoughtfully. "His spirit animal was, as I have told you, an eagle. He was able to send it soaring over the land in search of game, but I do not know how far it was able to travel."

"We must learn how to do this thing," said Hawk, chewing his lip and staring down into the fire, which was now burning brightly. "If we are to protect ourselves and know what is to come, our spirit animals must search out the land before us and find danger before it finds us."

Emri thought back on the time of sickness when his spirit had walked among the tribe, lending them strength and fighting for their lives. It had seemed a right thing to do and he had suffered no ill effects. Perhaps spirit travel would not be so difficult. Hawk spoke with wisdom. They would need to do all that was possible to protect themselves from Mandris as they drew closer to home.

"How and when shall we do this thing?" asked Emri.

"In a place of great safety," Hawk replied at length. "I think that the body must be very safe before the spirit is allowed to go wandering. And only one of us should do this thing; the other must remain behind and guard the body to make certain that nothing goes amiss. We will know the time and the place when they are right."

"Hawk, what if our spirits encounter the spirit of Mandris?" Emri asked in a troubled tone. "His powers are surely stronger than ours. To meet him in the spirit form would surely be as dangerous as encountering him in the flesh."

"Perhaps more so," said Hawk, "for if the spirit is defeated while out of the body, it will wander forever and the body will die as well."

The thought was chilling. Thinking back on Mandris's considerable powers, they were all but overwhelmed at the thought of this powerful enemy whom they were destined to fight.

The current was in their favor now and carried their floaters swiftly south. The last of the ice had vanished from the waters, and more and more often they were accompanied by the immense gray fish who were traveling in the same direction. Once, carried farther out into the waters than was their norm, they found themselves surrounded by a large group of the gray fish.

At first there was great panic and it was feared that the giant fish would eat them or break their fragile floaters and cast their bodies out into the cold waters. Dawn, frightened since she first stepped into the floater, was absolutely terrified. As the fish began to surface around the floater, she wrapped her arms around her swollen belly and began to cry, convinced that she was going to die.

They held their spears and their steering sticks ready, to fight the immense beasts. But although they came close enough to touch, they made no move to harm the floaters or the people inside. Instead they swam leisurely alongside and turned their tiny eyes on the people as though curious about the strange creatures who rode atop the waves rather than below them.

As it became obvious that the fish wished them no harm, the people lowered their sticks and their weapons and sat quietly, watching the great beasts as they swam and dove with grace and ease despite their huge bulk.

Emri, while attempting to comfort Dawn and urging her to open her eyes and watch the beautiful fish, noticed that Hawk was sitting quietly in his floater. His hands were folded neatly in his lap, eyes open yet seeing nothing. Only after the last of the gentle giants had vanished with a flip of their vast tails did Hawk stir. His body seemed to twitch, and then, turning his gaze to Emri, he smiled softly as though still wrapped in a wondrous dream.

That evening as they sat beside the fire, staring out over the dark waters, watching the luminous crests of the waves drift to shore, Hawk said, "I let my spirit fly and it touched those of the great fish. It was unlike anything that has ever happened to me before. I felt myself grow larger, swell from inside with a feeling of warmth and joy. We were wrong to fear them, Emri. There is no harm in them, no danger to man. They are like us, only more gentle, as gentle as the smallest girlchild who sees only beauty and wonder in the world. Their spirits had much beauty. They called to me and asked me to come with them on their journey. It was a sorrow to me that I could not do so. There is much that is good in spirit travel, Emri. Why did it take us so long to learn?"

"I think it is a gift that is given to the few." Emri looked deep into the flames, choosing his words carefully. "Every man has his spirit animal, but I think that many do not know how to use them and never come to know them as we have. Surely we are among the fortunate whom the Spirits have chosen to honor. It was not always so, if you remember. We have not always been able to know our spirits. There was a time of learning and a time of testing before we were judged as worthy."

"This is true." Looking back at the tall cliffs that rose behind them, rising to the grassy plateaus high above the shore, Hawk said, "I think this is a place that is safe. I think that we should send our spirits forth from

this place and see what we might see. I feel strong,
Emri. I feel ready to see the future."

Looking at him, his sharp profile outlined against the
ruddy fire, Emri could not help but agree.

*The tiger spirit that was Mandris pulled back sharply
from the burning brand. He moved quickly, but even so
his fur was singed and the stink of burned hair and the
pain of the injured flesh caused him to hiss aloud and
shake his great head.*

*How had it happened? How had they become aware
of his presence? Never before had it happened—although
the girl Dawn who had scorned him had twisted away
from him even as she slept, rejecting him still.*

*The spirit cat recoiled from the flames and spat out
its rage at being discovered, noting that the lion cub
and the two men were both staring at the spot that
marked his presence. He had watched them, kept track
of their progress, and whispered words of doubt and
fear in their unsuspecting, unguarded minds whenever
possible.*

*Now it appeared that such a thing would be more
dangerous. If they were aware of his presence, it could
only mean that their own powers were growing stronger.
They were still, as yet, far weaker than he. They were
but fledglings and would be unable to do any but the
most simple deeds. Still, it was a disturbing occurrence.
He had not expected it to happen at all, ever, and he
cursed himself for the oversight, for underestimating
his enemy. He turned and left the camp, bounding
across the sky in great leaps, returning to the safety of
his human body.*

*He would have to be certain that his hatred did not
blind him to the strengths of his enemies. They were no
longer the helpless adolescents that they had been. They
were men now and well versed in the use of weapons.
More importantly, their hatred was as strong as his and
they would not fail to call upon it in future encounters.*

*Still, the stakes were high: leadership of the tribe,
which was powerful and strong; their territory rich*

with game and groundfoods; and the woman, she who had been the old chief's woman. There was much prestige in her presence, no matter how unwilling, at his fire. He was admired and feared by all who knew him. He would not relinquish the position; he would keep it or die in the trying.

His lips curled back from his fangs as the ground blurred beneath his feet. There was no worry in his heart, no fear, no sense of danger. If there was dying to be done, it would not be he whose blood was shed. It would not be the blood of the tiger.

CHAPTER NINETEEN

Early the next morning Emri and Hawk began their preparations. They told the people that they would not be traveling that day. Instead Hawk would be taking a spirit journey and that all must be in order to allow him to do so in peace and safety.

The floaters were drawn up high on the sand and secured, which gladdened the hearts of both Mosca and Dawn. Mosca continued to be a problem, for his aversion to the floater was strong. It was necessary to catch him each morning and tie his paws, then place them in leather pouches so that he could not rip the skin of the floater with his claws. But unless they captured him while he slept, he ran from them and frequently delayed them for long periods while they attempted to trap him.

Dawn did not hate the floater so much as she feared it. Try as she might, she could not free herself from the belief that it would carry her to her death. The water terrified her. The farther from shore, the greater her fear. Even more than for herself, she was afraid for the child within who had grown big and would surely be entering the world soon.

But unlike Mosca, Dawn knew that the floater represented the fastest and easiest way for them to return home. They could not walk half so fast as the floater traveled, and even she had to admit that sitting in the floater was far easier on her physically than walking. Walking, as well as almost everything else between waking and sleeping, brought extreme discomfort these days. Her backed ached always and her feet and legs were badly swollen.

Dawn was fearful of the birthing. She knew all too well how many women and new ones died at this time, even with the benefit of other women and healers to help. Running Bird tried to offer comfort, holding her hand and telling her there was nothing to fear, but Dawn remembered the first birthing—the pain, the blood, and the new one who had not lived.

It would not do to discuss such things with Emri, for it was clear that he was doing his best and struggling with problems of his own. The time was fast approaching. Dawn knew that the child had turned. The head, which had lodged beneath her rib cage for so long, pressing against her heart, was now completely reversed so that it hung beneath her navel, pointing down. The time could not be far off, and more than anything, Dawn was afraid.

Emri was frightened as well, but for completely different reasons. Although both he and Hawk had tranced, only he had experienced the separating of spirit from self. He was worried that something might happen to Hawk. But it had been decided that it was Emri's place to remain with the tribe. Hawk himself did not seem afraid. If anything, he appeared eager to begin.

The place where they had made their camp was but an open strip of beach between two large folds in the land. The land rose up steeply on three sides, cradling them in a sandy cul-de-sac. A rivulet of fresh water trickled over the edge of the cliff, fell to the rocks below, and entered the Endless Waters. Emri guessed that it would dry up completely during the long, hot days of Warm Time. But for now, he was grateful for its existence.

The women and children were using the day of rest in various ways. The boys were scooping up handfuls of wet sand, forming balls and throwing them at each other.

Birdsong was babbling cheerfully to herself and

playing with a handful of shells that Dawn had gathered
from the edge of the waters. Occasionally she would
call out " 'ama, 'ama," and waddle over to Dawn and
present her with some small token of favor that Dawn
accepted gravely. Mosca lay at the child's side, enjoying
the warmth of the sand and tolerating Birdsong with
great forbearance as she placed shells and sand and bits
of twigs in his mane.

The women were searching the rocks for wood to add
to the fire, and several of the men were fishing from the
rocks, using lengths of thin leather and hooks fashioned
from bone, stone, and wood. Others lay asleep on the
sand next to their fires.

Everyone was doing their best to give Hawk and
Emri the space and the privacy that such a serious
occurrence required.

Hawk and Emri had removed themselves from the
camp itself and had found a sheltered spot at the base of
the cliff. Here they had built a fire of their own and
spread a furskin before it.

Hawk had taken no food or drink and sat down on the
furskin wearing only his loinskin. His clothes and the
two pouches that held the casting stones were placed to
one side, freeing him from any form of constraint.

He filled the small ivory pipe with a pinch of the
powdered herbs and pieces of the dried fungus. He lit
the pipe with a twig and took the smoke deep into his
chest. He smiled at Emri once, as though to reassure
him, then directed his gaze into the flames.

After a time the pipe held nothing but ashes, and
Hawk sat motionless, his hands resting quietly in his
lap. He stared into the fire still, although Emri doubted
that he really saw the flames, knowing that his gaze was
directed inward.

The crackle of the fire was very loud to Hawk's ears.
Everything was very loud. He could hear his own blood
pulsing through his veins, feel his heart beating in
his chest, and hear his every breath.

He could feel the breeze that played across his body

and separate it into strands of slightly different temper-
atures. The tang of salt was heavy in his nostrils as was
the scent of fish and the long green grasses that floated
on the waves. He heard the high, thin cries of the birds
as they wheeled overhead and the tiny skitter of a crab
as it crept from one place of hiding to another.

Slowly he directed his attention inward, shutting out
the distractions of the outer world and concentrating his
energies on the inner self.

His breathing slowed, became shallow. His eyes ceased
to acknowledge images, and his ears no longer heard
the sounds of life around him.

Inside, all was darkness. Then there was a spiral of
brilliance that began as a small dot of light and grew
larger and larger, circling out farther and farther until it
was larger than he himself. He sat at the very center of
the light with bands of light radiating from his chest.
He felt the heat from which the light flowed and it was
good.

Hawk sat for a time, growing accustomed to the
strange feelings, then he focused his thoughts on the
hawk who was his power animāl. He pictured it, proud
and alert with bright shining eyes, cruel curved beak,
and sharp talons.

He summoned it closer and the hawk opened its beak
and hissed at him, although no sound was heard. It did
not seem anxious to comply with his wishes. It opened
its wings and shook them as though preparing to fly,
disregarding his command. He abandoned his peremp-
tory tone and called to the bird softly, urging it to his
side.

The hawk placed its head over to one side and looked
at him curiously. It seemed to hesitate for a moment,
then it lowered its wings and folded them to its sides. It
took a step forward and stepped onto one of the golden
bands of light. Without moving, it was drawn closer and
closer to Hawk until its eye touched his. The small dark
eye looked into the depths of the larger eye, each
seeing the other, seeing themselves and knowing that
they were one and the same. And then the eyes merged

and they flowed together, absorbing each other's essence. And when they separated, they were one.

Hawk stretched his great wings and felt the flow of air stroke his feathers. He turned impatiently, angered by his ties to the earth and pecked at the bands of light that anchored him. Then suddenly the bands faded away and were gone and there was nothing holding him.

His wings rose and fell, cupping the air beneath them, forcing it down against the land, rising heavily at first and then more easily as the great wings thrust against the air. And then he was aloft, circling high above the puny, awkward creature seated on the sand who was his other self. A tremendous sense of power swelled in his breast as he spread his great wings and floated.

He opened his beak and uttered a harsh cry that could not be heard by the living, but projected a sense of presence for any who were sensitive enough to feel it. A gaggle of white sea birds wheeling nearby broke apart and dove for the safety of their nests, unwilling to answer his challenge. The birds held no interest for the hawk and he scanned the earth below him, searching out whatever was there to be seen.

He saw the land stretching below him in gentle curves, rising and falling softly, crisscrossed by streams that nourished the small stands of trees, the rich growth of grasses, and the abundance of life that fed upon it.

Long-necked camels grazed along the fringes of a huge herd of shaggy-haired bison, their great horns all but scraping the earth as they grazed. Slow-moving horny-backs waddled along the edges of the streams, prodding the mud with their long noses, feeling out the crayfish and burrowing insects with their clever hands. These were noted by the hawk but had no bearing on his needs. He angled his wings so they caught the wind and rose still higher.

The land passed beneath him like some strange furskin of gold and green, dotted with a variety of animals both large and small. Once his eye caught a flitter of move-

ment and he folded his wings and dove. He opened his
wings and locked the feathers along the edges as well as
lowering his tail to break his fall at the last instant. He
pulled up just above ground level and saw a grouping of
spirits, watery and pale in the full sun.

They were the spirits of a man and a woman and two
small children. Their faces raised to his and he saw that
they were thin and wasted, their bodies little more than
a collection of bone and sinew covered by skin. Their
eyes bore the look of desperation and deprivation, and
he knew that they had died during a Cold Time, caught
out on the empty rolling plains with no food and no
shelter.

He did not know how they had come to be there,
where they had come from, or where they had been
going. But they had died and there had been none to
say the words that would send them to their ancestors.

The hawk steeled itself against their mournful cries,
knowing that there was nothing it could do to aid them.
It rose into the sky once more, intent now on fulfilling
its own mission.

The land passed swiftly and the hawk scanned the
earth for any sign of the enemy, Mandris, the shaman
of the Tiger clan. The hawk had formulated no plan,
formed no images of action, but knew that it would act
when the time was at hand.

The land continued to unfold, the sameness made
different only by the animals that walked its surface.
Soon the river passed beneath his wings, so shrunken
in the heat of Warm Time that in places one might
easily cross it on foot.

The Hawk flew on, catching one current of air, then
the next as it followed the course of the river. It found
the broad rocky ledge at the edge of the river where
the Toad clan had made their camp, saw the multitude
of spirits that teemed over it in anger and despair, and
saw a small child, searching the shallows with anxious
eyes.

But the Toads were of no concern to him—curious as
it was to find one still alive, for he had been told that all

of the Toads had been killed. His prey still had not been sighted.

The way was more familiar now. As he traveled toward the Tiger encampment, his fierce spirit wondering what would be found, he noticed a stream that cut through the land. This stream was unaffected by the great heat that baked the land and flowed into a broad, shallow lake.

The hawk sailed above the clear waters, noting the lush vegetation that framed its edges and the large flocks of birds and beasts that fed along its grassy shores, and saw the great stands of trees that encompassed the whole. It seemed a place of great beauty and tranquillity, and the hawk was strongly drawn to it.

Then it was seized by a moment of dizziness, a faltering that left it feeling strangely diminished. The hawk's confidence was shaken and it felt a stab of fear. Then it steadied and continued on toward the Tiger encampment.

The camp was within the hawk's sight when the strange dizziness returned, blurring the landscape below, his keen vision gone in a blink of an eye. He was overcome by a whirling feeling. When it passed, he was falling through the air on his back, unable to open his wings to break his fall.

He knew that he must find a way, for his senses told him that the ground was rising fast beneath him, but his wings remained closed. He did not have the strength to halt the deadly plunge.

Sound returned and with it the sense of falling increased. The wind ripped through his feathers. There was a bitter taste in his mouth. He did not fear death but mourned the loss of life itself, and he knew that he would die.

There was a tremendous impact, accompanied by a flash of searing heat. Then everything was gone in a wash of red, which slowly faded to white, and then into the pale beige of nothingness.

For a long time the hawk floated on this pool of nothingness. There was no top, no bottom, no sides, no surface. It merely was. It existed. There were no demands, no motion, no movement, no life, only calmness and peace. Then slowly the pale light began to glow, to turn orange at the edges. The space around him grew brighter and brighter until it was the soft yellow of a flower opening to the first tentative touch of the morning sun. It was a soft yet vibrant shade of yellow, yellow of the sun, yellow of fire, yellow of life. It called to him, softly at first, then more and more insistently, urging, then commanding him to respond.

The hawk closed his eyes more tightly, closing his mind and heart against the persistent voice that demanded that he hear, feel, and act once more. But there was no escaping the sound; it was like a constant buzzing inside his head, calling him over and over, shaking him and pulling him back to life. The nothingness was nowhere to be seen. It was gone. Grieving over the loss of that great calm, the hawk opened his eyes.

"Hawk? Hawk, do you hear me?" asked a voice.

Hawk lay still, his cheek pressed against the shaggy furskin, looking directly into the red-orange heart of the coals. For a moment he did not speak, unable or perhaps unwilling to move. He wondered if it were possible to remain in that state. He wondered whether he could close his eyes and find that place of calm again.

But then the voice came again, calling his name and shaking his arm over and over again. He sighed deeply, knowing that the place of peace was no longer within his reach. And now, even as he thought of it, it withdrew from his memory, becoming distant and less real with every passing heartbeat.

He sighed and a tightness in his chest eased. It occurred to him that he had been holding his breath for a very long time. He took air into his chest, air that was rich with the taste of salt and smoke, air that was good to breathe.

He rolled over onto his back and looked up into the eyes of Emri, his friend, his brother, and knew that he had returned.

CHAPTER TWENTY

The tribe was gathered in a circle around the fire at the base of the cliffs. Hawk sat cross-legged in front of the fire, hugging the furskin to him and drinking the hot brew that Dawn had handed him. He was cold through and through and could not seem to stop shivering.

"What did you see, brother?" asked Emri. "Were you able to do it? Did you go to the Tiger camp?"

"I was one with the spirit," said Hawk. "We flew high above the land and saw much. There is one still alive at the Toad camp, a child I think." He recounted all that he had seen, including the spirits of the dead family. The people stirred nervously and looked around them as though worried that the spirits might have followed Hawk back to camp.

"We will say the words that will release their spirits." Emri knew that he did not care to encounter any more wandering spirits during his travels. "Mandris," he said, bringing the conversation back to the matter at hand. "Did you see the shaman?"

"I saw nothing. I was taken by a strange dizziness as I approached the camp and I began to fall through the air. I thought that I was going to die."

Mosca strolled through the crowd of people, insensitive to the cries that followed his passage as he stepped on first this person, then that one. He stood in front of Hawk and butted him gently in the chest with the top of his great head as he had done so often as a cub. Then

163

he sank to the ground and laid his huge head in Hawk's lap, a heavy, rumbling sound echoing deep in his chest.

"I, too, was afraid that your spirit would not return," said Emri. "Your breath stopped and your skin was cold to the touch and you gave no sign of life. I could not think of what to do."

"You did right by calling my name. It was your voice that I heard calling me. It was your voice that brought me back."

"What do you think caused this dizziness?" Emri asked.

"It was the shaman," said Proud Bear. "He put an evil sign on Hawk and brought him to the ground."

"It was the shaman's *spirit*," said Running Bird, unwilling to allow anyone else's opinion to go before hers. "Did you not see another spirit in the air beside you?" Running Bird was certain that it must be so even though she herself had never voyaged in the spirit world.

"No, I do not recall another spirit. But my mind is clouded and perhaps I do not remember truly. There was, however, a lake with much game and many trees that would be a good place for a camp. We could wait there while we send Broken Tooth to the Tigers with our message. Perhaps we are wrong, Emri, perhaps Mandris will not choose to fight."

"Ha!" cried Running Bird before Emri had a chance to respond. "That one will fight. Of that there is no doubt. He will not want you strutting around his camp, showing your muscles and your woman. Others will laugh at him and say that he is without courage. This, he cannot allow."

"You are right, old mother. But still we must send Broken Tooth to carry our greetings and ask for permission to return to the tribe. It is the way things should be done. If he says no, then our path is clear."

"It is clear now . . . waste of time," grumbled Running Bird.

"I will take the message," said Broken Tooth, "although I no longer think that it will do any good. Tell

me, this Toad . . . are you certain that it was not a
spirit?"

"No, it was a child," replied Hawk. "Quite alive,
although very thin. I cannot see how it could have
survived the Cold Time on its own or escaped being
eaten by animals. Surely the spirits of its ancestors are
watching over it."

"I have been troubled by our slaughter of the Toads,"
said Broken Tooth. "It was a wrong thing. Walks Alone
said that they were less than people and it was right to
kill them, but my mind has always thought back on
them and sorrowed. If this one is still alive, I would
take him to my woman and give him a home at my
fire."

Hawk was deeply touched that one of the Tiger clan
would speak so and wish to give shelter to a Toad whom
he had once tried to kill.

"Do you know of this lake?" asked Hawk. "If our
quarrel with Mandris is not resolved, it would be a
good place to make our home."

"I have never heard of it," replied Emri, "but it does
not matter. This time I will not walk away, and our
quarrel will be resolved once and for all by the death of
one of us."

"You will not be alone, my brother," said Hawk. "We
are many and our spears are sharp. Your fight is our
fight. You will not be alone."

"You have the spirit of the hawk, my brother," Emri
said with a smile, "but this is a thing that I must do
myself. This fight is between Mandris and me. It is I
who must deal with him."

"And what of me?" asked Hawk. "His fight may be
with you, but his actions have certainly affected my life
as well as yours. It is by luck alone that I am still alive.
Had it been left to him, I would have been dead long
ago. What am I to do while you are bravely fighting?
Am I to sit by and watch, idly marking your success or
loss as though you were but a stranger?"

"No," replied Emri, realizing that much of what Hawk
said was truth. "You must guard the tribe. We cannot

know that Mandris will not have brought others with
him who would attack our people. If anything happens
to me, they are yours to guide."

"And what of Mosca," asked Hawk. "Is he to sit and
watch as well? You know that he will not do so, and
your arguments will have little influence on his actions."

"I had not thought of this," admitted Emri, "but
Mandris did not hesitate to send the tiger against us. I
think it only fitting that Mosca be allowed to help finish
this one."

"Well, that will certainly alter the balance," murmured Hawk, a smile tugging at the corners of his
mouth. "Mosca could take on the shaman by himself
and end the battle there."

"Do not underestimate our enemy," said Emri. "I
feel that he is dangerous in ways that we have yet to
learn. He is as sly as a weasel, as fast as a snake, and as
dangerous as an angry bear. Never forget it."

"And we are brothers to the lion and our hearts are
strong and brave." Hawk's boasts were echoed by the
people around him. "I respect his powers, but I no
longer fear him."

"I have hunted and killed many a bear," said Proud
Bear. "My spear is sharp and thirsts for his blood!"

"Weasels are good only when dead and skinned,"
cried Tusk. "My club cries out for his head and I would
strip that weasel of its pelt!"

"And I would grind the snake beneath my heel,"
added Dawn. "Too long have his actions caused us
grief."

"If the Gods wish it and the ancestors guide our way,
it will be done," said Emri. "Now we must plan our
days and form the message that Broken Tooth must
carry."

"Do not say that we will come crawling back," said
Hawk. "I will not beg."

"I will not say such a thing," said Emri, "but it will
not do to be openly hostile. There are still many there
whom I care about and who would feel the shaman's
wrath, should our words anger him. I had thought only

to say that we are returned; that we come with the
People of the Deer, a tribe who has much to offer in
skills and abilities; that we are willing to rejoin the tribe
and live in peace, setting aside our differences for the
good of all."

"And do you think that he will agree to such a thing?"
Hawk's dark eyes glittered like shards of black obsidian.

"I cannot imagine that he would," Emri said disarm-
ingly, "but such a thing must be said."

"Good," said Hawk, "for I do not wish to live with
him in peace." And this thought was echoed by those of
the entire tribe.

Emri looked from one grim face to the next and knew
that even if he was to fall, Mandris would not live long
enough to enjoy his victory.

They slept one last night around their fires on the
beach and then set forth early the next morning, as
soon as the mists had lifted from the cold gray waters.
Their progress was good and within three days they had
covered all the land that Hawk had seen in his vision
and entered the mouth of the river.

The river was so low with the heat of Warm Time
that it was necessary to gauge the passage of the waves
and ride the crest over the mouth of the river. Just
below the level of the water, there were great ridges of
sand that could easily rip through the thin skins of the
floaters.

These same waves helped them through the giant
rocks that stood like silent sentinels in the narrow place
between the two headlands. There was far less water
than there had been on their previous voyage, yet it
was no less dangerous. Sharp barnacles and openmouthed
bivalves lay thick upon the rocks, their edges as sharp
as any knife. Water-men clung to these rocks and watched
them with wide, curious eyes.

They passed between the rocks and allowed the current from the Endless Waters to propel them into the
wide bay that lay beyond the headlands. Here the
current dissipated. So weak was the flow of the river

itself that they were able to drive the floaters upstream with little difficulty.

Emri looked around him, noting that the water had fallen far below the tops of the banks, which rose a full man-height above their heads on both sides of the river. He remembered that when they had made their perilous escape from the Toad camp with Hawk lying unconscious on the bottom of the floater, the water had run level with the banks and in many cases overflowed it, the current racing far, far faster than a man could run. A look from Dawn told him that she too was remembering that terrible day.

They camped that night beneath a large oak tree. The men were fortunate and cornered a fat female squealer in a narrow ravine where it was rooting in the damp soil. The female was accompanied by two small babies. They stared at the men out of tiny round eyes instead of running away, which was their first and last mistake.

The female was far more difficult to dispatch, and her high-pitched squeals rang against the steep walls of the ravine. Finally a well-aimed spear caught her in the ribs, and she ended her life with a scrabble of hard-pointed hooves on the muddy earth.

They gave their thanks to the Gods and carried the squealers back to camp, where they were welcomed with excited cries. None of the women, with the exception of Dawn, had ever seen a squealer before, and they examined the animals from the tips of their blunt snouts to the last curl of their hairless tails. Their curiosity satisfied, they allowed Emri and Hawk to butcher the animals and set them to roast above the fires.

The succulent white meat was a treat that was enjoyed by all. Birdsong glistened with grease, her chubby cheeks shone in the firelight as she sucked sleepily on a bone. Mosca, too, gnawed on a large joint. Even Dawn appeared happy, the little lines of worry that had recently crept across her face were now erased by the warmth of the flickering firelight and the comfort of friends. She stretched, easing the ache in her back, and pushed back the tangle of dark curls from her face. Feeling Emri's eyes upon her, she smiled at him, and the smile remained even after she turned back to the fire, hauling the sleepy but protesting Birdsong onto her lap.

Emri looked at the faces of the people whom he had brought so far, the people whom he had come to care about as though they were members of his own family. Then it came to him that they were no longer merely a group of strange people who had come under his protection, people whom he did not really know or care about.

He thought about Proud Bear's arrogant demeanor that merely cloaked a vulnerable soul. He thought about Running Bird, with her pithy comments and sly, humorous insults. He thought of the quiet, steady reliability of Tusk and Broken Tooth and of brave Otuk whom they had lost to the angry spirit of the old one. He thought of Brunk and the courage that far surpassed his young age, and of Leaping Fawn, whose love had saved her mate. Then he knew that these were no mere strangers, but friends who had become his family.

CHAPTER TWENTY-ONE

The morning mists had not yet lifted from the waters when they loaded the floaters and set off. It was judged that they were not far from the place that had been the Toad encampment. They knew that the Toad child would flee if he saw them and felt that approaching under cover of the mist was the only way to slip up upon him.

The rocky spit from which Emri and Dawn had launched their previous journey appeared out of the fog far sooner than they had expected. Had they but known, they could have walked to the camp the previous evening.

They slipped from the floaters silently, lifted them out of the water, and placed them on the ledge, noting the wreckage of the single floater that had been destroyed in the violence of their previous visit.

The camp was a desolate shambles. There had been little to mark it as a site of human habitation before, but now there was even less to see.

The mist lay heavy on the rocky ledge as they spread out and began their silent search, looking for the child whom Hawk had seen in his vision. There were many bones. Most appeared old and all had been cracked to get at the rich marrow contained within. Worse, most seemed to be of human origin. Emri shuddered but closed his mind to the implication. A starving child on his own during Cold Time would have little compunction about the source of his food.

They searched the ledge diligently, but nothing was found that would indicate the presence of a living being. Emri looked at the mists that floated above his head and shivered, wondering if angry Toad spirits lurked within them. He was all but ready to call off the search when Dawn touched his arm softly and nodded toward the wall of the embankment that rose steeply to the land above.

Emri followed her, signaling Hawk to join them. Emri had forgotten the shallow caves that the Toads had carved into the bank, and this was where they finally found the child.

The boy had been very enterprising, making the cave deeper and wider as well as lining it with soft grasses that gave it the appearance of some giant mouse nest. A fire smoldered in the entrance, and it was this smoke that had betrayed his presence. A large boulder was wedged in front of the opening and could be pulled back, protecting the cave's resident from the worst of the elements as well as roving predators. Nonetheless, it would not have protected him from cold or hunger or fear. Emri felt his heart going out to the unknown youngster who had survived on his own against overwhelming odds.

He knelt down in front of the small opening and looked inside. The child was curled into a small ball. He was covered with an assortment of tattered furskins that Emri could only assume were the garments of his less fortunate tribal members.

Emri reached in and shook the child gently. The child erupted in a wild flurry of arms and legs. As Emri drew back, startled, there was a sharp pain in his hand. Something had clamped down on his hand, and even as he struggled to free himself, the point of a knife was jammed into the flesh of his forearm. Emri yelled. Wedging his feet against the base of the embankment, he pulled hard, yanked the child out of the hole, and dropped him still squalling and flailing out with his knife upon the ground.

The child scrambled to his feet and tried to run, but

found himself ringed by adults. He raised his hand and
curled it into a claw, the other hand still clutched the
stone knife with which he had stabbed Emri. His lips
were drawn back in a snarl, revealing teeth that appeared ready to bite anyone who ventured near. His
hair was a matted snarl of dirt and filth and hung about
his face and shoulders like dirty rags. He stood his
ground bravely and turned, searching for a weak spot, a
place of escape.

Emri examined his hand, noting the half circle of
deep impressions that marked the flesh at the base of
his thumb. Fortunately the skin was not broken, but it
was painful. Even more painful was the place where the
child had stabbed him. This was no surface flesh wound
but was bleeding profusely. Emri knew that he would
have to see to it soon so that an angry spirit did not
enter the wound and prevent it from healing. But for
now, he merely wiped the blood away and then knelt to
speak to the child.

"Stop," he said gently. "We have not come to harm
you but to help you. We wish to take you with us, make
you part of our tribe. Lay down your weapon so we
might talk."

But the child either did not understand Emri's words
or chose to ignore them. In any case, he did not lay
down his weapon but continued to circle, an angry,
animallike growl issuing from his mouth. Emri looked
at Hawk and a silent message passed between them.

Hawk placed himself where the child could see him
and began to speak to him in the tongue of the Toads.
This language was similar to that which Emri spoke,
and if he listened carefully, he could understand what
was being said.

"Ho, brother Toad, I see you," said Hawk. "Do you
not recognize me? I am Hawk, son of Glarn, who was
of this tribe."

The child did not lay down his weapon but turned to
face Hawk and snarled again. "You are not my brother,"
he spat angrily. "You are but a weasel in the night who
tried to trick us out of all that was ours. You killed Trog

and Fish and Big Stick and led the others to us, and they killed all the rest, even Old Woman."

"It is a long and complicated story, young one," Hawk said gently. "It is a story that begins before you had memory and involves much that you do not know. We have nothing but sorrow in our hearts for the deaths that have occurred and would do what we can for you. We offer you our friendship and the safety of our fires. If you would join us, the story will be told and you will understand, even if you do not forgive, what has gone before."

The child seemed to hesitate, to ponder. He lifted his knife and waved it toward Hawk. "If your are a Toad, why are you with these others? Toads need no one. I need no one!"

"I am sure that that is true," Hawk said gravely. "It appears that you have managed very well on your own. Old Woman would be very proud of you, as am I. I am sure that you could continue on your own without our help, but it would make us feel better if you joined us. It would allow us to show the Spirits that we are sorry for their deaths.

"And yes, I am really a Toad. And these three are Tigers, and the rest are People of the Deer from the land of ice and snow. We are together because it is better than being alone and all men need someone. Still, it is your decision. If you chose not to join us, then we will respect that decision and leave."

Hawk rose and made as though to leave. Emri saw the child's eyes fill with sudden fear, and he leaped forward and grabbed at Hawk's arm, the knife dangling, forgotten at his side.

"Do not go," he said, attempting to appear nonchalant. "I will come with you if it will make you feel better. But it is not because I am afraid or because I need you, 'cause I don't need anyone."

"I understand," Hawk said seriously, and he touched the child on the shoulder and drew him to his side. The others stood aside and allowed the two of them to pass. The child held his head high and looked each of the

men in the eyes, daring them to speak out against him
or make some hostile move, but no man did so. Only
when they had passed out of the circle and gone to
stand by the floaters did the others turn back to Emri
and begin to talk among themselves in subdued voices.

The child was far from the sad, lonely thing they had
expected. They had never stopped to think that their
offer of friendship and inclusion into the tribe—which
they had come to think of as magnanimous—would be
rejected or that they themselves would be regarded as
anything other than rescuers by the child.

But as Dawn rubbed healing unguent into his bloody
wound, Emri had ample time to reflect upon the child's
words. All he had said was true, yet Emri had viewed
the sequence of events from his viewpoint only. Never
mind the fact that they had not intended to kill anyone,
it had happened. Nor could they have known that Broken Tooth and Walks Alone would find the camp and
kill everyone with the single exception of this child.
That too had occurred. From the child's viewpoint,
they were indeed the enemy. Emri could see no reason
for his agreeing to join their tribe.

Yet that was exactly what happened. Late in the
morning, after much talk, Hawk and the child rejoined
them. It was obvious from the child's bearing that he
had come to view them in a different manner.

"My brother the Hawk has told me your story and I
understand that you did not mean to cause my people
to die. If you will say the words for Old Woman, who
was always good to me"—here the boy's words faltered
and his lip began to tremble—"I . . . I will go with you
and take your tribe for my own."

"You would do us a great honor," Emri said, and
indeed he felt it to be true. "We will do this thing and
say the words for Old Woman and all the others so that
their spirits will not wander this sad place but will join
their ancestors. Soon, after their journey is done, their
spirits will look down on you and see that you are well
and they will be at peace.

A small shy smile stole across the boy's face, and
Emri could see that the thought gave him much pleasure.

The bones were gathered, all those that had survived
the long Cold Time and had not been stolen and scattered by animals. They were placed in the boy's cave
along with an assortment of other possessions—a stone
bowl, a stone club, two spears whose points were nothing but wood hardened in the fire, fishhooks, an awl,
and a stone hide-scraper. Many of the people added
items of their own. When they were done, the boulder
was wedged in the entrance of the cave and the edges
sealed with mud.

Everyone gathered around Emri as he said the words
that would send the spirits on their way to the next
world. The words were said with all the care that Emri
could muster, and Hawk and the People of the Deer
added words of their own to help send the spirits on
their way.

The boy, whose name was Empty Belly, stood by
proudly, his eyes shining with happiness as the ceremony concluded. He turned to Hawk and Emri and
nodded his thanks with an awkward bobbing of his head.

There followed a brief busy time as the tribe emptied
their floaters and carried them high upon the ledge
where they covered them with layers of branches and
grass gathered from the land above. It would seem that
their usefulness was over, but the floaters had been
made with much time and great care. They needed to
be preserved so that they might be used again if the
need arose.

Then, as the sun rode just above the edge of the
world, throwing its brightest rays and casting the longest shadows, they climbed the steep trail that led to the
top of the embankment and left the empty ledge that
was the Toad camp for the last time. The boy paused
for a moment, looking down on the world that was no
more, and then he too turned and followed his new
tribe onto the rolling land.

CHAPTER TWENTY-TWO

In spite of Dawn's ministrations and all of Running Bird's advice, Emri's arm did not heal as expected. By evening it had begun to throb painfully and the entire arm was swollen, stiff and tender to the touch. By morning, long red lines spidered out from the wound and reached halfway up the length of his arm.

"This is not good," Running Bird said with a frown. "Did you keep the salve on it all night as I said to do?"

"Yes, I did as you instructed." Emri grimaced in pain as Running Bird probed the inflamed edges of the wound with her fingers.

"Hmmm," muttered Running Bird as she and Dawn and Hawk moved away from Emri to confer among themselves.

Emri looked down at his arm and did not like what he saw. He did not need Running Bird to tell him that an angry spirit had entered his body through the wound and was preventing it from healing.

The boy, Empty Belly, stared at him with large frightened eyes across the circle of the camp. Emri could read fear in the boy's eyes, for it was he who had caused the injury allowing the angry spirits entry. Emri did his best to smile at the boy, knowing that he had only been trying to protect himself and that had Emri himself been in the boy's position, he would have done no less. Again, the boy seemed surprised at the reaction and smiled back shyly, then turned and darted away.

Emri closed his eyes and rested his arm on the furskin as close to the fire as possible. It was paining him far more than he would have thought possible. He tried to ignore the pain, but it broke through his concentration and soon it was all that he could think of. Emri knew that something would have to be done to draw the evil spirit out or he would surely die. He hoped that Dawn and Hawk and Running Bird would know of some cure. He could not leave the tribe leaderless now, nor did he wish to die.

After a short time Hawk returned to the fire with a handful of plants that he held upside down and far away from his naked skin. Emri saw that he had wrapped a bit of furskin around the stalks of the plants to keep them from touching his skin.

". . . now strip the leaves from the plant and place them in a cooking sack with some water," advised Running Bird as Hawk placed the plants on the ground in front of the fire. Emri could see that Hawk was none too pleased with Running Bird's commentaries, but he did as he was instructed, stripping the leaves from the thick stalks, using his knife to cut them away and place them in the cooking sack. Emri recognized the plant and knew that the leaves and the stalk were covered with tiny hairs that burned if they were touched by naked skin. If solid contact was made, blisters rose. Emri was even less anxious than Hawk to come in contact with the awful stuff.

After a time the brew was removed from the tripod over the fire and the leaves were fished out, a sodden, dark-green mass. These Running Bird slapped on top of his wound before Emri even realized what she was going to do. The heat of the scalding leaves caused Emri to rise up with a loud shriek. But Running Bird merely cackled and chastised him for disturbing the steaming poultice.

Emri fumed as Running Bird bound the leaves in place with a wide strip of furskin. "I may survive the wound yet die of the cure, old mother," he said between gritted teeth. Running Bird grinned at him, her eyes all but disappearing in the folds of fat that had once again filled out her cheeks.

"Ah, Emri, little chief, why do you whimper so?" she asked cheerfully. "Everyone knows that a medicine cannot help you if it feels good or is pleasant to the tongue. And pain is better than death, any day." As the pain and the shock of the hot leaves slowly diminished, Emri noted with surprise that the heat was actually easing the pain of the wound and he held his tongue.

Emri was not the only one to receive the old woman's ministrations. As Dawn knelt beside him and checked the advance of the red lines, Running Bird handed her a shell filled with the dark evil brew that had cooked out of the leaves.

"What is this?" Dawn asked, startled. "I have no injury."

"This is true." Running Bird shook the shell in front of Dawn's face, demanding that she take it. "But I have seen the pain on your face and remember well how heavy the child drags on your back in these final days. This will help the hurt. Now drink it down."

Protests helped Dawn no more than they had Emri. With many a shudder and grimace, Dawn was forced to drink two shellfuls of the awful stuff before Running Bird was satisfied.

Within a short period of time the poultice had drawn off much of the pain, and Emri got to his feet over Running Bird's protests, determined that they would travel that day. They said their good-byes to Broken Tooth, who was to leave them and travel on to the Tiger camp, where he would deliver Emri's message. Hawk gave him detailed instructions on how to locate the lake where they would make their camp, so that he could rejoin them and carry word of the shaman's reply.

With great sadness they watched the brave figure vanish in the distance. They had all come to know and care about Broken Tooth and his presence would be missed.

Emri said a prayer for his safety, begging the spirits of his ancestors to protect him from the shaman's wrath. The boy, Empty Belly, would accompany them until Broken Tooth's return, for it would not do to antagonize the shaman needlessly by bringing a second Toad into his camp.

The boy himself was more than willing to stay with them. He was openly fearful of the Tiger clan and could not believe that they would accept him gladly. Tigers and Toads had been enemies for time beyond memory.

Broken Tooth had merged with the dark blue line that marked the horizon before they broke camp and began their journey to the lake that Hawk had seen in his vision. Although they had no way of knowing, it was more than two days distant and would take them north and west of the Tiger camp.

The poultice helped for a time, and then the severity of the evil spirit overcame it and the pain returned once more. Emri knew that no good would come of stopping, for he feared that once he fell he would not rise again. A great heat rose within him as his spirit fought with the evil spirit. He could feel them as they waged their warfare inside his body. His head ached with their efforts and his limbs dragged with the weight of their added presence.

Dawn and Hawk walked on either side of him, supporting him when it seemed that he might fall and helping him over rough terrain. Mosca slunk alongside, often all but under his feet, wuffing low in his throat. His eyes were nervous as though scenting some danger in the air.

Emri would have said something to comfort the cat, but his tongue lay thick and heavy in his mouth, and it seemed too much trouble to speak. For a time he formulated the words, then could not remember whether he had spoken them aloud or not. The day was endless, a constant succession of low hills, one after the other, of placing one foot before the other and going on and on, long after his body cried out for him to cease.

They made camp early that night, and the people moved about silently, fearful, and uneasy over Emri's illness. What did it mean? If the evil spirit won out over Emri, it would be an omen that their journey was ill-conceived. Surely this was a sign from the Gods that they were doing the wrong thing.

"We have to do something, Hawk," Dawn said quietly as they lowered Emri onto his furskin in front of the fire. "The people think that we are doing the wrong thing. We must convince them otherwise. We cannot face Mandris by ourselves."

"Surely they would not desert us?" Hawk said. "They would not abandon us so easily. We have come too far and meant too much to each other."

"This is true," said Dawn, "but this is not their quarrel. They believe that Emri's wound is a sign from the Gods that we are wrong. They might not leave us, but they might not help us either. They may just stand back and leave the decision to the Gods."

"I cannot believe that they would do this." But even as Hawk said the words, he knew in his heart that it was true.

During the course of the day he had watched the land carefully, searching out those plants that he knew to be helpful in the curing of wounds. These he now prepared while the people busied themselves with the preparation of food.

After the potion was ready, he removed the furskin from Emri's arm and was shocked to see how ugly the wound had become. The wound itself was no longer than half a finger's length, yet the edges had not drawn together or begun to heal and were dark and discolored with shades of green and yellow tinting the flesh. The inside of the wound was swollen and oozed a thick, nasty fluid that stunk like carrion lying too long in the sun. The red lines had returned as well and streaked upward from the wound, reaching nearly to Emri's armpit. The entire arm was grossly swollen from fingers to shoulder and was extremely painful to Emri, who cried out at the lightest touch.

Dawn and Hawk stared at each other, alarmed over

the rapid advance of the damage. Both of them had seen people die of simple wounds and knew that they had to drive the evil spirit out soon or Emri would die.

Mosca pressed himself up against Emri's side and panted with his mouth open, a sign of extreme nervousness. He hissed whenever anyone came close, and his eyes were wild and glinted in the firelight.

Hawk applied the hot herbal tea to Emri's arm as gently as possible, then dusted the edges of the wound with a powder he had made by grinding up a root that was thought to be effective. Next he wrapped the entire limb with rabbit pelts, fur side in to cushion it. Before the pelts were bound to the arm, Hawk slipped three stones out of his pouch and placed them around the wound. These stones represented Dawn and Emri and himself, and he hoped that their power would lend Emri strength.

They had kept Running Bird away, unwilling to let her see how bad the wound had become. Although she was their friend, her mouth knew no enemy and would talk to any who would listen. Doing so earned them the sharp end of her tongue, but even that was preferable to allowing her tongue to wag over Emri's true condition, increasing the people's fear.

"Cast the stones, Hawk," said Dawn. "Let us learn if the Gods are against us. Perhaps there is some other course of action that we have not considered."

"I cannot cast the stones," Hawk replied, since he had included the three that were most important in the wrappings of the pelts. "But I will trance and try to speak to the spirits and learn whether we are favored or not."

"There is danger in this trancing," Dawn said nervously as she rubbed her belly. "Without Emri, there is only me to stay by your side and guard the connection. What if the connection is broken? What if your spirit is lost? What am I to do? I'm afraid, Hawk. Do not leave me here alone."

"I am afraid too, Dawn," Hawk said simply, "but there is no other way. We must do what we can to save

Emri. I must trance and you must help me and there is
no more to be said."

Dawn bit her lip and lowered her head so that Hawk
would not see the tears that came to her eyes. Although
she had not told anyone, she knew that her time was
near. The child had dropped farther still and the ache
in her back, although initially eased by Running Bird's
foul brew, had grown more intense after this day of
walking. She was afraid that Emri would die and that
Hawk's spirit would not return to his body and that she
would be left to face the birth and the shaman by
herself. She did not know which thought frightened her
more. Nor could she imagine life without Emri and
Hawk, for she loved them both and wanted them beside her always. Yet Hawk had spoken truthfully. They
had done all they could for Emri and it had not been
enough. There was nothing left to do but speak to
the spirits directly and pray that they would lend their
guidance.

The preparations were quickly made, and once more
Hawk took the smoke into his lungs and felt his spirit
separate from his body. This time, there was a rough
transition-a strange bumpiness as though the spirit were
passing through turbulent air. Then it was over and the
hawk flowed out of the top of his head and sat there for
a time, spreading his wings and opening and closing his
beak, as though glad to escape the confines of the body.
His talons gripped the top of Hawk's head and punc-
tured his forehead, but there was no pain, no sense of
fear. He and the hawk were one.

The hawk knew the mission without a word being
spoken. He uttered a high, thin cry that no one but
Mosca seemed to hear—although Dawn shivered and
looked around her with wide eyes.

The hawk leaped into the air and sought the heights
immediately, rising at a sharp angle until the camp was
but a small bright eye winking up through the darkness.

The hawk found the cold currents of the higher elevations and spread his wings wide and allowed himself

to soar along with them, letting them take him where they would. If the Gods were with him, they would take him where he needed to be and show him what he needed to learn.

Time passed and the winds continued to blow, carrying the hawk with them. The darkness was complete both above and below him. There was no moon and no fire denoting the presence of man. The hawk was alone in the black night.

Soon, or perhaps not soon, for the passage of time was strangely warped by the darkness, the hawk was circling over the lake that he had seen in his earlier vision. He sensed the presence of many animals below him and scented the richness of water.

Suddenly an image of the lake formed in his mind as it had appeared to him in daylight. He saw the rich vegetation and the multitude of animals and the glint of the sun on the water. But there was something else, something that he knew he should see, some message that he was missing. He studied the image more closely and the water zoomed toward him, growing larger and larger and larger until he saw that which he had missed before. Along one edge of the lake, in a small inlet, the mud at the edge of the water was not brown as mud should be. Nor was it the color of sand. Rather, it was the color of night, black as black could be.

The hawk was not interested in mud, no matter what the color, and shook its head impatiently, but the image would not fade and he looked upon it once more with exasperation. The image became larger and he looked at it more closely, anxious to do whatever was needed then be on his way, searching for the answer to their problems.

As the image grew larger, he saw that the mud was not mud at all but some curious substance that seemed to have a life and movement of its own. Suddenly the hawk became alert, interested. The black substance lined the edges of the inlet, lying in thick ridges. As he studied it, the hawk saw that it flowed beneath the clear water as well, yet so clear was the water that the

blackness appeared as nothing more than the bottom of
the lake. As he watched, a bubble began to form. It
grew larger and larger, and when it was as wide as the
space between fingertip and elbow, it broke and disappeared beneath the surface of the water, only to be
replaced by another, which slowly repeated the previous sequence of events. The hawk was fascinated and
watched as bubble after bubble formed, broke, and
disappeared.

Then a movement at the edge of the image broke his
concentration. A bird, as tall as a man and clad in white
feathers, dropped down out of the air, reaching for the
water with its long, thin legs. It landed in the shallows
and the hawk watched, expecting the bird to begin
probing the waters with its long beak, searching out the
tiny fish and frogs that were its diet. But the bird did
not do so. It began to struggle. The hawk watched
intently, wondering if the bird had been caught by
some large fish or perhaps a water-loving snake. But
there was no sign of life other than the bird.

As the hawk watched in puzzlement, the bird's actions became more frantic as it jerked in this direction
and then the other. It lunged back, and as it did so, one
foot came clear of the water trailing long webs of the
black goo. But the bird lost its balance and fell backward into the water, which seemed to absorb it and
draw it down.

The bird struggled a while longer, but it was futile.
First one wing, then the other was covered with the
sticky black stuff, and long before the glazed eyes and
gasping beak vanished under the surface of the water, it
was obvious that the battle was lost.

The vision vanished as swiftly as it had appeared, and
once more the hawk circled above the dark lake. And
now he could pick its scent out from all the others, that
of the strange black substance. It was different from
anything he had ever smelled before. It was an acrid
smell, rather like the scent of burning, yet somehow
sweet as well, not unpleasant but unlike anything else
in his vast encyclopedic storehouse of smells.

Then there was nothing but the night around him—no spirits, no hint of the Gods, no other messages—and he knew that whatever message there was, was contained in the image he had been given, the image of the strange black goo.

The hawk returned to the body beside the fire and after a moment of hesitation, reentered the body that held his spirit when he walked as a man.

Hawk opened his eyes and saw Dawn staring at him intently, twisting a piece of leather in her hands. Seeing his eyes open, Dawn flung herself at him with an anxious cry and began sobbing as though he had died, leaving only the empty husk of his body behind. Hawk patted her on the back and smoothed her hair. Mosca growled.

"Hush, little mother, everything is all right.. I have returned safely as you can see."

"I . . . I was so afraid," sobbed Dawn. "I was afraid that you would not come back."

"But I have returned," Hawk said calmly, "and the spirits have given me a vision, although I do not understand its meaning."

"Tell me." Dawn wiped her eyes with the furskin and tried to still her labored breathing.

Hawk related the vision from beginning to end while Dawn listened closely.

"It is a medicine," she said when Hawk was done with the telling. "It is a medicine that will cure Emri's wound. That is what it means. We must go there with all speed."

"A medicine?" Hawk said dubiously. "It did not seem a medicine. Rather a method of death, a trap in which we might catch the shaman. This is what I think."

"Then it is both," Dawn said with great confidence, her earlier fears vanished. "The Gods would not have given you the vision had they not wished to heal Emri."

"But, Dawn, the shaman is as big a problem as Emri's wound, and it is he whom we must defeat. I believe that this black stuff was shown to me so that we know how to use it for our protection."

"Hawk, it may be a weapon, but it will heal Emri as well," Dawn said firmly. "It was your vision, and you may interpret it in any way that you wish, but my heart tells me that I am right too. We must leave as soon as it is light and travel to this place, for it is there that the Gods wish us to be."

Wrapping herself in her furskin, she lay down beside Emri and was soon asleep. Hawk remained awake longer, stroking the nervous cat and studying the feverish face of his friend. He was filled with doubts and examined the vision from beginning to end trying to bring it into focus, extract the last bit of meaning from it.

He wanted Dawn to be right but saw no sign that it was so. The black stuff had killed, not healed. But sometimes things did not always make sense, ran contrary to the way they ought. For the sake of them all, he prayed that it was true.

CHAPTER TWENTY-THREE

The shaman was restless. Something was wrong. The woman made a small move behind him and he struck out, clubbing her with his fist as punishment for disturbing his concentration.

He could feel that something was wrong, much as a cat feels the approach of a storm through the buildup of electric current in the air. He was not alone in this feeling. The entire village was alert. Men and women alike had taken to scanning the horizon searching for sign of game, hairy tuskers, or bison, something that would explain the feeling of waiting that had seized the camp.

Snarling, he ordered the woman out of the dwelling. She obeyed quickly, knowing all too well the danger of disobeying him.

He closed the door flap and then stared into the tiny flickering fire, determined to seek out the cause of the disturbance, to find out what was wrong.

He breathed deeply, concentrating on reaching that inner space, that spark of power that was the real source of his existence. He focused on it, drawing upon it until it swelled larger and larger, expanding into his body and then beyond, becoming more than mere self yet far less tangible. There was a moment of hesitation as though the spirit feared the actual moment of separation, and then it moved beyond and where there had been one, there were now two.

The spirit of the tiger sat silently for a moment as

though communing with the empty shell of the man
who contained its essence when it was not free to roam.
The man looked into the tiger's eyes and it rumbled
deep in its tawny chest as though to assure the man that
it would not fail. Turning, it slipped through the hide
covering of the dwelling and was gone.

Having loosed his spirit, the shaman rested against
one of the pole uprights and waited for it to return. He
thought about walking around the village and calming
the people, directing their attention elsewhere, or sending the men on a great hunt. In the end he did nothing.
Though it was possible for him to function while his
spirit roamed free of his body, it was not a thing that
was to be done without thought. Should the spirit encounter anything unusual, it would draw upon him for
strength, strength that he must hoard against the need.

Separation of spirit and body was always dangerous.
If something were to happen to the body while the
spirit was absent, there would be nothing for it to
return to and the spirit would be forced to wander . . .
lost.

Always to be feared was the possibility that the tiger
might encounter another spirit while roaming free. In
such a case there were but four possible outcomes. The
spirits would see each other, yet choose not to make
contact. Or they would enter into conflict. If the tiger
won, it would seriously weaken the second spirit's body.
If the opposing spirit had no body, it would disappear
into the void that lay beyond the death of the spirit.
The worst possible outcome would be for the shaman's
spirit to be defeated. Then the hostile spirit would
supplant the shaman's spirit with its own, taking over
his body and forcing the shaman's spirit to wander the
earth.

Such a thing was always a possibility, but until now
the shaman had never encountered a spirit that was as
strong as his own. Emri's father—he who had been
leader and shaman of the Tigers—had had a formidable
spirit. But in the end he had died like any other man.
Even a spirit could do little against a knife in the back.

Mandris smiled bitterly, remembering Crow's death, which had allowed him to gain his position of power.

He had come to the Tigers as a young man, eager to learn all that could be taught under the tutelage of the older man. But he had not reckoned on the son, on the boy, Emri, upon whom Crow had directed all of his love.

Crow had agreed to take the young stranger on as an apprentice, and he had taught him much. Mandris had idolized the older man, loved him as the father he had never known. But while Crow was always pleasant and careful to praise the younger man's efforts, there was something missing, something held back. After a time Mandris came to realize that it would never be different. No matter how hard he worked, no matter how hard he strove to please, he would always be an outsider.

Crow reserved his affections and his attention for his son, Emri. He too sat in on the lessons. Mandris came to hate the child's eager face and the light that filled his eyes when he mastered some skill or understood a difficult lesson.

And always he learned a heartbeat before Mandris. A surge of rage filled Mandris's chest at the memory, and his face flushed with anger.

Everything had come so easily for Emri. His mind was quick and handled the strange new concepts with ease while Mandris had struggled to master them. He was well liked by everyone in the village and would have been popular even if his father had not been the chief; his sunny disposition and open caring endeared him to both young and old.

Mandris had been accepted by the clan because the chief had deemed it so, but his painful shyness and fear of rejection had been taken as coldness. The villagers were polite, but barely so.

Nor had he won acceptance among the women, who teased him openly and then laughed aloud at his discomfort. He had hunted and then slain a great bear, alone, with only his spear and knife, thinking to win the love and respect of a young woman named Laughing

Water. The deed had earned him great merit and for a
time Laughing Water had looked on him favorably. But
in the end she had chosen another, and their bodies
warmed the bearskin while Mandris slept alone.

Still, with the passing of the years, Mandris had
mastered all that he was taught and more. He learned
to protect himself from what he viewed as the gibes and
cuts of the villagers. They in turn, hurt and rebuffed by
his distant manner, gave up their tentative efforts to
make him a part of their lives.

Mandris had always known that the boy, Emri, was
being groomed by his father to fill his role as chief, but
over the years he had come to hope, to expect, that he
would be given the position of shaman.

Mandris knew that Crow had watched him carefully
over the years and had come to respect his abilities—
the fierce determination, the strong pride that held him
to a difficult task and drove him on long after others had
given up, and the courage and bravery that far out-
stripped his years.

He hoped that Crow recognized the painful shyness
and knew it to be but a mask, the reason for his seemingly cold manner. And he ignored the small warning
voice that told him that these were not the qualities one
looked for in a shaman.

If Crow was the head of the clan, the shaman was its
heart, its spiritual guide. More than courage, more than
pride, more than fierce determination, a shaman needed
to be caring of others and able to understand their
needs. Mandris closed his ears to the inner voice, promising that when he was made shaman and accepted by
the people, he would open his heart to them and be all
that they could wish for.

Crow had attempted to talk to the younger man
many times, to share his concerns and offer sugges-
tions, but Mandris had stared at him with tied tongue
and burning cheeks, unable to reply, to reassure him
that all would be well when he was shaman. He thought
that Crow would understand what was in his heart
despite his inability to speak.

But Crow began to pull away and spent less and less time with the younger man. After a time he let it be known that Emri would inherit both roles upon his death.

It seemed to Mandris as though the world had come to an end. The words, small, tiny sounds that they were, had put an end to his dreams, to his life for a second time, and this time was more cruel than the first.

Mandris had come from a small hunting tribe far to the east. He had watched his people sicken and die, coughing and spitting up blood. Only he had been spared. He had wandered the plains for a long time, alone and fearful, terrified of the many predators and even more frightened of the many wandering spirits whose presence he felt around him throughout the empty days and endless nights.

Finding the village of the Tiger clan and being allowed to remain had seemed a gift of the Gods. Now the Gods were exacting payment and the price was harsh. He had no family, no other place to go.

His heart pounded in his chest and his head ached at the thought of being alone, of being without a tribe again. There had been no mention of his leaving, but Mandris knew that the day could not be far off when such a thing would be said. Crow would not wish for his son to face a potential rival, even if his position was firmly established.

More to the point, Mandris was unwilling to be relegated to a position of nothingness. There was no other place for him in the tribe. He had devoted himself to his shamanic studies. His arm was strong and his aim was true, but he had no real liking for hunting and would not find favor among those tightly knit ranks.

There was a terrible reluctance in him to be anything other than shaman. He had come to look upon it as his due. He wanted it so much that he could not bear to think of its being otherwise. A resentment began to grow, small at first, no more than a trickle of anger, directed at himself for his own shortcomings.

But Emri's face was before him always, cheerful and content in the knowledge that he belonged, knowing that no matter what happened, his life and his future were secure. No one could rob *him* of *his* birthright.

But the more Mandris thought about it, the more wrong it seemed that Emri should have so much simply by an accident of birth, while he, Mandris, should have so little in spite of having worked so hard to achieve it. Everything came easy to Emri: study, friends, honor, and even love. It was at that moment that Mandris began to hate Emri and Crow and to plan their downfall.

In the beginning it was no more than a wish that Emri would disappear. It seemed that every time he turned around, he saw Emri's happy, smiling face. Soon Mandris was having to force himself to turn and walk away so as not to strike the younger man. Next he began to dream about what it would be like if Emri did not exist, had never been born or was perhaps to die in some unfortunate accident. If Emri were gone, then Crow would turn to him and he would inherit the mantle of love and respect. Then Crow would realize how sadly mistaken he had been.

Unfortunately, dreams are not reality, no matter how much one wishes them to be true. More and more often now, Crow turned his face from Mandris and devoted his full attention to his son. Mandris knew that it would only be a short time before he was excluded completely and asked to leave the tribe. He also knew that he would do anything to prevent that from happening.

His chance came one bright day when Crow, perhaps realizing what little attention he had paid to Mandris in recent days, suggested that they journey to the lowlands. Mandris agreed reluctantly, knowing that the moment he had dreaded had come at last.

The publicly stated purpose of the journey was to collect herbs, which grew in profusion along the banks of the river. These herbs were useful in preventing pain and were highly prized by the people of their tribe. But Mandris knew that the herbs were but a subterfuge, a cover for the real reason of the trip, telling him that he

must leave the tribe. His heart ached in his chest and
the blood roared and pounded in his ears. His inner
voice cried out in anguish, demanding that he do something. Outwardly Mandris smiled and remained calm,
saying only that he would be glad to accompany Crow
in search of the herbs.

Of late, Crow had taken to mixing the herbs with bits
of meat that he then fed to the great saber-toothed tiger
who was the totem of their tribe. The tiger was old and
one of his great fangs had broken halfway up its length.
Crow knew that the huge animal was suffering. He had
begun feeding it the mixture in order to spare it pain,
and when the time came, to ease its passage into the
land of the Spirits.

The tiger had become a familiar sight around the
village, having learned that the man could be counted
on to provide him with food. Even now it walked in
their tracks and followed them as they made their way
along the shallow riverbed that bordered the village.

The words that Mandris so feared did not come and
Crow seemed friendlier than he had been in some
time. But far from putting Mandris at ease, he became
even more nervous, waiting for the blow to fall.

They were away for three days and nights and still
Crow did not speak of any save ordinary matters. The
herbs were gathered from where they grew at the base
of large oak trees and then spread in the sun to dry.
Next, they were crumbled and packed away in leather
pouches.

Crow showed Mandris the proper proportion of meat
to herbs, that which was the most effective for dulling
the tiger's pain, and then watched as the younger man
molded the mixture into small balls that the tiger could
swallow without difficulty. Then, surprisingly, he allowed Mandris to approach the tiger and feed him.

It was an exhilarating experience. The tiger was immense, longer than Mandris himself. The head was
twice as large as a man's, and the single intact fang was
longer than a man's hand and curved far below the
tiger's jaw.

The tiger watched Mandris approach through amber eyes, a low rumble like distant thunder rolling through its massive chest. Mandris was afraid—the tiger could kill him easily with one blow of its immense paw—but below the fear was a feeling of excitement such as he had never known before. The tiger's gaze was hypnotic and Mandris stared into its eyes as he drew closer, holding out the offering on the palm of his hand.

Crow hissed a warning, urging him to stop, but Mandris continued on, drawing closer and closer to the huge beast. The tiger's lips drew back, exposing yellowed teeth, teeth that could cleave through flesh and grind his bones. But even this did not stop Mandris and he drew closer still until he stood directly in front of the great beast.

They stood staring at each other for a time, yellow eyes meeting brown, and it seemed to Mandris that the world stopped. There was no sound, no thought, no movement, nothing except the man and the beast linked by the gaze that looked beyond the vision of flesh and form as each recognized themselves in the other.

There was a sharp crack as Crow in his concern for the younger man's safety, stepped forward onto a twig and the spell was broken. The tiger dropped his eyes and shuffled backward moaning *"unnhhh, unnhhh, unnhhh,"* from deep in his chest. Mandris placed the ball of meat on the ground before the tiger and then returned to Crow's side with downcast eyes and an apologetic manner.

"You must never do that again!" cried Crow, taking his arm and pulling him away. "The tiger is no tamed bird to be petted and fed by hand. Never forget that it would as soon kill you as look at you. You were very, very lucky."

Mandris murmured his apologies, concealing the excitement that filled him. He knew that the tiger would not kill him, not now and not later—and it had nothing whatsoever to do with luck. The Gods had sent him an omen; now he knew what was to be done.

As though fulfilling that prophecy, Mandris found the

upper jaw of a saber-toothed tiger lying at the edge of a stream bed later that afternoon. From the look of the bones scattered among the rocks, it was an old kill and had been there since the previous Cold Time. Most of the bones were broken, but the jaw was intact and the two great fangs were still firmly lodged in the bone. He stood looking at the jaw and knew that the Gods had placed it there where he would find it, almost as though they were directing his actions. He would not wait for Crow to speak, but would seize the initiative and act first.

Still listening to his inner voice, which had grown more strident, more demanding, Mandris waited until the following morning to make his move. Crow took the lead as was his nature and began to retrace their steps, toward home. Then Mandris took the jawbone from his pouch. Moving up behind Crow, he brought it down in one swift movement, slamming it into the man's back powered by all the strength of his hatred and fear.

Crow stumbled forward, dropped to one knee, and half turned toward Mandris. His eyes were open wide and even at that moment held no more than wonder and sadness. He opened his mouth as though to speak and raised his hand, but a great gout of blood rushed from his mouth, choking off the words. His hand fell, scrabbling uselessly at his chest. Slowly, his eyes still staring into Mandris's, he toppled forward onto the ground, his head twisting at an awkward angle.

There was no joy, no instant release of tension such as he had yearned for; instead, Mandris was filled with nervous energy that set his limbs aquiver and his muscles twitching as though he were possessed by an evil spirit. And still Crow lived, his eyes watching Mandris, his silence worse than any words.

And then Mandris lost control, unable to bear the silent scrutiny that did not damn him for his actions but held only understanding and compassion.

Mandris kicked out, showering Crow with a thick layer of forest debris, covering the man's head and staring eyes with dead leaves and bits of twigs. He began to giggle, the awful sounds pouring out between clenched teeth and contorted lips. He heard the sounds as though at a great distance and wondered where they were coming from.

Then a great fury seemed to take him and he began to throw things at the fallen man, anything and everything that came to hand: leaves, a broken branch, stones. The giggles turned to gasps and then to a kind of hysterical laughter. When the man's form was all but buried, Mandris fell to his knees as though he had been struck, all the strength suddenly gone from his legs. Unable to support his own weight, he collapsed on the ground and lay there, clutching himself and shivering although the day was warm. He vomited and then lay there with the spittle hanging from his mouth in long strands, tears coursing down his face, unable to move.

It was dark before he stirred. When he finally moved, it was only to the base of a nearby tree. He sat holding himself, all but overwhelmed by a sense of loss and grief such as he had never known before. For once, even the inner voice that had driven him on for so long was silent. He was truly alone.

When the first gray mists of morning lighted the wood, he rose to his feet shakily and moved to Crow's side. Crouching down amid the disturbed soil, he brushed the debris away gently, almost hoping that the man was not dead. Punishment or even banishment would be preferable to the way he felt.

Crow was dead. His open eyes still stared at Mandris, but they were vacant and unseeing. Gone was the look of understanding and compassion that was more painful than words or even a fatal blow. Mandris saw himself strangely distorted in the dead man's eyes and drew back in horror. Gingerly he prized the jawbone from Crow's back, careful not to touch the spill of blood that had crusted on the cold flesh.

He buried the jawbone in a deep hole and covered it with earth and stones and a layer of leaves, anxious to remove it from sight as well as existence.

He returned to find the tiger, whom he had all but

forgotten, snuffling at the body. Then, before he could stop him—if such a thing were even possible—the tiger hooked the dead man's arm with his claws and drew the body toward him. Mandris closed his eyes and turned away, sickened, as the tiger began to feed on Crow's body.

The cat's actions disturbed him deeply and it was all that he could do to prevent himself from rising and trying to take the corpse away from the cat. Unable to watch the desecration, he walked into the forest and wandered about without direction until the sun burned red on the ground and the cool breezes of evening began to rise. Only then did he turn his footsteps back to the clearing..

The tiger had vanished, its belly filled with the soft flesh of the man who had honored him throughout his life. A plan had begun to form in Mandris's mind, and now as he viewed the ruined corpse, it took on greater definition.

To any but the most practiced eye, it would appear that the tiger had killed the man. Close examination would reveal the two deep fang marks in the man's back. Any knowledgeable hunter would know that a tiger would not choose to attack that portion of a man's anatomy, preferring the neck or the head or even a limb. But that was hindsight now. He could but hope that the wounds would be overlooked in the greater horror of the deed itself. There might be suspicions, but there was no reason for anyone to think that Mandris might have killed Crow himself. Since no man could command the tiger who was their totem, the act must have been directed by the Gods. No man could quarrel with that.

Mandris walked into camp two days later with Crow's blood-caked body draped over his shoulder. Those two days had taken their toll on him. He had paid a heavy price for his awful deception. It was as though he had lost his youth overnight. His eyes burned with a terri-

ble fevered light and his steps were heavy and dragged
along the ground.

Amid the terrible outcry of grief that followed his
return, throughout the weepings and wailings that accompanied the burial, it was seen that the tiger followed close on Mandris's steps and attended his every
move. It was seen that he fed from Mandris's hand and
made no move to harm him. It was as a sign from the
Gods.

No man spoke the words that he most feared; no
woman accused him. Nor was he opposed as he donned
the skull and furpiece of the shaman and took up the
polished thighbone that was the sign of that office. As
was fitting under the circumstance, since Crow had
outlived his brothers, Mandris took the man's family to
his fire. Thus did he become chief as well as shaman of
the Tiger clan.

So rapidly had the events transpired that many seemed
to pass their days in a state of shock. How had it
happened, this awful thing? What had they done to
cause the Gods to become so angered with them as to
strike down one who was beloved by all, one who had
led them so admirably. Among those who were most
affected by the death of Crow were Emri, his mother,
and his two younger sisters. They could not understand
what action that gentle and generous man could have
made to draw down the wrath of the Gods and given
them into Mandris's keeping.

If any among them suspected all was not what it
should be, it was Emri. But even he held his silence,
for the tiger's allegiance was obvious. Not even his
father had commanded the beast so completely. Grief
and shock also played their part, and when doubt and
suspicion finally rose, it was far too late to act. The
thing was done.

Mandris opened his eyes wearily, gaining no joy from
the memory of those distant events. He had reigned as
chief and as shaman, gaining prominence in his clan.
He had tried to rid himself of Emri as well, the last
threat to his security.

But there had been no pleasure. After all this time, there was no joy in him, only the heavy, ever-present weight on his heart and shoulders. Sometimes at night, unable to sleep, he thought he heard the coughing grunt of a cat prowling outside his dwelling, although the tiger had been dead now for nearly two Cold Times.

Sometimes it seemed to him that he was but passing his days, waiting for something to happen. It was almost as though he had heard a story without an end and could not continue his life until the thing was done. Emri was the end of the story. Some part of him had always known that, and the story would not end until Emri himself was dead. Emri with his knowing eyes and sharp words could undo the life that he had created for himself. Mandris was determined that such a thing would not happen.

He had sent the tiger against Emri and the Toad and they had killed the tiger. He had sent the two men, Walks Alone and Broken Tooth, to kill them and neither had returned.

He had searched for them with his spirit and he knew they were near. Soon there would be an end to the story. If the Gods were with him, it would be told with words of Mandris's own choosing.

CHAPTER TWENTY-FOUR

They had reached the lake that Hawk had seen in his vision. It was larger than they had expected and was surrounded by stands of tall trees draped with moss. Between the trees and the water was a thick, lush expanse of grass dotted with bright yellow flowers whose fragrance hung heavy on the still air.

There was much animal life. Small creatures scuttled through the grass, causing Mosca to bound after them. Small horses, delicate and nervous, browsed among the grasses, which rose nearly as high as their backs. Antelope and deer, long-necked camels and a single bison, grazed side by side. A male squealer, his long, curved tusks gleaming wickedly, rooted under the nearest trees. All, even the deer, gave the squealer wide berth.

Long-legged, white-plumed birds stalked the thick reeds at the edge of the lake, searching out the tiny frogs and minnows that were their mainstay. Birds no larger than Birdsong's small hand, the color of rainbows, darted through the air and hovered above the flowers on whom they fed. Raucous cries rent the air as huge colonies of black birds fought among themselves on the branches of the trees. A lone condor circled high overhead, waiting for the summons of death.

They set up camp under the edge of the trees and Dawn sank to the ground wearily, allowing the other women to perform the necessary chores. The pain was gathered at the base of her spine now, like a solid lump of fire. Running Bird took the child from her and set her down to play with a pile of stones.

Hawk lay Emri down gently on a mound of grass covered with a furskin. Emri's arm was a mass of black, blue, purple, and a sickly shade of yellowish green. Dark purple lines snaked their way up the length of his arm and reached as far as his armpit. One did not have to be a healer to know that the arm was filled with poison. Unless something was done to drive out the evil spirit, it seemed likely that Emri would die. This knowledge dampened their spirits, and the feeling of the camp was one of quiet watchfulness as they waited to see what would happen.

Hawk wasted no time after he settled Emri but set out along the lake, searching the perimeter for the place that he had seen in his vision. The water appeared to be clear with a fine sand bottom at the point where they had made their camp. But a short distance away, Hawk found one of the long-legged birds floating on the surface of the water, its beautiful plumage saturated with water and shining with an oily iridescence that did not come from water alone. Although the bird's body was floating on the surface, its feet seemed to be mired in the sand. Hawk could not understand how the bird had come to be so trapped, but he did not stop to investigate.

After a time he began to notice small, round black balls floating at the water's edge. He picked them up and found that they were neither heavy nor firm and could be mashed between thumb and forefinger releasing a sharp, acrid aroma. Hawk had never seen anything like them and wondered what they could be and where they had come from.

The black balls grew more numerous, and finally he saw a thin line of the black material edging the shore itself. Then he saw it, the small cove of his vision. The surface of the water was drawn with swirls of the strange shining iridescence. The water itself seemed clear, and it was possible to see to the very bottom. Only when one looked very closely could it be seen that what first appeared to be the bottom was not solid at all, but some shadowy, murky stuff that hung suspended below the surface.

Hawk found a stick and probed the water, careful not to step off the solid ground. When he pulled the stick back, it was draped with a smooth black goo. He touched the stuff with his finger and found that it was warm, almost hot, and possessed a sharp smell that was not totally unpleasant.

Hawk crouched near the edge and peered into the water touching it cautiously with a finger, noticing for the first time that there were no fish in the water and that the water itself was unnaturally warm. His stomach twisted as he looked into the depths and he knew that the vision had been no mistake. Somehow the strange blackness was to play a role in their survival.

As he hurried back to camp to tell Dawn of his finding, he studied the lake more carefully and noticed that all of the reeds were coated with bits of blackness. He surmised that the black goo was present throughout the lake even when it was not clearly visible.

Dawn was curled up alongside Emri, her hand clutching his uninjured arm. Hawk did not even stop to take note of the fact that she was resting at midday, an unusual occurrence for any of the women.

"I have found the blackness that I saw in the vision." Hawk dropped to the ground beside her and handed her one of the semi-solid balls that he had gathered on his return.

The words roused Dawn from the light sleep into which she had fallen, and she sat up and examined the ball.

"How is it to be used?" she wondered aloud. She broke off a bit and placed it in her mouth, only to spit it out and wipe her tongue on the back of her hand with a grimace. "No, surely it is not eaten! Yet it is soft. Perhaps it can be placed in water and heated to make a poultice that will draw the evil spirit out of his arm."

Unable to think of any other method in which the stuff might be used, Hawk filled a cooking sack halfway to the top with the black balls and then covered them with water. The sack was then placed above a cooking fire. After a time a harsh, burning smell began to waft from the bag. When the mixture was stirred, the stick came away coated with the black substance. Still not knowing if what they were doing would do any good, they continued on for lack of any other choices. None of their medicines had worked, none of their prayers. If the black substance failed to heal Emri, it seemed likely that he would die.

Emri's arm was unwrapped and the furskins laid aside. The arm was thick and swollen to more than twice its normal size and gave off a terrible stench. Taking the red-and-black-streaked obsidian knife that hung at Emri's side, Hawk slashed the arm in six places between wrist and armpit. Immediately dark blood and yellow pus began to ooze out of the wounds. Dawn turned her head, sickened by the sight and the gagging smell.

Hawk swallowed hard and then stirred the contents of the steaming sack. When he thought that it was cool enough to apply, he began to spread it on Emri's arm. Even though Emri was no longer conscious, the great heat caused him to writhe and thrash on his furskin, crying out with words that had no meaning. Mosca bounded up to them, growling and looking about for signs of danger. Dawn let go of Emri's shoulders in order to calm the cat, assuring him that all was well.

Hawk called to Proud Bear and Tusk and soon there were enough hands to hold Emri firmly, allowing Hawk to smear the steaming mixture on the afflicted limb. He coated the arm liberally from wrist to shoulder, missing no portion, and not stopping until the cooking sack was empty.

The black substance had not mixed with the water, and what little had not dispersed as steam now dribbled out onto the ground. The sack itself had become stiff and hard and it seemed unlikely that it could ever again be used for cooking. Several of the men were examining the curious black stuff, pinching it and pulling it between their fingers.

Emri had lapsed back into the stupor that had overtaken him two days earlier. His arm, now coated with a
thick black crust, looked like something out of a night-
mare, and everyone averted their eyes.

"You must come with me," Running Bird said to
Dawn as she helped her to her feet. "Your time is near
and you will do neither your man nor yourself any good
if you lie here on the ground and sicken."

Dawn protested, but in truth the pain was growing
more and more intense with every passing heartbeat. It
did not seem as though Emri even knew that she was
there.

"I will stay with our brother," said Hawk, sensing her
reluctance to leave. "Do as Running Bird says." Dawn
did as she was bid, allowing herself to be led to a pallet
of furskins where she drank a mixture of flower tops and
herbs that Running Bird vowed would ease her pain.
Running Bird sat beside her and stroked her forehead,
crooning to her in soft tones that seemed to lighten her
burden of worry and pain. Comforted by the older
woman's presence, knowing that others were watching
over Emri and the child, she allowed herself to sleep.

When she wakened, the sun had gone to its rest and
risen yet again. The camp was filled with people hurry-
ing about with new purpose and energy, and there
were smiles on faces that had known only frowns and
tension for days past. Dawn sat up quickly, her own
problems all but forgotten. "Emri . . . ?" she asked,
reaching out to one of the women.

"Awake!" the woman replied happily, "and asking for
food and drink!"

Dawn threw back the furskin and ran to Emri's pallet, only to find it empty. He was seated on a log a
short distance away, wan and thin as though he had
shrunk during his illness, but his eyes were bright and
he appeared to be much improved. His arm was still
coated with blackness, yet it now appeared as though it
were a too large garment and hung from his shoulder
like the hard shell of an emerging larva that no longer
fit the host.

"Oh, Emri," cried Dawn, and she sat down beside him and touched him gently as though he might vanish. "I thought that you would not waken . . . I thought that you would journey to the ancestors. I was so afraid."

"I would not leave you," Emri said with a smile, as he smoothed the shining mass of curls away from her face, "nor did the spirits want me. They have sent me back and told me to finish what I have started."

Hawk approached and made his way through the crowd that had gathered around Emri. "Ho, brother. I see that our vision has cured you just as Dawn said it would."

"If this is your vision, then it must be so." Emri lifted his blackened arm slightly. "But I am not certain that there is still an arm inside this shell. It feels very strange. What now? Must it remain still longer or can it be removed?"

Dawn and Hawk looked at each other and shrugged. The vision had not given them this information.

"Come, brother, take pity on me. I would see if there is still an arm inside this thing. I am as a bird trapped in a snare. Say that you will set me free!"

Smiling, Hawk took up the red-and-black blade once more and began to cut away the stiff shell. Emri bit his lip and held his arm braced against his thigh, allowing Hawk to free the imprisoned limb.

A great stench, like that of rotting meat, assaulted their nostrils as the black shell was pierced. Fearing that the arm had begun to rot, Dawn felt her heart plummet—although she was careful to keep all signs of despair from her face. But as the shell was peeled away like bark from a tree, she saw that the interior was caked with pus and sickness that had drained from the arm.

The arm itself was red and angry looking, the flesh puckered and blistered. But it seemed that this was a result of the heat contained in the black substance and not evidence of further sickness.

A thin, clear fluid flowed from several of the cuts. Others had already begun to scab, but the dark blood

and the pus had vanished as had the ugly red lines that
had streaked ominously upwards. It seemed that the
evil spirit had been vanquished.

Now Mosca, drawn by their happy cries, left off his
attempts at stalking one of the long-legged white birds
and came bounding toward them. Pushing his way
through the throng of people, he butted Emri in the
chest and growled gruffly, a sign of happiness.

Emri reached up and scratched the cat behind his
ears. As Mosca moaned with pleasure, Emri looked
across the top of his head and nodded to the people
clustered around him.

"I thank you for your efforts. The Gods have seen fit
to spare me and lead us to this place. Now we must
ready ourselves, for there is a purpose at work here
whose meaning we cannot see. I feel that the time of
confrontation is near. The shaman is coming, and when
he arrives, we must be ready."

CHAPTER TWENTY-FIVE

Broken Tooth had returned to the Tiger clan. His woman clung to his side and touched him as though she had not believed she would see him again. His children ran through the village, crying aloud that their father had been to the land of ice and snow. They told everyone of his journey to the distant Cold Lands that were more myth than reality, as though his feat had somehow given them new stature. Indeed, it had.

Soon he was surrounded by a large crowd who followed him as he directed his steps toward the shaman's dwelling. They called out his name and asked after Walks Alone, his companion on the long trip. But Broken Tooth, much as he would have preferred to stop and talk with his friends, knew that his duty lay first with the shaman. It was to him that the story must first be told and told carefully, if there were to be any hope of a bloodless reconciliation.

Alerted by the noise, Mandris emerged from his dwelling, looking even more drawn and haggard than the last time Broken Tooth had seen him. His eyes were ringed with red and his cheeks were deeply scored. Although he was younger by far than Broken Tooth, he appeared to be much older. Still, he had about him a sense of quiet menace like that of a black sky before the release of rain that he wore like a cloak, intimidating all who came near.

"You have returned," he said simply, and made as though to return to his dwelling, gesturing for Broken Tooth to enter as well. But Broken Tooth, drawing strength from the mass of people behind him, old friends and men of good reason, stood fast and dared to speak out.

"It is a long story and one that should be heard by everyone. Let us sit outside in the sun and I will tell the story once, for all to hear, while enjoying the sight of my family from whom I have been separated for so long."

Mandris was displeased by these words, as Broken Tooth had known he would be, but cries of assent broke out all around him as friends and family supported his suggestion. Then, before Mandris could utter an objection, Broken Tooth had been carried toward the central fire, that which was always kept burning and around which all village activities of any importance were centered. Women hurried to their dwellings in search of food and drink. The morning had taken on the feeling of a day of celebration, and with any luck the story would last long into the night.

When all had gathered around the fire, Broken Tooth seated himself on a large, flat, centrally positioned rock that was used in ceremonies and important announcements. He spent a great deal of time arranging himself comfortably, making certain that he had a skin of water at hand to wet his throat and that he could be seen by all around him. It was obvious that he was enjoying his moment of importance. His woman was seated on the ground below him. She fussed with her braids and beamed pleasantly at all of her women friends—those same women who had pitied her aloud and within her hearing during Broken Tooth's long absence.

Mandris stood to one side all but ignored by those around him, yet it was his burning gaze that eventually brought Broken Tooth back to the matter at hand and caused him to begin his long tale.

He told how he and Walks Alone had followed Emri,

Hawk, and Mosca from the place where the tiger who had been their totem had been killed. He told of the great fire that had been set in the hopes of throwing them off the trail. He told of finding the third set of footprints and following all three to the river's edge. Sharp gasps and cries of horror sprang to his listener's lips as he told of the carnage they had found upon entering the Toad's encampment. And then he spoke of the death they had brought to those Toads who had survived. Nor did he seek to place himself in a more favorable light, but spoke truthfully of his part in the slaughter.

Strangely, his listeners did not seem to view his actions with any degree of disapproval. Rather, they cheered his actions loudly as though he had done something worthy and deserving of merit.

Before his journey Broken Tooth himself would have shared their opinion. Something had changed since and he was no longer the man he had once been. Remembering Empty Belly, he looked down and waited for the rude comments to end before he continued.

He felt Mandris's hot eyes on him. He raised his head and looked directly at the shaman without fear, holding his gaze without flinching until the crowd quieted and he was able to speak again.

He talked throughout the long, hot day, telling of their dangerous journey and of all that had transpired. At the first mention of her son's name, Emri's mother had begun to cry, the tears running down her cheeks in silent streams. Then, as it appeared that he was both safe and well, the tears dried and she moved closer and closer to Broken Tooth, unaware and uncaring of the shaman's extreme displeasure.

The dark blue shadows of night had crept up on them all but unnoticed, and still the story continued. Wood was heaped upon the fire and women hurried to their dwellings for additional supplies of food and drink, reluctant to miss even the slightest detail of the exciting saga.

They shivered and huddled together even though the night was warm during the telling of the long, cold winter, locked in the land of forever ice. They murmured over the miracle of love that had transformed their own cold clansman, Walks Alone, and they wept with real sorrow as they learned of his death in the collapsing mountain of ice.

Sleepy-eyed, chubby-cheeked children were bundled into their furskins and rocked in the arms of their mothers while the story of starvation, deprivation, and death unfolded. Broken Tooth spoke of their long journey south, with Emri and Hawk leading the way. Several women whose bellies swelled with the beginnings of new life stroked their own mounded abdomens and hugged their men close, realizing perhaps for the first time how fortunate they really were.

Now they heard of the return to the Toad camp and of the finding of the child, Empty Belly. They looked at the abundance of food spread before them, knowing that even the smallest scraps would have been a feast for the starving child, and felt guilt and sadness at their own well-being.

They learned further of the spirit journeys of the two men, of their growing mental and physical prowess, and felt pride that Emri was of their clan, overlooking the fact that none of them had opposed the shaman when he had cast the boy out.

Finally, as the moon rose high in the night sky, Broken Tooth spoke of the lake where the tribe was camped, saying that it had been shown to them in a vision. He made no mention of the fact that Emri had been injured, unwilling to allow the shaman to know that they were anything less than strong.

The telling had gone well. Broken Tooth knew that the clan's sympathy lay with Emri and Hawk and Dawn and those of the new tribe. He knew that had the decision been theirs alone, the outcasts would have been welcomed into the tribe without a second thought, but he also knew that the decision was not theirs alone.

This was why he had dared to risk the shaman's anger and told the story to the entire gathering.

The shaman's dark gaze, which had never once left his face during the entire telling, told Broken Tooth that the man knew what he had done and for what purpose. Whether he had achieved anything other than the shaman's displeasure was yet to be seen.

No sooner had the story ended than he was besieged by questions. Foremost among the queries was the question of what would come next: would the tribe set up a village of their own beside the vision lake?

"It is Emri's wish to come home," said Broken Tooth, turning to face the shaman, looking him directly in the eyes while drawing courage from the support of those around him. "He wishes nothing other than to return to his village, bringing his woman and those who have followed him. It is felt that they have much to offer and would be no burden on the clan. Nor have they any wish for trouble. They have asked me to convey their desires and pray that you will allow them to return."

The clan grew silent and all eyes turned to the shaman. Then for the first time, some of them realized what Broken Tooth had been trying to accomplish with the public telling of the shaman's mission. Even those who did not fully realize what was happening could sense the shaman's anger and feel the cold undercurrent of his hatred. Thus it was with great surprise that they heard him speak.

"I can see no reason why our brother should not be welcomed back into the clan. And the others as well. Yet this is not a thing that can be done casually. It is an occasion of importance and should be treated as such. You are to be commended for your bravery, Broken Tooth. Do not think that I will forget your part in this venture. And now, I must think upon this matter and decide what is to be done." Then, turning his back on the gathering, he returned to his dwelling and lowered the doorflap.

A sense of oppression seemed to lift with his departure, and the villagers turned back to Broken Tooth, closing in on all sides and plying him with questions.

But Broken Tooth was not deceived by the shaman's mild manner and pleasant reply. Not for a heartbeat did he believe that the man intended to allow Emri and the others to enter the camp. He alone knew that the man had not given up his insane hatred and would not rest until Emri and all of Emri's companions were dead. And now, he had placed himself squarely in their midst. By his storytelling he, too, had become the enemy.

CHAPTER TWENTY-SIX

Mandris paced back and forth in his dwelling, his hands knotted into fists and his face contorted in rage. Curses rose to his lips and he spat them out like stones. How had this happened! Never did he think that things would come to such a pass. How had they survived? They should have died many times—and better men such as Walks Alone had perished in their stead. Suddenly he came to a halt and wondered for the first time if the Gods themselves were protecting them and for what reason. But he could think of no reason why the Gods would trouble themselves over so small a matter and dismissed the thought from his mind.

Broken Tooth's story had ruined any hopes he might have had of dispatching Emri and his followers without the tribe's awareness. Now all attention was focused on them and the clan's sympathy was with them as well.

Now more than ever Mandris was aware of how little he was liked and the fact that the clan had never really accepted him. Even the fact that he had never gotten the woman with child was whispered about with amusement. It was through no lack of trying on his part, but it was a difficult and joyless matter. The woman cried and turned her face from him, and her quiet, ongoing hatred was a thing you could all but touch. Mandris suspected that had she found herself with child she would have drunk some herb or done herself some damage to prevent the birth.

His anger vied with sadness. In the end he sat before the fire, arms hugging his legs to his chest, rocking back and forth like an unhappy child while angry thoughts buzzed in his head like maddened wasps, stinging him with their poison.

It was clear that he could make no obvious move toward the outcasts. The feeling of the clan would go against him. Whatever he did would have to be done with subtlety so that no suspicion would fall on him.

Mandris took deep breaths, staring into the flames and calming himself. Success would require a cool head. And now there was the immediate need of seeing the enemy for himself, to view them from the safety of his power animal, the tiger.

His breath came slower and slower, his pupils opened wide and took in the light of the flames. He listened to the drumming of his heart beating in his ears and slowed his breathing to match it.

Eager to be free, the tiger slipped from the top of the shaman's head, looked around him, and snarled, dewlaps twitching. Then it slunk forward and passed through the wall of the dwelling, vanishing like a puff of smoke. It bounded forward in great leaps that saw the miles flow beneath its body like a river in flood. Guided by Broken Tooth's words as well as its own heightened senses, it soon reached the lake of the vision.

All was quiet. A few fires flickered to keep the night-stalking carnivores at bay, but there was no guard set that might prevent one such as he from entering the camp. He would not have been caught out, knowing that danger lurked nearby, and his fear of Emri was somewhat diminished by seeing the camp unguarded.

He stalked through the camp sniffing at this one and then that. A sense of power filled him, knowing that he could kill them where they lay and it would be thought but an act of the Gods. He bared his fangs as the idea took hold, growing stronger. Yes! That was the way! Kill Emri as he slept, an unfortunate incident that could never be blamed on him. Then, after they returned to the village, he would take the woman, Dawn,

and dispose of the others at his leisure. He padded
forward, searching out his enemy.

The cry of a night bird walking at the edge of the
water disturbed his concentration and he looked up in
time to see a shadowy form, that of a weasel or an otter,
slither forward into the rushes and seize the bird by the
legs. The two figures fell into the water, struggling.
Then their actions took on a more frantic note and their
struggles intensified, grew more erratic, more troubled.

The tiger waited, expecting to see the killer emerge
from the water, clutching the bird between its jaws, but
this did not happen. Instead, there was only a vague
heaving and then silence.

Intrigued, wondering if the creature had swum away
with its prize, the tiger drifted to the water's edge.
There he was greeted with a sight that held him wrapped
in puzzlement. The otter, a powerful creature, adept on
land or water, lay on its side near the shore. Its eyes
rolled wildly and it attempted to rise, but could not
seem to do so. It appeared to be held in some mysterious manner. Its body was covered with some black
substance that gleamed in the light of the moon.

The bird, or what little could be seen of it, was also
trapped by the blackness. Its head and feet were already submerged, and its body settled deeper and deeper
as the tiger watched in bewilderment. A large bubble
rose to the surface and popped. When it subsided, the
bird was gone. Even now the otter sank lower and
lower. With one last wild shake of its head, one last
look of white-eyed terror, it too was swallowed by the
blackness.

The tiger moved closer and peered into the water,
taking in the sharp, burned smell that rose from the
lake. There beneath the surface he could see the otter
and the bird, struggling no more, with bands of blackness wrapped around their bodies. And then even as he
watched, they sank lower still and disappeared completely.

The tiger stepped back a pace and sat down to ponder this strange new event. It would seem as though
some form of deadly quicksand lay beneath the surface

of the lake. He thought about this new fact and wondered if it had figured into Hawk's vision. But no matter; he was warned and although he might use the lake
for his own purposes, never would he step foot in it
himself.

His thoughts returned to his original plan. He slipped
into the camp once more, treading lightly and subduing
all emanations of his presence as he cautiously approached Hawk, Dawn, and Emri. Of the cat, there
was no sign and he assumed that it was away hunting,
for nighttime was the time that cats sought their prey.
Just as he was doing now.

The woman was restless, twisting and turning on her
pallet of grass and furskins with a small, plump girlchild
lying at her side. The tiger could tell that her time was
near, could sense the child within her and feel its
strength. The Toad, who was called Hawk, lay on Dawn's
left and was wrapped firmly in sleep. Emri lay on the
woman's other side and he too appeared to be deeply
immersed in sleep.

The Tiger hesitated, studying his prey. His searching
eyes saw the pucker and shine of newly formed skin,
sensed the weakness of the limb, and knew it to be a
sign from the Gods, a sign that his half-formed plan had
met with their approval. Emri would die and his death
would be blamed on the injured arm and whatever
illness had caused it.

The tiger slunk nearer and nearer his prey, making
himself small, dissipating to the point of appearing to
be no more than a drift of vapor in the night. His
essence slipped through the air and allowed itself to be
drawn up into the man's nostrils—flowing smoothly,
smoothly into his body; invading gently; probing stealth-
ily for head and heart, where it would wrap itself around
those vital organs and sink claws and fangs into them,
stealing and stilling their life force.

Perhaps he moved too quickly in his desire to have it
done. Perhaps he made some untoward move that roused
the sleeping spirit. Whatever the reason, the effect was
the same: the man began to waken.

Sensing that he would soon be discovered, the tiger abandoned all attempts at concealment and flung himself forward through the narrow strictures of the body, stretching, reaching for head and heart.

Emri wakened with a start, clutching his head in his hands, his body arching upward, head and heels pressed against the ground as spasms of pain ripped through him. It felt as though hot, glowing embers were being forced through the inner passages of his body. He screamed aloud in agony, waking those who slumbered beside him as well as most of the others in the camp.

"Emri, what's wrong? Tell me!" cried Dawn as she knelt as his side and tried to touch him. But his body was as taut as a fully extended sling, the muscles standing out as hard as frozen trees. She pulled her hand back swiftly as though it had been burned by fire.

Hawk kneeled at Emri's side, noting the contorted expression and the spasms of pain that racked his friend's body. Already Emri's face had taken on a bluish tinge, and tongue and eyes were bulging from his head. His body started to shake and Hawk was certain that he was near death. Dawn began to scream, throwing herself across Emri's chest and calling his name over and over.

Hawk knew that there was little time. If Emri were to be saved, Hawk would have to lend him strength, pull his spirit back from the land of the spirits. Quickly Hawk allowed himself to slip into the trance state, forcibly blocking out all that was occurring around him, drifting into, taking on, becoming, the spirit of the hawk.

The hawk stretched its wings and stepped free of the heavy body of its host. Instantly it was struck by the pervasive aura of evil that floated on the air and hung around his friend's body like the stench of carrion. Mandris! The shaman had a part in this, it was no natural happening. And then he saw it, the smallest bit of gold mist hovering outside of Emri's nostrils like a pinch of pollen inhaled with the scent of a summer blossom. But this was not pollen, no harbinger of beauty, but a messenger of death. Even as he started forward, the last threads of mist were disappearing up into Emri's nostril with an anguished gasp of breath.

The hawk's head thrust forward and seized the bit of mist in its beak much as it would the tail of a snake. It pulled backward, wondering if the mist were too insubstantial or if there were really some form of concealed solidity.

The spirit that was the tiger felt a sharp, unexpected pain and knew that its presence had been detected. Feeling victory within its reach, it ignored the pain and surged on, forcing itself toward its goal despite the resistance both within and without. But it had not reckoned on the fierce determination of its attacker and found that no matter how hard it pulled, it could go no further.

Anger pulsed through the spirit tiger. Turning, it retraced its passage and burst out of the nostrils in a flood of gold and flung itself at the hawk, claws fully extended, fangs ready to crush and maul whatever or whomever had thwarted its efforts.

As the hawk hurtled into the dark sky, it noted that Emri had collapsed upon his furskin. The tiger stretched to its fullest and clawed the air, roaring aloud, rending the air with expressions of rage.

The hawk plunged downward with all the speed of those of its kind, talons outstretched. It caught the cat by surprise and drove its claws into the tiger's eyes, blinding it with its own blood. The tiger squalled, dropped onto its haunches, and pawed at its eyes.

The hawk seized its brief advantage and ripped and pecked at the tiger's head, knowing that its moment would not last, that the tiger would soon rally and drive it away. The hawk increased its efforts, knowing that it could not hope to win out against the tiger's greater strength.

The tiger, bleeding from many wounds on its head and ears, blinded by its own blood, shook its head, attempting to clear its vision long enough that it might rid itself of the attacking spirit. But now the thing had attached itself to the tiger's back, slicing the skin with its claws and clinging to the flesh itself with its talons as its knife-sharp beak sought out the great artery on the side of the tiger's neck.

The tiger flung itself to the ground and rolled on the hawk, knowing that he must dislodge the giant bird of prey before it found the vital mark. He brought his full weight to bear on the plumed fury and rolled back and forth.

The hawk was unable to take the punishment. Releasing his hold on the tiger's back, the hawk slipped out from under the huge animal and rose up into the air, screaming out the cry of the hunt.

The tiger heard the terrible cry and felt his spirit waver. Still blinded by his own blood, aching and burning from a multitude of wounds, he gained his footing and fled, vowing to return, and marking the hawk for death.

CHAPTER TWENTY-SEVEN

It was some time before Mandris was able to travel, so grievous were his wounds. During this period of recovery he refused to admit the woman who had become his mate. She and her daughters gladly took refuge with Broken Tooth's family.

The shaman gave no explanation for his behavior, nor would he allow any others to attend him. He preferred to sit alone with his pain and his thoughts, planning the death of his enemies.

When at last he emerged from his dwelling, the members of the clan stared at his ruined features with shock. Heavy brown scabs crusted with dried blood covered his eyelids, his nose, and even his lips and ears. There was little of his face that was unmarked, yet no man dared to ask him what had caused the damage. After the first moment they averted their eyes and continued on about their activities as though nothing had happened.

Mandris took this as another sign of their lack of caring, never thinking for a moment that his own fierce manner and glinting eyes might have dissuaded their natural expression of concern. He made no mention of anything, gave no hint that anything was amiss. He directed his woman to prepare a pack for him, saying only that he would be gone for several days.

The woman was quick to obey, yet sought out Broken Tooth before the shaman had passed the outer edges of the village and told him that the moment had come.

Broken Tooth had suspected that the shaman might attempt to slip away unnoticed and had been waiting for such a thing to occur. Never did he think that the man would leave so boldly, in broad daylight, almost as though he did not care whether they knew of his intentions. He wondered briefly at the shaman's terrible wounds and then put the thought away as he gathered the group of men who had volunteered to go with him. These men would not bow down before Mandris this time, but would stand fast in the face of his anger and protect those whom they had harmed by their neglect.

The shaman had journeyed south, traveling on a line opposite to that which would take him to the vision lake. Broken Tooth and his party waited until the man had dropped below the line of the horizon before they followed, sacks of provisions hanging from their shoulders, spears and clubs held at the ready. They set themselves an easy pace, yet one that would eat up the distance and leave them fresh for battle if it should come to that. Broken Tooth did not understand why the shaman had chosen such a route, but knew in his heart that no matter what its beginnings it would undoubtedly have its end in Emri's camp.

Although he never looked back, never paused in his steady lope, it seemed that the shaman had chosen his path knowing that he would be observed. He stopped only briefly during the day and then, at some point during the night, switching his course, turning sharply northwest. Although Broken Tooth and his party had been expecting such a thing, they missed the actual point of departure, their eyes being heavy with the need for sleep and their minds clouded with exhaustion.

Broken Tooth cursed, yet knowing the man's destination, he allowed his men to sleep. They could cut across the land at a sharp angle and arrive at the lake even sooner than the shaman, who could but guess at its location. There was no way that he could have known that the shaman had been there in his spirit form and would have no trouble locating it as a man.

Things had gone better for those who camped beside

the lake, for they now knew that their presence was
known to the shaman and they were on their guard.

Emri had suffered no permanent damage, and other
than a shortage of breath that came on him at times,
accompanied by a feeling of terrible anxiety, he was
unharmed.

Dawn, however, had taken to her furskin and lay
there still, her belly cramping with pain. A sheet of
moisture had drenched her legs on the second night of
the shaman's journey, and the long-awaited, long-feared
time of birthing began. Women clustered by her side
uttering words of advice and holding her hands through
the worst of the pains. Now, a night and a day had
passed since the breaking of the water, and still there
was no sign of the child, although Dawn was weak and
racked with pain.

Hawk had gone in search of a specific flower that was
known to increase the spasms, coaxing even the most
reluctant child into the world. Hawk was still bruised
and sore following his battle with the spirit tiger, but he
gave no thought to his own aches, all of his concern
being focused on Dawn.

Running Bird was anxious as well, for she had seen
far too many women during her long life succumb to
the rigors of childbirth. It was not good that the child
refused to come. Nor was it good that the girl had so
little strength. Strength was needed for birthing and
for surviving afterward. If only Hawk could find the
flower . . .

Emri could do little but stroke Dawn's brow and let
her know that he was there. Then, when the times of
pain came and the women drove him away, he and
Mosca and the child walked by the edge of the lake—
the lake that had now taken on a more ominous feeling
as he watched numerous creatures, birds, mice, small
carnivores, and once a large dire wolf, go to their
deaths. Each was drawn to the water by the sight or
sound of struggling victims and then lured in turn to
their own death, mired in the sticky black substance.

Emri was much afraid that the child would escape

him and be caught in the lake herself, for she was an inquisitive creature and often did that which she was specifically forbidden. Mosca was little better, for he had not lost interest in the great white birds. Never did he seem to understand that their slow, long-legged pace concealed their ability to rise into the air at the least suspicion of attack. Although they were the most frequent victims of the treacherous lake, they had little to fear from the clumsy, heavy-pawed cat.

And now, as he stared out across the quiet surface of the lake, Dawn's whimpers cutting across his consciousness like blows, he felt a subtle change in the air around him, almost as though there were to be some ominous change in the weather. But the sky was clear and there were no signs of clouds, dark or otherwise. Yet he knew that he was not wrong. The birds had fallen silent in the trees and even the deer had lifted their heads and were staring into the forest. The shy horses wasted no effort on looking, but took to their heels and thundered away. Even a giant sloth, never the brightest of creatures, left off its browsing on the tender tips of a young tree and stood up on its immense haunches, sniffing the air with its long, flexible snout. A vague look of terror crossed its dull face, and bleating aloud, it dropped to all fours and ambled away with all the speed its bulky body could attain.

And then, suddenly, intuitively, Emri knew that the moment had come. The shaman had arrived.

CHAPTER TWENTY-EIGHT

Mandris had chosen his moment well. The Toad, Hawk, was away from camp and could not lend Emri his assistance. The men were spread out around the far edges of the camp acting as sentinels to warn against his arrival. He had noted their presence and avoided them easily, slipping through their ranks and advancing to the heart of the camp and his prey. There he found Emri and the cat at the edge of the water, the lake that would somehow play a role in the coming drama.

Mandris watched as Mosca balanced on his hind legs and then pounced forward in a series of high leaps, attempting to catch a long-legged white bird. The bird allowed the cat to draw quite near before it opened its wings and casually flapped away. The cat teetered, almost plunging into the water before it regained its balance.

Mandris watched for a time, concealed deep in the shadows of a tree whose trunk was far wider than his body. Then another bird came stalking out of the grasses with its peculiar stiff-jointed gait. It was uncertain whether or not the bird saw the humans and the cat, but being of small intelligence and perhaps believing in its own ability to escape, the bird drew closer still.

Mandris focused his attentions on the bird and willed it to turn in the opposite direction, away from the camp. The bird did so—although whether influenced by Mandris or obeying some dim thought in its own small brain, it was impossible to know. Then, just as Mandris had hoped, Mosca began to stalk the bird.

The bird paced onward with Mosca, Emri, and the child following in its wake. The child shrilled aloud in her high, piercing voice. Breaking lose from Emri's grip, she ran to pick some desirable object up off the ground. The quick movement startled the bird, and it darted forward into the rushes at the edge of the water rather than taking flight. Mosca, unable to curtail his excitement and ignoring Emri's warning cries, dashed after the bird into the dense stand of rushes.

Emri ran after the cat, screaming aloud for him to stop. The cat, caught up in the excitement of the moment and unaware of his danger, ignored Emri. Mosca plunged farther and farther into the shallow lake, stopping only after the bird—lighter and perhaps not so stupid as it had seemed—took to the air, trailing its long legs behind.

The cat, realizing that he had lost the bird, growled and pawed at the air, then turned and began to swim back to shore. Emri held his breath, his hand pressed against his chest, hoping that the cat would somehow avoid being mired in the deadly blackness. Perhaps this portion of the lake was not tainted with the awful stuff.

But it was not to be. While still more than two man-lengths from shore, the cat's movements became slower and slower until it seemed that he was swimming in place. Emri felt his heart grow heavy in his breast and he took a step toward the water, and then another, as though by his presence he could somehow help the cat extricate itself.

Birdsong came running to his side, clutching a bunch of bright blue flowers in her fist. She laughed aloud and held the flowers up to be admired. Emri thrust her behind him and spoke to her harshly, terrified that she too might fall into the water.

Birdsong lost her balance and fell onto her plump bottom, her mouth a circle of astonishment. Her eyes pooled as tears spilled down her chubby cheeks and loud wails were not far behind. When Emri did not rush to take her in his arms and console her, she clambered to her feet and toddled toward camp, her cries growing in strength and volume, searching for someone who would take her grief more seriously.

Emri shut Birdsong out of his thoughts, knowing that he need not worry about her now, that someone would console her and hopefully grow curious over Emri's absence and come searching for him. Now, all of his efforts could be directed toward saving Mosca from the lake.

He thought swiftly, realizing that it would do no good to enter the lake himself. What was needed was something that the cat could grasp. As yet his head and shoulders and nearly half his body remained free of the water.

Emri looked around him and saw nothing. Then his eyes fastened on the forest behind him. A branch, a fallen tree, these would give the cat purchase, a way of climbing out of the water and making his way to shore. Emri hurried into the thick wood, searching for a broken limb or a sapling that he might uproot.

But for all its density, the forest was young. With ample water from the lake and good soil in which to sink its roots, there was little die-off, and Emri found no broken limbs, no dead trees that would suit his purpose. Nor was he able to uproot any of the saplings. Growing desperate, he pulled his blade from its sheath and began hacking at a tree, bending it fiercely, commanding it to break. A crack appeared near the base and then rose, vertically. Emri cursed. Dropping the blade to the ground, he seized the tree with both hands and began whipping it back and forth, pulling upward all the while.

The tree gave up its hold on the earth reluctantly and came up with a shower of dirt. Emri ran through the trees and dashed toward the lake, dragging the sapling behind him.

Mosca had sunk farther, his hindquarters were now completely submerged beneath the surface of the water. His eyes were rolling wildly and his mouth was open, panting, his tongue lolling out the corner of his mouth. He was panicked and seemed not to hear Emri command him to be still.

Emri positioned the sapling as best he was able, with its roots trailing along the bank and with the farthest edge of the slender branches reaching the cat. He also realized what he had always known, that the slender branches would not support the cat's weight. His breath rasped in his throat and he stood on the bank, shivering with the need to do something, yet unable to think of what.

Mosca bawled, a terrible sound that struck straight to Emri's heart. He all but cried, unable to think of a single thing that would save the cat who meant as much to him as Hawk or Dawn.

Emri looked back at the camp and knew that he would never reach it and return in time. The cat would be swallowed by the waters. He had to make do with what little was at hand.

Mandris watched the unfolding events from behind the tree, grinning with grim pleasure. He could see no way that Emri could rescue the cat. Mandris hoped that Emri would be foolish enough to try, that his love might be strong enough to vanquish reason and send him into the water in a futile attempt to save the animal. If so, Mandris would accomplish the main portion of his goal at absolutely no risk to himself.

Emri's eyes fastened on the long grass that grew in thick abundance at the water's edge. He began to rip up huge armfuls and toss them onto the water, directly atop the sapling, all the while calling out calm words to quiet the cat. Mandris could not see that such a thing would help but watched with interest, noticing that the cat had ceased struggling and for the moment was no longer sinking.

Emri struggled to control his shaking voice while pulling up as many of the weeds and grasses as possible, then laying them across the sapling. It appeared to form a firm path, although he knew that it was anything but. Next he began to rip up the rushes, feeling in their heavy, hollow stems and coarse leaves some of the strength that was needed. These were added to the trail, yet it became more and more difficult to place the reeds upon that span that was farthest from the shore. This was the stretch that was the most critical, for it was here that the cat would most need support if he were to free himself from the deadly, clinging goo.

Mosca began to struggle again, thrashing back and forth, heaving his chest out of the water and making swimming motions with his front paws in a desperate attempt to gain the shore. Emri began to scream at him, begging him to cease, but his words only served to drive the cat on to even greater efforts. When at last he became too exhausted to continue, it was obvious that he had sunk much deeper into the water. Only his head, neck, and the top of his shoulders remained above the surface.

Emri was frantic. Another such struggle would plunge the cat below the surface of the water. He had to do something or Mosca would die. A dangerous plan began to take shape in his mind. Knowing that there was little chance that he would succeed, yet knowing that he could but try, Emri began to gather reeds. Each armload was added to those already lying atop the sapling. Now there was a great mound of them reaching more than halfway to the cat. And still he continued to rip them up by their roots, talking continuously to the cat in a soothing tone, urging him to remain quiet.

But it seemed that the cat had entered into a catatonic state. He did not move—not even his glazed eyes—and he did not appear to see Emri or anything else around him. His mouth was open and he was panting in soft, shallow breaths. Emri was alarmed but quickly concluded that it was far safer for the cat to remain in this state than to struggle.

Now he had reached that point where he had to decide whether to continue or to withdraw. The rushes presented a thick, buoyant platform that might well support his weight, allowing him to reach the cat. He realized that he could not afford to ponder the question. There was no wisdom in it at all, and to think on it for any length of time would be to decide not to do it. Yet it was Mosca's only hope for survival.

Shoving wisdom and caution aside, Emri stepped out onto the trail of reeds, carrying yet another bundle in his arms, testing his footing, ready to spring back toward the safety of the land at the first feeling of movement. The reeds dipped gently beneath his feet yet did not give way. Instead, he felt the sturdy base of the sapling, well cushioned by the reeds and seemingly resting on a firm bottom. Encouraged, he edged his way farther along, still murmuring in reassuring tones to the all-but-submerged cat.

The feeling of stability remained until he was nearly halfway to his goal, then abruptly the trail shifted beneath his feet and bobbed up and down as though rocked by some action of waves, which did not exist on the calm waters. Emri had expected such a thing to happen and was well prepared for the occurrence, merely spreading his feet wide and keeping his balance until the movement ceased.

Finding that his plan was actually working gave him the courage to continue. When he was within reach of the end of the trail, he tossed his bundle of reeds before him, seeing them land in just the position he had chosen. Then he returned to the shore and before his courage could fail, picked another bundle of reeds and made the trip a second time. Again and again he repeated the process, gaining more and more confidence with each trip until he all but raced over the slender bridge.

At last he had extended the mat of reeds to reach the trapped cat. This last section was barely anchored, for the widespread tips of the branches were still half an arm's length from the cat's head. Emri had attempted to overlap the reeds, making them stronger with the stems of dried woody weeds that he had found among the grasses, but he was worried that while they might support his weight, that of the cat would prove too much.

Mosca had begun to stir once more, perhaps encouraged by Emri's presence. Emri spoke to him sternly, commanding him to be still. It was not a command that the cat had ever obeyed before, yet strangely he heeded Emri and settled quietly, his muzzle touching the water.

Emri lay down upon the reeds, stretching himself out on the tentative surface, and wrapped his arms around Mosca's neck, murmuring soft words of encouragement. Slowly he began to exert pressure, pulling the cat toward him. Mosca lay his head on Emri's shoulder and moaned softly, a sound of fear such as he had made long seasons ago as a round, furry infant.

The reeds bowed beneath the additional weight and Emri felt the moisture creep onto his abdomen. He wriggled backward, placing his hands behind the cat's forelimbs, and tugged harder. Again the reeds dipped and now Emri felt the wetness along the length of his entire body. Mosca was clinging to him now, his claws digging into Emri's back. Emri could feel the cat trembling beneath his hands, and the great heart pounding so hard as almost to be heard.

Already the farthest edge of the mat was coming unraveled and sinking below the water. Emri knew that he had to get the cat out quickly before the entire support gave way beneath them. Trying to spread his weight out evenly with no single portion poking through, he pulled on the cat as hard as he could, gripping the loose folds of the thick pelt and exerting a steady pull.

And then it seemed to him that he felt the cat move. Quickly he slithered backward on the swaying, bobbing mat, never loosing his hold on the cat even though it moaned aloud in fear or perhaps pain.

And now the cat reached for the reeds with a hind leg coated with black slime. Hooking his claws into the fragile mat, Mosca lunged forward and broke through. The reeds came loose and floated free. Even so, Mosca was free of the clinging bottom and half the length of his body was still supported by the remaining reeds.

A thrill of excitement lanced through Emri as he realized that they would make it. There was just a short distance between them and the most stable portion of the bridge. If they remained calm, they would reach the land in safety. Drawing a deep breath and speaking calmly to the cat, urging it forward, he inched backward toward safety.

Mandris watched the efforts of the younger man with an amused expression, wondering how Emri could think that such a thing could succeed. Then, almost incredibly, it began to seem even to him who wished it to fail, that Emri would succeed. The reeds appeared both buoyant and strong and they supported Emri's weight until he had all but reached the cat.

Surely the cat will struggle, thought Mandris, struggle and take them both to their deaths. But even though the cat sank his claws into Emri's back, the blood running down his skin in rivulets, neither cat nor man panicked. Slowly but surely, they began to work their way toward land.

Mandris watched a while longer, hoping that he was wrong, the taste of defeat bitter in his mouth. Then he knew that his enemy would win out against certain death yet again.

His rage and his hatred rose up before him, blurring the sight of the enemy. And then, knowing that he would never get a better chance, he gripped the heavy throwing spear with its keen-edged stone point and strode toward the water's edge, determined to put an end to the one whom he had hated for so long.

CHAPTER TWENTY-NINE

Emri concentrated on their progress, slipping, scrambling, edging, balancing precariously, trying to center his weight and that of the cat on the slender sapling. It was difficult, whole sections of the mat broke off under their exertions and floated away, yet still, they were gaining. Improbable as it had seemed, it now looked as though they would reach the land.

Foremost in their favor was the fact that the cat was so terrified that it was hard to make him move at all. He only moved when Emri pulled him forward and dragged his front paws into place. Had he exhibited any of his normal enthusiasm, they would both have sunk long ago.

Moving backward with his back to the land, all of his attention focused on the cat and the problem at hand, he neither saw nor sensed anything amiss. Had it not been for a widening of the cat's eyes, he would never have turned his head and would have died on the spot. Turning, he saw Mandris running toward him, spear held high, ready to throw.

A single swift glance told him that he would never be able to reach the land and gain his footing before Mandris cast his spear. Yet if he did not move, he would be skewered like a frog on the end of a bird's beak. Spear or water, the choices were not good. Knowing that he could not hope for the spear to miss him and hoping to escape the water a second time, Emri hurled himself off the floating bridge of reeds and flung himself into a shallow dive paralleling the shore.

He had scarcely entered the water when he felt the spear lance the water beside him, felt the pressure of its impact on the bottom below him. Then, reacting more than thinking, he turned in the water and grasped the haft of the spear before it could sink. Holding it with one hand, he extended his other arm, flexed his legs, and propelled himself through the water. Two short, powerful strokes and he had gained the rushes at the edge of the shore.

Cautiously he allowed eyes, nose, and mouth to break water at the base of the rushes. He held the spear concealed beneath the water. The usually clear water had become roiled and murky from all the activity. Mud, sediment, and bits of the sticky blackness concealed Emri's presence from the shaman, who was even now peering intently at the water.

Emri lay still and breathed slow and steady, calming his racing heart. He did not take his eyes off the shaman, but he sensed that Mosca had not relinquished his grip and was still clinging to the reeds. Even as the cat came to his mind, Emri heard him begin his low, repetitive, bawling moan, an indication of his distress. There was nothing he could do for the cat now except draw Mandris's attention away and allow the cat to continue the short distance to shore.

Emri could feel the warmth of the black goo beneath him, yet as long as he permitted the water to support him and did not attempt to place his weight in any one place, he thought that he would be safe.

Mandris took a tentative step onto the floating bridge, his fury and bafflement clear even from Emri's poor vantage point. He scanned the water intently, wondering if Emri could have been seized by the sticky bottom and drowned. But much as Mandris wanted to believe that it was true, he could not. There had been no bubbles, no sign of struggle, and there was no body. Mandris knew that he would not be content until he was able to gaze on the body of his enemy with his own eyes.

His eyes flicked toward the lion, sparing it but half a heartbeat of his attention. The lion did not matter. It seemed to be a creature of little courage, and it amused him to think of it clinging to the reeds, unable to move forward, until the reeds finally broke beneath his weight and deposited him in the treacherous water.

He turned back toward land and walked along the shore in the opposite direction from Emri's hiding place until he was certain that Emri was nowhere to be seen. Then he returned and examined the rushes on Emri's side of the bridge.

It was a simple matter to take a deep breath and submerge until the shaman had gone past, although the man nearly touched him with the point of a second spear. Had the reeds not been so thick, Emri knew that he would have been seen.

After a time the shaman moved away and seated himself in a central position where he could keep the entire stretch of shoreline within his sight. Then, perhaps realizing that he could be seen by those in the camp, he moved back under the cover of the trees and waited. Sooner or later, if he was but patient, Emri would be forced to show himself.

Emri pondered his position. It was possible, he supposed, to pull himself along the edge of the reeds until he reached the safety of the camp. But the camp was a good distance away and he feared that the lake might not be so gentle with him were he to impose himself on it much longer. His presence could prove to be too great a temptation to the evil spirits who inhabited the lake bottom and they might reach up and pull him down to devour him at their leisure. The sooner he left the lake, the better.

He thought about moving a short distance away before emerging, but even that was of no real merit. The longer it took for him to reach the shaman, the longer the man would have to ready himself for the attack. The only thing that would be in his favor would be surprise.

The quicker he could attack the man, the greater the sense of surprise which could only act in his favor.

Lying in the warm muck was strangely restful, the heat of the black goo leaching the tension out of his muscles. Had he not been in such danger, it would almost have been pleasant.

Emri brought one hand up out of the water and grasped a clump of reeds, then started back in surprise. He nearly cried out loud with shock, for his hand was black! It had become coated with a diluted layer of the sticky goo and was completely black! Emri laughed inwardly. He could see no way in which it could help him, but if it startled Mandris half as much as it had himself, then it might gain him a few precious heartbeats of time. Grinning to himself, Emri rolled carefully on the bottom. Then, using his hands, he worked the stuff into his hair, face, ears, and neck, trying to imagine what he must look like.

But even as Emri was preparing himself for the coming battle, Mandris had decided to wait no longer. Yet he had no wish to expose himself to discovery if it could be avoided. Emri must be located, then he would decide what measures were to be taken. Slipping into the trance state, Mandris freed his power animal, the tiger, and sent it to roam in his stead.

The tiger leaped free, shaking itself violently, always anxious to rid itself of the clinging confinement. Needing no direction, being one and the same with the shaman's thoughts, it began to stalk toward the bridge of reeds. It knew that the man had not died and sensed that he had not left the area.

Emri came alert with the sound of Mosca's growls. Cautiously peering through the reeds, he saw nothing, but Mosca's growls increased in depth and strength and the cat began to drag himself forward, moving for the first time since Emri had left him.

The cat's growls were throaty and ominous; his dewlaps were twitching, revealing his fangs and half-open jaws. He was watching something that appeared quite close, but Emri could see absolutely nothing at all. The

shaman had not moved from his position beneath the
trees where he sat in almost total stillness. This was
puzzling as well, for surely Mosca's growls would have
brought him to investigate. Unless the shaman already
knew what the cat was growling at. Unless he himself
had caused it.

Suddenly suspicious of the shaman's lack of movement, Emri turned his eyes back to the man, studying
his strange immobility, noticing the chin resting on the
man's chest, the slow, steady rise and fall of his chest,
almost as though he were asleep—yet it was too slow
for sleep. The man was in a trance state! The spirit of
the tiger was out! Instantly all became clear. Even
though he was immersed in water and covered in goo,
Emri felt the short hairs on the back of his neck rise up
and prickle with imminent danger.

Thoughts, plans, strategies, raced through his mind.
His first thought was of rising out of the water, racing
over to the shaman, and plunging the spear into the
man's breast, but then he realized that that was the
most dangerous thing of all. To do so would be to loose
the man's spirit on every innocent person within its
range. There would be no protection against its evil and
it would kill and destroy with impunity. No. The only
way to protect them was to kill the man and vanquish
his spirit as well.

Taking a firm grip on the spear, wedging himself
firmly in among the reeds, Emri closed his eyes and
concentrated, directing his awareness inward, relaxing,
opening himself, touching his inner consciousness, and
allowing that which was within to flow, to expand, to be
released.

The cat separated from the man and took form. It
padded through the dense reeds more softly than the
most gentle of breezes, not even stirring them with its
passage. It crouched in the dense vegetation, just short
of the shore and gazed upon the shaman, confirming
what was already known, that his spirit was loose on the
land. No longer a matter of interest, the cat turned its
immense head away from the man and sought out his

enemy, the tiger. It was not difficult to find. It crouched amid the torn, waterlogged bits of vegetation at the base of the bridge as though daring Mosca to come any closer, its long tail thrashing back and forth.

Mosca was snarling and hissing, his ears plastered flat against his skull. Although he had moved still closer to land, he did not attempt the final distance, perhaps intimidated by what he could not see but only sense.

Hunched in the reeds, the spirit cat that was Emri dug his claws in, pushed down with his powerful hind legs, and launched himself toward the spirit tiger. There was a blur of gold and then he landed atop the tiger's back, all four sets of claws extended.

Taken by surprise, the tiger yowled loudly and flung itself on its back in an attempt to dislodge the cat, to prevent it from wrapping its long front paws around its neck and biting into its neck with its great curved saber teeth.

The lion landed on its feet and dove in toward the exposed throat, but the tiger was too swift. It rolled to its side and sprung to its feet in one swift movement. Then its great jaws and long, curving canines seized the lion by the back of its neck as it pulled back from its abortive attempt at the tiger's throat. Fortunately for the lion, the tiger was unable to get a firm grip and merely came away with a mouthful of fur and loose skin.

Blood dripped down the lion's neck, staining its golden pelt with crimson. The two cats faced each other, mouths agape, teeth and fangs glinting in the bright morning light, eyes flashing. The tiger lowered its great head and its skin wrinkled into innumerable folds over the bridge of its nose as it hissed and snarled.

The lion lowered its head as well and swayed back and forth in a smooth, snakelike manner as though unwilling to give the tiger a stable target. The two immense creatures circled each other in a deadly dance, searching for an opening, a weakness in the other's defense. Then, as though unable to wait, thinking to create its own advantage through the use of its greater size and weight, the tiger rushed across the short dis-

tance that separated it from the lion and crashed into
the cat, bowling it over and then falling on it with
slashing claws and stabbing fangs.

The lion was taken by surprise, not having expected
the rush. It was all he could do to avoid serious harm in
those first few heartbeats, but his smaller size worked to
his advantage and he rolled into a ball and slipped out
from under the tiger before it realized that it had lost
its prey.

The two cats did not separate as they had before, but
rose up onto their hind legs, using their open-clawed
paws to strike at each other. The tiger, taller by far and
with the longer reach, used both paws simultaneously,
while the lion with its shorter limbs held one paw still
as though to stabilize itself while it clawed at the tiger
with the other. Although the blows were powerful enough
to do great damage, neither cat connected and there
was no bloodshed. Dropping to all fours, they began to
circle once again.

Mandris, from his position beneath the tree, had
seen the spirit lion emerge from the reeds and now
knew where his enemy was concealed. He thought of
recalling the tiger spirit but decided against it immediately. It would not do to leave himself open and unpro-
tected against an attack by the lion.

Although there were great risks involved, Mandris
decided at length to attempt to kill Emri. Although
Emri had developed a power animal of his own and
knew enough to call it forth and release it at will,
Mandris did not think that Emri would be strong enough
to function on the physical level as well. This skill was
not learned so easily and took many seasons to develop
and control. Rising to his feet, he grasped his spear and
began to stalk toward Emri.

The lion saw the man climb to his feet and begin
walking toward Emri. Emri-the-spirit-lion squalled aloud,
the cry that signaled imminent danger and saw Emri-
the-man's head appear between the rushes before he
himself was charged by the tiger again and forced to
turn his attention to his adversary.

Emri saw the shaman advancing toward his hiding place, spear in hand, and knew that the moment of confrontation had come. It could not be delayed, for to do nothing would be to die. Yet he did not know that he could move while the spirit was out of his body since he had never attempted such a thing before. Obviously the shaman had no such problem. He was gliding forward and would soon be upon him.

Calling on all the spirits of his ancestors and the Gods as well, Emri slithered forward on all fours and then rose up to face the shaman, spear in hand.

Mandris stopped in shock, confronted by a dripping black apparition that was surely not human. Yet even as he hesitated, the frightening thing bared its teeth in a grimace, raised its spear, and threw it at him

Mandris had enough presence of mind to duck. Perhaps thrown off by the clinging mantle of black goo, the spear passed harmlessly to one side and landed somewhere behind the shaman. This action served to shock him to his senses. If the thing could use a spear, it was human. Mandris closed in, his own spear at the ready.

Emri cursed his hasty action as he paced in step with the shaman. He watched the man's eyes, looking for the telltale tightening of the lids that signaled an attack a half heartbeat before it occurred. His hand reached for his knife, but he realized with a sickening lurch that he had used it to cut the sapling and had not replaced it in its sheath. He was weaponless!

Mandris realized it as well. Smiling, he took his time, drawing out the moment of revenge. Having finally recognized his enemy beneath his coat of grime, Mandris was not anxious to cut the moment short. Then, perhaps careless because of his great advantage, or perhaps merely less observant because his attentions were focused on Emri, the shaman stepped into a dip in the ground. His ankle twisted beneath him, throwing him off balance for less than a heartbeat. But it was all that Emri needed. He flung himself on the shaman, one hand going for the man's throat, the other reaching for the spear.

Down they went, crashing onto the ground, grappling for the advantage. Of similar size and build, Emri and Mandris were evenly matched. The shaman was taller and more heavily built, but he was older by at least five Cold Times and knew more about fighting than did his opponent.

But Emri was driven by the knowledge that this was his single opportunity to avenge his father's death and regain all that he had lost. He was also aided by the strength of his youth.

Still, fueled by the fact that to lose was to die, both men fought with an intensity that was not normally seen during hand-to-hand combat.

At first it seemed that Emri had gained the upper hand, but then, driven on by the strength of his incredible hatred, Mandris seized the advantage and rolled on top of Emri and brought all of his weight to bear upon Emri's still-weakened arm. Emri tried to rise and could not. With sinking heart he felt something in his arm give way. The bone snapped as though it were but a twig broken beneath the weight of a footstep.

A cold, bright light in the shaman's eyes told him that the man had heard and knew that the battle was all but won. But knowing that there was far more at stake than his own life, knowing that others whom he loved would suffer at the hands of the shaman, Emri fought on stubbornly, hoping against hope that something would happen to turn the battle in his favor once more.

CHAPTER THIRTY

Hawk had found the flowers that he had searched for so diligently, knowing that they came to a full blossom during the greatest heat of Warm Time. They grew on tall stalks, nearly as tall as he himself, the flowers hard, flat rounds of gold no larger than his thumbnail. They appeared most insignificant, being nowhere as attractive as other flowers, and their scent was harsh and almost unpleasant. Yet, when steeped in boiling water, the resulting infusion could bring on the birth of a child while easing the mother's pains.

Hawk stripped the plant of its largest and firmest flowers and then turned his footsteps toward camp without pausing for rest or nourishment.

It had taken far longer to find the plant than Hawk had thought possible, for it was common and generally found in most locations. He had been gone since earliest light and was all but consumed with fear for Dawn. His stride lengthened, his pace increased, driven by the need, the compulsion, to get back as quickly as possible.

The sense of urgency was overwhelming, and soon he became convinced that either Dawn lay near death or that some new, terrible disaster had overtaken the camp. Clutching the pouch of flower tops to his chest, he drove himself to even greater speed and did not stop until the glimmer of the lake could be seen through the trees.

He was hailed by the cries of the sentries, posted around the edges of the forest to warn them of any danger, especially any sign of the shaman. He did not stop to acknowledge their welcome, knowing that had there been some new danger they would not still be watching in the forest, but the feeling of danger did not abate.

He collapsed beside the fire, heart pounding in his chest, slamming against his ribs, and handed the pouch to Running Bird. She emptied it instantly into the waiting cooking sack, the water already on the boil.

Hawk drew breath into anguished lungs and huddled on the ground looking over at Dawn's still form. She was surrounded by women, all of whom did some small chore—wiping her pale brow, moistening her lips with cool water, rubbing her distended belly. Yet Hawk could see the downward turn of their lips and read the frightened look in their eyes. He did not need to be told that all was not well.

He looked around for Emri but saw him nowhere. This in itself was most strange, for even when the women drove Emri off, he was always within calling range. A stab of fear, a premonition, struck at Hawk. He looked around once more and his eyes fastened on the child, Birdsong. Her tearstained face and pouting lip reinforced his fears. Hawk rose quickly, feeling the ache in his legs, and hobbled to her side. He pulled her up and settled her on his hip. He removed her thumb from her mouth and said, "Where is Da, Birdsong?"

Without a word she pointed behind him, in the direction of the lake.

Hawk turned and followed the direction of her soggy finger. He could see nothing but trusted that the child knew what she was saying, so swift was her response. He knew as well that something had gone wrong from the tremble of her lower lip. Kissing her on the forehead, Hawk swung the child down to the ground and then hurried off in the direction she had indicated. His hand clenched the handle of his knife. He paused only to grab up a spear in passing.

At first he saw nothing. The lake itself was clear of

any activity, and the grassy strip around it was empty as well. It was this very emptiness, the lack of animals, that alerted him to the danger. Never since they had taken up residence beside the lake had the land been vacant of animals.

His eyes swept the land and the forest beyond as he searched for Emri, for Mosca, and for whatever danger was at hand. He had gone some distance from camp and had turned the far circle that formed the western border of the lake when his eye caught a blur of movement. He increased his pace without even knowing what he was seeing, somehow realizing that this was the danger he had sensed.

As he came closer, he saw Mandris and then made out the figure of Emri pinned beneath the weight of the older man. Farther along at the edge of the shore, his mind's eye took in the wavering nearly transparent images of two spirit-cats, that of an immense tiger as well as Emri's cat, locked in a battle of their own. Farther still was Mosca, teetering on some unseen surface half a man's length from shore.

Hawk wavered in mid-stride, wondering how such a thing could happen so close to camp and yet be unobserved. What was he to do? Should he attack the spirit cat or the shaman himself? Both were dangerous and both were to be feared. The only answer seemed to be that he must attack them simultaneously. Otherwise, if one were vanquished, the other would fight all the more strenuously.

Hawk was no less worried than Emri at the thought of separating body and spirit and acting independently— for he had never attempted such a thing—but it was obvious that such an effort was required.

Hawk drew as close as possible to the two human combatants—close enough to allow Emri to see him and hopefully draw courage from his presence, yet far enough to avoid easy accessibility to Mandris.

"Courage, my brother, I am with you," he cried. Then seating himself, he took deep breaths, trying to calm himself enough to free the spirit of the hawk.

Dimly he heard Mandris utter a deep, guttural growl and then felt the presence of the hawk growing stronger within him. Once again there was the curious bumpiness, the sense of turbulence, and then he was free. He looked up and saw the clear image of the hawk lifting free of his body, beating the air with powerful wings, searching, staring with its keen eyes, opening its cruel hooked beak in a strident yet silent cry.

For a moment Hawk stood immobile, then with a great wrench of mental effort, he forced himself into motion. First one foot and then the other, he pulled his body along like a great sluggish snail. Then suddenly it was gone—the resistance vanished with the very act of movement.

Swiftly he brought himself to the side of the struggling men and raised his spear to plunge it into the shaman's body. Mandris, seeing what was to happen, threw himself to one side and then pulled Emri close in a fierce embrace, presenting no clear target for Hawk's spear.

Over and over they rolled with Hawk dogging their every movement, waiting for the opportunity to kill the man who had caused them such hardship. Emri had one hand locked around the shaman's neck, squeezing and pulling as though he would rip the man's throat out if he could.

The shaman slammed his chin down on Emri's hand, trying to dislodge it while attempting to drive his own fingers into Emri's eyes as well as bring his knee up into Emri's groin. All efforts were accompanied with wild, erratic moves that spun them in one direction and then the other, preventing the completion of most maneuvers. Then, even though Hawk cried out in warning, the two men rolled over and over in a sudden frenzy of activity and plunged into the shallow waters of the lake!

The hawk circled high, all but invisible against the bright sky, then keening its wild cry, it plunged straight down, talons outstretched, wings streaming behind it.

It struck with all the force of its dive behind it, driving its long, cruel talons deep into the eyes of the spirit-tiger.

The tiger reared up on its hind legs and sought to smash the hawk, the pain-giver, with its great paws. But the hawk had aimed well. Even as the tiger brought up its paw to crush the bird, it drove its talons in farther, piercing the retina and plunging into the brain itself, slashing and tearing, bringing death with its sharp tines.

The tiger paused in mid-motion, its paw falling harmlessly and dangling limply on its chest. Dark rich blood, thick with the scent of salty death, poured out of the tiger's ruined eyes. It crumpled in on itself and slowly, slowly toppled to the ground. The hawk, unable to free itself from the fatal grip, was borne to the ground crushed beneath the tiger's great bulk. The spirit-lion, stunned into immobility by the lightninglike attack, rushed to the hawk's assistance, gripping the neck of its fallen foe between powerful jaws and tugging it free of the crumpled bird of prey allowing it to crawl free.

At the very moment of impact, Mandris rose up out of the water and gasped, his eyes going wide with agony. Emri, not yet realizing what had happened, seized the moment of advantage. Using the shaman himself as leverage, Emri swung himself atop the man, his legs wrapped around the shaman's waist, and forced his head below the water.

Eyes starting from his head with the shock of the attack on his spirit, mouth open wide with the intensity of the mental pain, the shaman was unable to protect himself from the attack. He slipped beneath the water unable to move or strike back. Water, hot and bitter-tasting, poured down his throat. Without thinking he breathed in, gasping for air, and drew in more water.

Emri had never relinquished his grip on the shaman's throat. He tightened his grip still further following the inward rush of air and forced Mandris's head still deeper beneath the water. He felt a tremor pass through the man's body and another and still another. Still he did not let go. The body grew stiff. The shaman's fingers, rigid as stone, rose up out of the water disembodied, and clawed at Emri's arms, gouging long bloody lines in the flesh. Nothing could break Emri's grip. He held on long after the arms had fallen back into the water to float limp and listless just below the oily surface.

Finally, something broke through his deadly concentration. Releasing his grip on the man's throat, Emri lifted his head to listen.

On the shore, Hawk-the-man, merged with the fierce bird who was his spirit, his strength. He moved to the water's edge and assisted Mosca as he leaped the final distance to shore. Together they turned toward Emri as the spirit of the lion rejoined its human host.

Eyes all but unseeing, focused on that which could not be seen, but only heard, Emri strode from the water, abandoning the body of his enemy as though it had little or no meaning. He joined the man and the cat who were his brothers and as they turned toward camp, the sound came again, hanging high and thin on the clear bright air—the cry of a newborn child, as strong and proud as the spirit of a hawk.

About the Author

Rose Estes has lived at various times in her life in Chicago, Houston, Mexico, Canada, a driftwood house on an island, a log cabin in the mountains, and a broken Volkswagen van under a viaduct.

She presently shares her life with an eccentric game designer/cartoonist, three children, one slightly demented dog, and a pride of cats that are unfortunately not saber-tooths.

While it is true that she did not live in a cave and eat roots and berries while writing this book, a great deal of research has gone into its making.

Ms. Estes lists reading, movies, animals, kids, tropical rain forests, and good coffee as the things that make her most happy.

She currently makes her home in Lake Geneva, Wisconsin.

"There will be born to the Royal House one who is dead
yet will live, who will die again and live again.
And when he returns, he will hold in his hand
the destruction of the world . . ."

THE DARKSWORD TRILOGY
by
Margaret Weis and Tracy Hickman

☐ **Forging the Darksword** (26894-5 • $3.95/$4.95 in Canada)
begins the adventures of the angry young Joram, born into
a world where his lack of magic powers means an instant
death sentence. When he meets the catalyst Saryon, destiny
makes them allies and they find themselves delving into
ancient technology, forging a sword capable of absorbing
magic.

☐ **Doom of the Darksword** (27164-4 • $3.95/$4.95 in
Canada) Determined to learn the truth of his heritage,
Joram travels to the royal city of Merilon. There he finds
not only the answers to his questions but treachery in the
palace and a battle for the throne.

☐ **Triumph of the Darksword** (27406-6 • $3.95/$4.95 in
Canada) Rising to power he never dreamed of, Joram finds
himself faced with the greatest challenge of his life: leading
the people of Thimhallan against powerful and ruthless
invaders.

Buy **Forging the Darksword, Doom of the Darksword** and
Triumph of the Darksword now on sale wherever Bantam
Spectra books are sold, or use this handy page to order:

A spectacular new series of adventure and magic.

Philip Jose Farmer's
THE DUNGEON
volume one: The Black Tower
by Richard Lupoff

When Neville Foliott disappears in the African rain forest, his brother Clive follows his footsteps in an attempt to find him. What he finds is the Dungeon, a multi-level helix of beings from distant galaxies and hidden pockets of time. Once there, neither Neville nor Clive can go back the way they came, so they must venture forward, in search of each other . . . and in search of a way out.

Packed with excitement, suspense and the wonders of other times and worlds, **The Black Tower** is the first volume in this six-volume fantasy series.

Buy **Philip Jose Farmer's The Dungeon volume one: The Black Tower** on sale now wherever Bantam Spectra Books are sold, or use this handy page to order:
